# Dick Merriwell's Aëro Dash

## OR
## WINNING ABOVE THE CLOUDS
### By
### BURT L. STANDISH
Author of the famous Merriwell stories.

**WILDSIDE PRESS**

Originally published in 1910.
wildsidepress.com

# CHAPTER I.

## THE CATASTROPHE.

A glorious midsummer morning, clear, balmy and bracing. An ideal stretch of macadam, level as a floor and straight as a die for close onto two miles, with interminable fields of waving wheat on either side. A new, high-power car in perfect running order.

It was a temptation for speeding which few could resist, certainly not Brose Stovebridge, who was little given to thinking of the consequences when his own pleasure was concerned, and who had a reputation for reckless driving which was exceeded by none.

With a shout of joy, he snatched off his cap and flung it on the seat beside him. The next instant he had opened the throttle wide and advanced the spark to the last notch. The racing roadster leaped forward like a thing alive and shot down the stretch—cut-out wide open and pistons throbbing in perfect unison—a blurred streak of red amidst a swirling cloud of dust.

Stovebridge bent over the wheel, his eyes shining with excitement and his curly, blond hair tossed by the cutting wind into a disordered mass above his rather handsome face. The speedometer hand was close to the fifty mark.

"You'll do, you beauty," he muttered exultingly. "I could squeeze another ten out of you, if I had the chance."

The horn shrieked a warning as he pulled her down to take the curve ahead, but her momentum was so great that she shot around the wide swerve almost on two wheels, with scarcely any perceptible slackening.

The next instant Stovebridge gave a gasping cry of horror.

Directly in the middle of the road stood a little girl. Her eyes were wide and staring, and she seemed absolutely petrified with fright.

The car swerved suddenly to one side, there was a grinding jar of the emergency and the white, stricken face vanished. With a sickening jolt, the roadster rolled on a short distance and stopped.

For a second or two Stovebridge sat absolutely still, his hands trembling, his face the color of chalk. Then he turned, as though with a great effort, and looked back.

The child lay silent, a crumpled, dust-covered heap. The white face was stained with blood, one tiny hand still clutched a bunch of wild flowers.

The man in the car gave a shuddering groan.

"I've killed her!" he gasped. "My God, I've killed her!"

He would be arrested—convicted—imprisoned. At the thought every bit of manhood left him and fear struck him to the soul. He knew that every law, human or divine, bound him to pick up the child and hurry her to a doctor, for there might still be a spark of life which could be fanned into flame. But he was lost to all sense of humanity, decency, or honor. Maddened by the fear of consequences, his one impulse was to fly—fly quickly before he was discovered.

In a panic he threw off the brakes, started the car and ran through his gears into direct drive with frantic haste. The car leaped forward, and, without a backward glance at the victim of his carelessness, Stovebridge opened her up wide and disappeared down the road in a cloud of dust.

The child lay still where she had fallen. Slowly the dust settled and a gentle breeze stirred the flaxen hair above her blood-stained face.

Then came the throbbing of another motor approaching, a deep-toned horn sounded, and a big, red touring car, containing four young fellows, rounded the bend at a fair speed.

Dick Merriwell, the famous Yale athlete, was at the wheel, and, catching sight of the little heap in the roadway, he stopped the car with a jerk and sprang out.

As he ran forward and gathered the limp form into his arms, he gave an exclamation of pity. Then his face darkened.

"By heavens!" he cried. "I'd like to get my hands on the man who did this. Poor little kid! Just look at her face, Brad."

As Brad Buckhart, Dick's Texas chum, caught sight of the great gash over the child's temple, his eyes flashed and he clenched his fists.

"The coyote!" he exploded. "He certain ought to have a hemp necktie put around his neck with the other end over a limb. I'd sure like to have a hold of that other end. You hear me talk!"

Squeezing past the portly form of Bouncer Bigelow, Tommy Tucker leaned excitedly out of the tonneau.

"Is she dead, Dick?" he asked anxiously.

Merriwell took his fingers from the small wrist he had been feeling.

"Not quite," he said shortly. "But it's no thanks to the scoundrel who ran her down and left her here."

His eyes, which had been looking keenly to right and left, lit up as they fell upon the roof of a farm house nestling among some trees a little way back from the road.

"There's a house, Brad," he said in a relieved tone. "Even if she doesn't belong there, they'll make her comfortable and send for a doctor."

4

With infinite tenderness he carried the child down the road a little way to a gate, and thence up a narrow walk bordered with lilac bushes. The door of the farm house was open and, without hesitation, he walked into the kitchen, where a woman stood ironing.

"I found——" he began.

The woman turned swiftly, and as she saw his burden, her face grew ghastly white and her hands flew to her heart.

"Amy!" she gasped in a choking voice. "Is—she——"

"She's not dead," Dick reassured her, "but I'm afraid she's badly hurt. I picked her up in the road outside. Some one in a car had run over her and left her there."

For an instant he thought the woman was going to faint. Then she pulled herself together with a tremendous effort.

"Give her to me!" she cried fiercely, her arms outstretched. "Give her to me!"

Her eyes were blinded with a sudden rush of tears.

"Little Amy, that never did a bit o' harm to nobody," she sobbed. "Oh, it's too much!"

"Careful, now," Merriwell cautioned. "Take her gently. I'm afraid her arm is broken."

"Would you teach a woman to be gentle to her child?" she cried wildly.

Without waiting for a reply, she gathered the little form tenderly into her arms and laid her down on a sofa which stood at one side of the room. Then running to the sink for some water, she wet her handkerchief and began to wipe off the child's face.

"You mustn't mind what I said," she faltered the next moment. "I didn't mean it. I'm just wild."

"I know," Dick returned gently. "A doctor should be called at——"

"Of course!"

She sprang to her feet and flew into another room, whence Dick heard the insistent ringing of a telephone bell, followed quickly by rapid, broken sentences. As the handkerchief fell from her hand he had picked it up and was sprinkling the child's face with water.

Presently the girl gave a little moan and opened her eyes.

"Mamma," she said faintly—"mamma!"

The woman ran into the room at the sound.

"Here I am, darling," she said, as she knelt down by the couch. "Where do you feel bad, Amy dear?"

"My arm," the child moaned, "and my head. A big red car runned right over me."

5

"Red!" muttered Merriwell, his eyes brightening.

"My precious!" soothed the mother. "The doctor'll be here right off. Does it hurt much?"

The child closed her eyes and slow tears welled from under the lashes.

"Yes," she sobbed, "awful."

Dick ground his teeth.

"It's a crime for such men to be allowed on the road," he said in a low, tense tone. "I'm going to do my level best to run down whoever was responsible for this, and if I do, they'll suffer the maximum penalty."

"I hope you do," the woman declared fiercely. "Hanging's too good for 'em! My husband, George Hanlon, ain't the man to sit still an' do nothing, neither."

"They—wasn't—men," sobbed the child. "Only one."

"One man in a red car of some sort," Dick murmured thoughtfully. "He must belong around here; a fellow wouldn't be touring alone."

Then he turned to Mrs. Hanlon.

"I think I'll be getting on," he said quickly. "I can't do anything here, and the longer I delay the less chance there'll be of catching this fellow. I'll call you up to-night and find out how the little girl is doing."

"God bless you for what you've done," the woman said brokenly.

"I wish it might have been more," Dick answered as he walked quickly toward the door. "Good-by."

As he hurried out he almost ran into a slim young fellow, who was running up the walk. He was bare-headed, and his long black hair straggled down over a pair of fierce black eyes that had a touch of wildness in them.

Catching sight of Dick he glared at the Yale man, and hesitated for an instant as if he meant to stop him. Then, with a curious motion of his hands, he brushed past Merriwell and disappeared into the house.

"I've found a clue, pard," Buckhart announced triumphantly, as Dick reached the car.

"What is it?"

The Texan held up a cloth cap.

"Picked it up by the side of the road," he explained. "Find the owner of that and you'll sure have the onery varmit who did this trick. You hear me gently warble!"

Dick took it in his hand and turned it over. The stuff was a small black and white check and was lined with gray satin. Stamped in the middle of the lining was the name of the dealer who had sold it:

"Jennings, Haberdasher,
Wilton."

Wilton was a good-sized town they had passed through about four miles back.

"I thought he belonged around here," Merriwell said as he rolled up the cap and stuffed it into his pocket. "Look out for a fellow without a hat, alone, in a red car of some sort, Brad. That's all we've got to go by at present, but I shouldn't wonder if it would be enough."

He stepped into the car and started the engine, Brad sprang up beside him and they were off.

They had not gone a hundred feet when the black haired youth rushed out of the gate to the middle of the road. His eyes flashed fire, and as he saw the car moving rapidly away from him his mouth moved and twisted convulsively as if he wanted to shout, but could not.

Then, as the touring car disappeared around a turn in the road, he clenched one fist and shook it fiercely in that direction. The next moment he was following it as hard as he could run.

# CHAPTER II.

## THE COWARD.

With pallid face and nervous, twitching fingers, which his desperate grip on the wheel scarcely served to hide, Brose Stovebridge flew along the high road between Wilton and the Clover Country Club.

Now and then he looked back fearfully; at every crossroad his eyes darted keenly to right and left, as he let out the car to the very highest speed he dared, hoping and praying that he might reach his goal without encountering any one.

All the time fear—deadly, unreasoning, ignoble fear—was tugging at his heart-strings.

He had gone through just such an experience as this little more than a year ago in Kansas City. How vividly it all came back to him! The unexpected meeting with two old school chums whom he had not seen in months; their hilarious progress of celebration from one café to another, which ended, long past midnight, in that wild joy ride through the silent, deserted streets.

He shuddered. He thought he had succeeded in thrusting from his mind the details of it all: The sudden skidding around a corner on two wheels; the man's face that flashed before them in the electric light, dazed—white—terrified. The thud—the fall—the sickening jolt, as the wheels went over him. Then that wild, unreasoning, terror-stricken impulse to fly, to escape the consequences at any cost, which possessed him. He gave no thought to his unconscious victim. He only wanted to get away before any one came, and somehow he had done so.

A few days later, in the safe seclusion of his home near Wilton, when he read that the fellow had succumbed to his injuries in the Kansas City hospital, his first thought was one of self-congratulation at his own cleverness in eluding pursuit.

His two chums he had never seen since that morning. Only a few weeks ago one of them had declined an invitation to visit him. He wondered why.

Once in his prep school days, when the dormitory caught fire, he had stumbled blindly down the fire escape and left his roommate sleeping heavily. Luckily the boy was roused in time; but it was no thanks to Brose that he escaped with his life.

For Stovebridge was a coward. In spite of his handsome face and dashing manner; in spite of his popularity, his athletic prowess, his many friends—in spite of all, he was a moral coward.

Few suspected it and still fewer knew, for the fellow was constantly on his guard and clever at hiding this unpleasant trait. But it was there just the same, ready to leap forth in a twinkling, as it had done this morning, and stamp his face with the brand of fear.

As the great, granite gateposts of the club appeared in sight, Stovebridge breathed a sigh of relief. By some extraordinary luck he had encountered no one on his wild ride thither. He had passed several crossroads, any one of which he was prepared to swear he had come by, and for the present he was safe.

Slowing down, he turned into the drive, and as he did so he took out a handkerchief and passed it over his moist forehead. He must compose himself before encountering any of his fellow members.

He carefully smoothed his ruffled hair with slim, brown fingers, and reached over for his cap.

The seat was empty. The cap had disappeared.

The discovery was like a physical blow, and for an instant his heart stood still.

Where had he lost it?

The spot where he had run down the child was the only feasible one. The cap must have fallen out when he put on the emergency, and probably lay in plain sight, a clue for the first passerby to pick up.

For a moment he had a wild idea of going back for it, but he thrust this from him instantly. It was impossible.

Then the clubhouse came in sight. He must pull himself together at once; he would get something to steady his nerves before he met any one.

Instead of continuing on to the front of the clubhouse, where a crowd was congregated on the wide veranda, he turned sharply to the right and drove his car into one of the open sheds back of the kitchen. Then he dived through a side door into the buffet.

"Whisky, Joe," he said nervously to the attendant.

A bottle, glass and siphon were placed before him, and even the taciturn Joe was somewhat astonished at the size of the drink which Stovebridge poured with shaking hand and drained at a swallow.

He followed it with a little seltzer and, pouring out another three fingers, sat back in his chair and took out a gold cigarette case.

As he selected a cigarette with some care, and held it to the cigar lighter on the table, he noticed with satisfaction that his fingers scarcely trembled at all.

"That's the stuff to steady a fellow's nerves," he muttered, blowing out a cloud of blue smoke. "There's nothing like it."

He took a swallow and then drained the glass for the second time.

Presently his view of life became slightly more optimistic.

"It was a new cap," he remembered with a sudden feeling of relief.

"I've never worn it here, and there's an old one in my locker. All I've got to do is to swear I never saw it before if I'm asked about it—which isn't likely."

When the cigarette was finished he went into the dressing room and took a thorough wash. There was no one there but the valet, who gave his clothes a good brushing, so he had no trouble in getting the old cap out of his locker and placing it at a becoming angle on his freshly brushed hair. Then he strolled out onto the veranda.

Three or four fellows, lounging near the door, greeted him jovially as he appeared.

"Rather late, aren't you, Brose?" one of them remarked, as he joined them.

"A little," Stovebridge returned nonchalantly. "It was such a bully morning I took a spin along the river road."

"Alone?" the other asked slyly.

Stovebridge laughed.

"Well, I happened to be—this time," he answered, a little self-consciously.

Being very much of a lady's man, it was rare for him to be unaccompanied.

"How I do love a hog!" drawled one of the fellows who had not spoken. "Why the deuce didn't you 'phone me? I've been sitting here bored to death for two solid hours."

Stovebridge was looking curiously at a big, red touring car which had just driven up to the entrance.

"Er—I beg pardon, Marston," he stammered. "What did you say?"

"Really not worth repeating," returned the other languidly. "You seem to have something on your mind, Brose."

Stovebridge gave a slight start as he turned back to his friends.

"I was wondering who those fellows are that just drove up," he said carelessly. "They're talking to old Clingwood."

Fred Marston turned with an effort and surveyed the newcomers.

"Don't know, I'm sure," he drawled sinking back in his chair. "Never saw them before."

For some reason the strangers seemed to interest Stovebridge extremely, and he continued to watch them furtively. There were four of them. The one who had driven the car, and with whom Roger Clingwood was doing the most talking, was tall and handsome, with dark hair and eyes, and the figure of an athlete. The fellow who stood near him was good-looking, too, and much more heavily built. Behind them, a short, wiry youth was talking to a tremendously stout fellow with a fat, good-humored face.

Presently Stovebridge left his friends and wandered along the veranda, pausing now and then to exchange a remark with some acquaintance, and before long he had reached the vicinity of the strangers, where he leaned carelessly against a pillar and looked out across the golf links.

"Very glad you could get here this morning, Merriwell," Roger Clingwood, an old Yale graduate was saying. "You'll be able to look around a bit before the race this afternoon."

"Merriwell!" exclaimed Stovebridge under his breath. "I wonder if that can be Dick Merriwell, of Yale."

Suddenly a hand struck him on the shoulder and a voice exclaimed heartily:

"Hello, Brose, old boy! Wearing your old brown cap, I see. What's the matter with the one you got at the governor's shop yesterday?"

Stovebridge wheeled around with a sudden tightening of his throat and saw the grinning face of Bob Jennings, son of the haberdasher at Wilton, who had been in the store when he bought that wretched cap the day before. Here was the first complication.

Stovebridge forced himself to smile.

"Left it at home, Bob," he returned carelessly. "This was the first one I picked up as I came out this morning."

In the pause which followed Roger Clingwood stepped forward.

"I didn't notice you were here, Stovebridge," he said pleasantly. "I'd like you to meet my friend Merriwell, who has come up with some of his classmates to spend a day or two at the club."

"Delighted, I'm sure," Stovebridge said with an air of good fellowship. "I know Mr. Merriwell very well by reputation, but have never had the pleasure of meeting him."

"Dick, this is Brose Stovebridge," Clingwood went on. "We claim for him —and I think justly—the title of champion sprinter of the middle West."

Merriwell smiled as he held out his hand.

"Very glad indeed to meet you, Mr. Stovebridge," he said heartily.

Stovebridge gave a sudden gasp and faltered; then he took the proffered hand limply.

"Glad to meet you," he said hoarsely.

Instead of meeting Merriwell's glance, his eyes were fixed intently on the corner of a checked cap which protruded from the Yale man's pocket.

It was the cap he had lost out of the car that morning, or one exactly like it. Apparently it did not belong to Merriwell, who held his own in his left hand. Where had he picked it up? Where could he have found it but in that fatal spot? Stovebridge's brain reeled and he felt a little faint. Then he realized that Clingwood was speaking to him—introducing the other Yale men—and with a tremendous effort he forced himself to turn and greet them with apparent calmness.

For a time there was a confused medley of talk and laughter as some of the other members strolled up and were presented to the strangers. Stovebridge was very thankful for the chance it gave him to pull himself together and hide his emotion.

Presently there was a momentary lull and Dick pulled the cap out of his pocket.

"Does this belong to any of your fellows?" he asked carelessly. "We picked it up in the road this morning."

Bob Jennings pounced on it.

"Why, that looks like yours, Brose," he said as he turned it over.

Stovebridge glanced at it indifferently. He had himself well in hand now.

"Rather like," he drawled; "but mine is a little larger check; besides, I didn't wear it this morning, you know."

"I could have sworn that you bought one exactly like this," Jennings said in a puzzled tone.

Stovebridge laughed.

"I wouldn't advise you to put any money on it, Bob, because you'd lose," he said lightly. "I'll wear mine to-morrow, and you'll see the difference."

"Where did you find it, Dick?" Roger Clingwood asked.

Merriwell paused and glanced quietly around the circle of men. Most of them looked indifferent, as though they had very little interest in the cap or its unknown owner.

"It was picked up in the road about four miles this side of Wilton," he said in a low, clear voice. "It lay near the body of a little girl who had been run over by some car and left there to die."

There was a sudden, surprised hush, and then a perfect volley of questions were flung at the Yale man.

"Where was it?"

"Who was she?"

"Didn't any one see it done?"

"Is she dead?"

The expression of languid indifference vanished from their faces with the rapidity and completeness of chalk under a wet sponge. Their eyes were full of eager interest, and, as soon as the clamor was quelled, Dick told the story with a brief eloquence which made more than one man curse fiercely and blink his eyes.

Once or twice the Yale man darted a keen glance at Stovebridge, but the latter had turned away so that only a small portion of his face was visible. He seemed to be one of the few to remain unmoved by the recital.

Another was his friend Fred Marston, a man of about thirty, with thin, dark hair plastered over a low forehead, sensuous lips, and that unwholesome flabbiness of figure which is always a sign of a life devoted wholly to ease.

As Dick finished the story, he shrugged his shoulders.

"Very likely she ran out in front of the car, and was bowled over before the fellow had time to stop," he drawled. "Children are always doing things like that. Sometimes I believe they do it on purpose."

Merriwell looked at him fixedly.

"That's quite possible," he said quietly, but with a certain challenging note in his voice. "But no one but a coward—a contemptible coward— would have run off and left her there."

Marston flushed a little and started to reply, but before he could utter a word, a number of the club members began to voice their opinions, and for a time the talk ran fast and furious.

Merriwell noticed that Stovebridge took no part in it. He stood leaning against a pillar, his hands in his pockets, apparently absorbed in watching a putting match which was going on at a green just across the drive.

Presently the Yale man strolled over to his side.

"Nice links you have here," he commented.

Stovebridge nodded silently without taking his eyes from the players.

"You have a car, haven't you," Dick went on casually.

The other's shoulders moved a little.

"Yes," he answered. "Racing roadster—sixty horse-power."

There was a curious glitter in Dick Merriwell's dark eyes.

"Dark red, isn't she?" he queried.

Stovebridge hesitated for an instant.

"Ye-s."

The players had finished their game and were coming slowly toward the clubhouse, but Stovebridge's eyes never left the vivid patch of close-cropped turf.

He was afraid to look up, afraid to meet the glance of the man beside him. He dreaded the sound of the other's low, clear voice. Why was he asking these questions? Why, indeed, unless he suspected?

"You didn't happen to run over the main road from Wilton this morning, I suppose?"

The guilty man could not suppress a slight start. It had come, then. Merriwell did suspect him. His tongue clove to the roof of his mouth and for a moment he was speechless. He moistened his dry lips.

"No," he said hoarsely. "I came—by the river road."

What was the matter with him? That did not sound like his voice. It was not the way an innocent man would have answered an unmistakable innuendo. If he did not pull himself together instantly he would be lost.

The next moment he turned on the Yale man.

"Why do you ask that?" he said almost fiercely. "What do you mean by such a question?"

His face was calm, though a little pale. His long lashes drooped purposely over the blue eyes to hide the fear which filled them.

Merriwell looked at him keenly.

"I thought perhaps we could fix the time of the accident, if you had gone over the road before me," he said quietly. "But I see we cannot."

He turned away, with a slight shrug of his shoulders, and joined the others.

Brose Stovebridge gave a shiver as he saw him go. He had the desperate feeling of going to pieces; unless he could steady his nerves he felt that in a very few minutes he would give himself away.

Without a word to any one, he slipped through the big reception hall of the clubhouse and thence to the buffet. Here he tossed off another drink and then hurried out the side door.

The attendant looked after him with a shake of his head.

"He's got something on his mind, he has," he muttered. "Never knew him to take so much of a morning—and the very day he's going to run, too."

Stovebridge walked over to the automobile sheds. He was not likely to be disturbed there, and if some one did come around he could pretend to be fussing with his car.

He scarcely noticed Merriwell's touring car, which had been put into the shed next to his own. At another time he would have examined it with interest, for he was a regular motor fiend. But now he passed it with a glance, and going up to his own car, lifted up the hood and leaned over the cylinders.

He had not been there more than a minute or two when he felt a hand grasp his shoulder firmly.

With a snarl of terror, he straightened up and whirled around.

He had expected to find Merriwell, come to accuse him. Instead, he saw before him Jim Hanlon, a deaf mute, who occasionally did odd jobs around the club. The fellow's face was distorted with rage, his eyes flashed fire, his slight frame fairly quivered with emotion.

Stovebridge stepped back instinctively.

"What's the matter with you?" he asked harshly. "What are you doing here?"

As the clubman spoke the deaf mute's eyes were fixed upon his lips. Evidently he understood what the other said, for his own mouth writhed and twisted in his desperate, futile efforts to give voice to his emotion.

The next instant he snatched a scrap of soiled brown paper from his pocket and produced the stub of a pencil.

Stovebridge watched him with a vague uneasiness as he scrawled a few words and then thrust the paper into the clubman's hand.

"Somebudy run over Amy an kill her."

As he deciphered the illiterate sentence, Stovebridge shivered. Until that moment he had forgotten that this fellow was the child's brother. What was he about to do? He looked as though he were capable of anything. Above all, how much did he know?

Looking up, Brose met the fellow's eyes fixed fiercely on his own. He shivered again.

"Yes," he said, with an effort at calmness. "I heard about it. It's too bad."

As the words left his lips he realized their utter inadequacy.

With a scowl, Hanlon snatched the paper from his hands and wrote again.

"I'll kill the man that did it—kill him!"

The word kill was heavily underlined in a pitiful attempt at emphasis.

As Stovebridge read the short line he felt a cold chill going down his back. He had not the slightest doubt that the fellow meant what he had written. But how had he found out? Who had told him? Was it possible that he could have witnessed the accident from some place out of sight?

He shot another glance at Hanlon and met the same malignant glare of hate. The fellow looked positively murderous.

The next moment the deaf mute had pulled a long, keen knife out of his pocket, which he held up before Stovebridge's terror-stricken eyes and shook it significantly. At the same time he nodded his head fiercely.

Brose gave a low gasp as he gazed at the wicked blade with fascinated horror. Why had he ever come out here alone and given the fellow this chance? Why hadn't he stayed with the others? No matter what else might have happened, he would have been safe. Arrest, conviction, disgrace—anything would have been better than this.

Overcome by a momentary faintness, he closed his eyes.

Suddenly the paper was twitched from his fingers, and, with a frightened gasp, he looked up.

The knife had disappeared and Hanlon was writing, again.

Desperately, as a drowning man clutches a straw, Stovebridge snatched at the paper.

"What's the name of the feller that came with three others in that car."

Puzzled, the clubman looked at Hanlon and found him pointing at Dick Merriwell's touring car. What did he mean? What could he want with Merriwell? Was it possible that he did not really know—that he wanted to get proof from the Yale man before proceeding with his murderous attack?

"Why do you want to know?" he faltered.

The other seized the paper from the man's trembling fingers, wrote three words and thrust it back.

"He killed Amy."

As Stovebridge read the short sentence, he could have shouted with joy. Hanlon did not know the truth, after all. For some unaccountable reason he suspected Merriwell. Perhaps it was because the Yale man had carried the child into the house; anyhow it did not matter, so long as he himself was safe.

Then another thought flashed into his mind. The fellow suspected Merriwell—not only suspected, but was convinced. He would try to kill the Yale man, and perhaps succeed. Well, what of that? With Merriwell out of the way Stovebridge would be safe—quite safe. No one else had the slightest suspicion.

He took the pencil out of the deaf mute's hand, and, after a moment's hesitation wrote, on the bottom of the paper:

"His name is Dick Merriwell."

Somehow, as he handed the paper to the wild-eyed youth, he had the odd feeling that he had signed a death warrant.

# CHAPTER III.

## A SCRAP OF PAPER.

The Clover Country Club had acquired a wider reputation than is usual with an organization of that description.

Intended originally as a simple athletic club, with out-of-door sports and games the special features, it had one of the finest golf links in the Middle West. Its tennis courts were unsurpassed, its running track unrivaled. There was a well-laid-out diamond which had been the scene of many a hot game of baseball, and which was used in the fall for football. Indoors were bowling alleys, billiard, and pool tables, a beautiful swimming tank in a well-equipped gymnasium.

But in the course of time other and less desirable features had been added. The younger set had developed into a rather fast, sporting crowd, and, slowly increasing in numbers and in power, they gradually crowded the old conservatives to the wall, until finally they controlled the management.

To-day the club was better known for the completeness of its buffet, than for the gymnasium; and it was a well-known fact that frequently more money changed hands in the so-called private card room in a single night than in the old days had been won or lost on sporting bets in the course of an entire season.

In spite of all this, however, out-of-door sports were still a feature, and now and then, when some especially well-known athletes were at the club, matches and contests of various kinds were arranged.

That very afternoon a mile race had been planned between Stovebridge and Charlie Layton—a Columbia graduate reported to have beaten everything in his class from Chicago to Omaha—who was coming on from the latter city especially for the occasion.

Fred Marston and others of his ilk usually did a great deal of sneering at such affairs, calling them farcical relics of barbarism, and made it plain that they only attended for the excitement of betting on the result; but this made little difference in the general enthusiasm.

For a time after the departure of Stovebridge the discussion of Merriwell's story continued with some warmth, and many were the speculations as to the identity of the brute who had run over the child and left her there. But even that topic could not hold the interest of such a crowd of men for very long, and presently they began to disperse, some seeking the card room, others the buffet, while the remainder found comfortable seats on the veranda to put in the hour before luncheon in indolent lounging and small talk.

Roger Clingwood hesitated an instant before the wide doors of the reception hall.

"It's too late for golf or tennis," he said regretfully. "Is there anything else you would like to do before lunch? Er—cards, perhaps, or——"

He was one of the older members who had fought vigorously, but in vain, against the introduction of gambling in the club; but his innate sense of hospitality made him suggest the only form of amusement possible in the short time.

Dick smiled.

"Not for me, thank you," he said quickly. "It always seems a waste of time to sit around a table in a stuffy room when you might be doing something interesting outside."

Clingwood's face brightened.

"I'm glad of that," he said warmly. "I enjoy a good rubber as well as the next man, but I don't like the kind of play that goes on here. How do your friends feel about it?"

He looked inquiringly at the others.

"Nix," Buckhart said decidedly. "Not for me."

Tucker and Bigelow both shook their heads.

"I used to flip the pasteboards in my younger days," the former grinned; "but I've reformed."

"Why not just sit here and do nothing?" Merriwell asked. "I feel that I'd enjoy an hour's loaf."

Bigelow evidently agreed with him, for he sank instantly into one of the wicker chairs, with a sigh of thankfulness.

The others followed his example, and their host took out a well-filled cigar case and passed it around. Tucker accepted one; the others declined.

"Layton ought to show up soon," Clingwood remarked, settling back in his chair and blowing out a cloud of smoke. "I believe he's due in Wilton at eleven forty-seven."

"Layton?" Dick exclaimed interestedly. "Not Charlie Layton, the Columbia man?"

"That's the boy. Know him?"

"I've met him. He's one of the best milers in the country. Stovebridge must be pretty good to run against him."

"He is," returned the older man. "He trains with a crowd that I'm not at all in sympathy with, but, for all that, he's not a bad fellow; crackerjack ten-

18

nis player, and has a splendid record for long distance running. He keeps himself in fair training and doesn't lush as much as most of his friends do."

"I see," Dick said thoughtfully.

This did not sound at all like a fellow who would run down a child and never stop to see how badly she was hurt. As a rule, good athletes are not cowards, though he had known exceptions.

At the same time, Stovebridge's actions had been suspicious. Dick had not failed to notice his consternation at the sight of the cap, though he had quickly recovered himself and his explanation had been plausible enough.

Later, during Merriwell's conversation with him, the fellow's agitation had been palpable. That he was laboring under a tremendous mental strain, the Yale man was certain. Of course, the cause of it might have been something quite different, but to Dick it looked very much as though Brose Stovebridge knew a good deal more about the accident than would appear.

And he had come to the club that morning alone in a red car!

All at once Dick became conscious that some one had paused on the drive quite close to the veranda and was looking at him.

As he raised his head quickly, he saw that it was the same dark-haired, sullen youth he had passed as he came out of the farmhouse that morning.

To Dick's astonishment the fellow's eyes were fixed on him with a look of fierce, malignant hatred which was unmistakable. His fingers twitched convulsively and his whole attitude was one of consuming rage.

As Merriwell looked up, the other seemed to control himself with an effort, and, turning his head away, slouched on along the drive.

"What's the matter with him I wonder?" the Yale man mused. "He looks as if he could eat me up with the greatest pleasure in life. I wonder who he is?"

He turned to Roger Clingwood, who was talking with Buckhart and Tucker.

"Who is that fellow that just passed, Mr. Clingwood?" he asked, when there was a lull in the conversation. "Did you notice him?"

"Yes, I saw him. That's Jim Hanlon; he occasionally does odd jobs about the grounds."

"Hanlon!" Dick exclaimed. "Any relation to the little girl?"

"Yes, her brother."

"Oh, I see."

Dick hesitated.

"Is he—all there?" he asked after a moment's pause.

Roger Clingwood looked rather surprised.

"Yes, so far as I know. He's deaf and dumb, you see, and has the reputation of being rather hot tempered at times; but I never heard that he didn't have all his faculties. Poor fellow! It's enough to drive any one dotty to have to do all one's talking with pencil and paper. I'm not surprised that he loses his temper now and then."

"I should say not," Tucker put in. "Just imagine getting into an argument and having to write it all out. I'd lay down and cough up the ghost."

"I opine you'd blow up and bust, Tommy," Buckhart grinned. "Or else the hot air would strike in and smother you."

"You're envious of my wit and persiflage," declared Tucker. "I'd be ashamed to show such a disposition as that, if I were you."

"When you're talking with Hanlon, do you also have to take to pencil and paper?" Dick asked interestedly.

"Oh, no," Clingwood answered. "He knows what you're saying by watching your lips. He's amazingly good at it, too; I've never seen him stumped."

At that moment Stovebridge strolled out of the clubhouse and stopped beside Clingwood's chair.

"Any signs of Layton yet?" he drawled.

"Haven't seen him," the other man answered. "He's had hardly time to get here from Wilton, has he?"

"Plenty, if he came on the eleven forty-seven. Sartoris went over with his car to meet him. I hope he's not going to disappoint us."

He turned away and walked slowly down the veranda toward Marston lounging in a corner.

As Dick followed him with his eyes, there was a slightly puzzled look in them.

Stovebridge was so cool and self-possessed, so utterly different from the man who had shown such agitation barely half an hour before, that for an instant Merriwell was staggered.

"Either I'm wrong and he's innocent," he thought to himself, "or he has the most amazing self-control. There isn't a hint in his manner that the fellow has a trouble in the world."

Then the Yale man's intuitive good sense reasserted itself.

"He's bluffing," he muttered under his breath. "I'll stake my reputation that, for all his pretended indifference, Brose Stovebridge is either the guilty man, or he knows who is. And I rather think he's the one himself."

Roger Clingwood pulled out his watch.

"Well, boys, it's about time for lunch," he remarked. "Suppose I take you up to your rooms and, after you've brushed up a bit, we'll go in and have a bite to eat."

"I'll get the bags out of the car and be with you in a minute," Dick said as they stood up.

"Wait, I'll ring for a man to take them up," proposed Clingwood.

"Don't bother," Dick said quickly. "They're very light, and Brad and I can easily carry them. Besides, I'd like to see just where they've put the car so that I'll know where to go if I want to take her out."

"Well, have your own way," smiled the other. "The garage is around at the back. Follow the drive and you can't miss it."

Leaving Tucker and Bigelow with their host, the two chums followed the latter's directions and had no difficulty in locating the automobile sheds.

Merriwell was glad of the opportunity, for he wanted very much to have a look at Stovebridge's car. In fact, that was his principal reason for coming out instead of having the bags sent for.

There were a dozen machines in the sheds, of all sizes and makes, but only two runabouts. One was a small electric, and the other—standing in the compartment next to Dick's car, the *Wizard*—was a new, high-power roadster, painted a dark red.

"That's the one, I reckon," he said aloud, as they surveyed it.

The Texan's eyes crinkled.

"I opine it is, pard, if you say so," he grinned. "Might a thick, onery cowpuncher ask, what one?"

"Stovebridge's car," Merriwell explained briefly.

The Westerner gave a low whistle.

"Oh, ho! A red runabout," he murmured. "So you think he's the gent we're after?"

As Dick stepped in to examine the car more closely, his eyes fell upon a scrap of paper which lay on the ground close by one of the forward wheels. Picking it up, he saw that it was a torn piece of common brown wrapping paper, very much mussed and dirty. He was about to toss it aside when he happened to turn it over. The next instant his eyes widened with surprise.

"What the mischief is this, I wonder?" he said in a low tone.

Buckhart stepped forward and looked at it over the other's shoulder.

"'His name is Dick Merriwell'," he read slowly. "Who's been taking your name in vain, partner?"

Dick made no reply. He was busy trying to decipher the illiterate scrawl which preceded the one legible sentence the Texan had read. Slowly, word by word, he made it out.

"Somebody—run over—Amy—and—kill her," he read at last.

"Amy—who is Amy?" he mused. "Why, that's the little girl we picked up this morning—Amy Hanlon."

21

He looked at the paper again, and then, like a ray of light, the solution flashed into his brain.

"Why, that dumb fellow—her brother—must have written this!" he exclaimed. "Clingwood said he had to do his talking on paper. But what on earth is my name here for? Wait a minute."

His eyes went back to the scrap of paper, and for a few minutes there was silence. When he looked up at Buckhart, his face was set and his eyes stern.

"Listen, Brad," he said rapidly. "On this paper there are four questions and one answer. The questions were written by an illiterate person; the answer—was not. It is evidently part of a conversation between this dumb fellow and some one else. Hanlon first informs this person that his sister had been run over and killed. How he got the idea I don't know, unless she had fainted when he went into the room, and he did not wait long enough to find out the truth. Then he proceeds to inform whoever he is talking with that he will kill the man who ran the child down. Then he writes: 'What's the name of the fellow that came, with three others, in that car?' Do you make any sense out of that, Brad?"

The Texan shook his head.

"I sure don't," he said decidedly.

"Well, I don't know as I blame you," Merriwell returned. "The next sentence is apparently the answer to a question by the other man. It is: 'He killed Amy.' Meaning that the man in a car with three others ran over his sister, which, of course, we know isn't so. There was only one, according to her statement. Then follows the line in another hand which you read: 'His name is Dick Merriwell.' Don't you see now, Brad?"

"Afraid I'm awful thick——"

"Why, it's clear as day," Merriwell interrupted. "This Hanlon has somehow got the idea that I ran over the little girl. He doesn't know my name and proceeds to ask this unknown person what it is, giving at the same time the reason why he wants to know. He gets the answer without a word of denial or explanation, and goes away with the firm belief that I am a murderer. That accounts for the look he gave me when he passed the veranda a little while ago."

"The miserable snake!" exploded the irate Westerner. "Wait till I put my blinkers on him!"

"He isn't to blame," Dick asserted quickly. "He thinks he's right. It's the other man I'd like to get my hands on—the fellow that let him go on believing a lie."

He paused and looked significantly at Buckhart.

"Who is the man most interested in shifting the blame to my shoulders?" he asked in a hard voice. "Whom have we suspected? Under whose car did I pick up this paper?"

"Stovebridge!"

The word came in a smothered roar from the lips of the irate Texan, and, turning swiftly, he started toward the clubhouse, his face flushed with rage and his eyes flashing.

"Stop! Come back, Brad," Dick called. "You must not do anything now. We have no real proof; he would deny everything."

Buckhart hesitated and then came slowly back to the shed. Dick went over to his own car and pulled out a couple of bags from the tonneau.

"Don't worry, you untamed Maverick of the Pecos," he said with a half smile. "We'll get him right before very long."

He folded the paper and put it carefully away in his breast pocket.

"I've got this, for one thing," he went on, "and I also have an idea in my head which I think will come to something."

# CHAPTER IV.

## STOVEBRIDGE FINDS AN ALLY.

Brose Stovebridge dropped down in a chair beside his friend Marston and pulled out his cigarette case.

"Have one?" he invited, extending it to the other.

Marston selected a cigarette languidly.

"How did this fellow Merriwell happen to honor the club with his presence to-day?" he inquired sarcastically.

Stovebridge struck a match and held it to the other's cigarette; then, lighting his own, he sank back in the chair.

"He's Clingwood's friend, I believe," he answered with apparent indifference. "You speak as though you didn't like him."

"I don't," snapped Marston. "I hate him—hate the whole brood."

The blond fellow raised his eyebrows.

"I didn't know you'd ever met him," he commented. "You certainly didn't greet him as though you had ever laid eyes on him before."

"I haven't," the other said bitterly. "I know his brother—that's enough."

"His brother?" queried Stovebridge.

"Yes, Frank Merriwell. I ran up against him at Yale, and of all the straight-laced freaks he took the cake—wouldn't drink, wouldn't smoke; wouldn't play poker, wouldn't do anything but bone, and go in for athletics."

"Humph!" remarked Stovebridge cynically. "I don't wonder you didn't like him. He wasn't in your class at all. But if he was as good an athlete as his brother, he must have been some pumpkins. I don't just see, though, how that accounts for your violent antipathy. Why didn't you let him go on his benighted way and have nothing to do with him?"

Marston's heavy brows contracted in a scowl.

"You don't suppose I cared a hang what he did, do you?" he snarled. "That didn't worry me any, but he had to get meddlesome and butt into my affairs. Got my best friend so crazy about him that he went and gave up cards and all that, and trained with Merriwell's crowd. Of course, he was no use to me after that. Do you wonder that I dislike Frank Merriwell, and his brother as well?"

Stovebridge hesitated.

"Don't know as I do?" he said in a preoccupied manner.

He had been thinking of something else.

They smoked for a few minutes in silence. Once or twice Marston glanced curiously at his friend, who was scowling at the floor.

"What's the matter with you to-day, Brose?" he asked presently. "You act like you had something on your mind."

The other looked up with a sudden start.

"Why, no; I——"

Marston shrugged his shoulders indifferently.

"Don't tell me, if you don't want to," he drawled. "But if it's something you want to keep to yourself, for goodness sake, wipe that scowl off your face and brace up."

Stovebridge eyed the other with a speculative glance. Why not confide in Marston? He hated Merriwell and would certainly never peach. Besides, he might suggest something helpful.

"I'll tell you about it, Fred," he said in a low tone, as he drew his chair closer to his friend. "I'm in a deuce of a scrape. I—I—was the one—who ran over that kid this morning."

His face flushed a little; his eyes were averted. He did not find it easy to tell, even to Fred Marston.

The latter gave a low whistle.

"By Jove!" he exclaimed. "You don't say! How did it happen?"

"It was at the bend by the Hanlon farm," Stovebridge explained. "I was hitting up a pretty good clip, and when I came round the bend she was standing in the middle of the road. There was plenty of time for her to get away, but she never moved. I tried to run to one side, but there wasn't room, and—the kid went under."

"I always said they didn't have sense enough to get out of the way," Marston remarked in a vexed tone.

Then he looked curiously at his friend.

"What made you beat it?" he asked. "Why didn't you stop and pick her up? It wasn't your fault—no one could have blamed you, if you only hadn't run away."

"I couldn't, Fred—I simply couldn't," Stovebridge confessed, without lifting his eyes. "My one idea was to get away before any one saw me. You know the beastly things they do to a fellow sometimes. Why, I might have been jugged for a year or more."

"Yes, I know," agreed the other. "Still——"

He stopped abruptly and looked out over the golf course in a meditative way.

"You managed pretty well, though," he said presently as he turned back to Stovebridge. "No one saw you on your way here, I suppose?"

The other shook his head.

"No; if it wasn't for that beastly cap I should feel quite safe. But Merriwell suspects me on that account."

Marston's beady eyes glittered.

"Let him suspect!" he snapped angrily. "We'll fix that all right. It wouldn't be safe for you to buy another, but there's nothing to prevent my doing so."

"Of course there isn't!" Stovebridge exclaimed in a tone of relief. "And you'll do it?"

Marston's teeth snapped together.

"I certainly will," he declared. "I'd do more than that to spite a Merriwell. Lend me your car and I'll go to Wilton right after lunch."

Stovebridge breathed a sigh of relief. How fortunate he had confided in Marston. With the question of the cap settled and Jim Hanlon sidetracked, he would have nothing to fear. Dick Merriwell might do his worst, but he could prove nothing.

Marston arose to his feet, yawning.

"Well, let's toddle in and get something sustaining," he suggested. "I feel the need of a little bracer."

"Don't forget to pick out a medium check," Stovebridge reminded, as they strolled through the reception hall to the dining room beyond. "I said mine was a little larger than the one he picked up, but if you get it too pronounced, Bob Jennings will smell a rat. He's a bit doubtful now."

"Trust me," Marston returned confidently.

They settled themselves comfortably at a small table near one of the windows, and a waiter hurried up.

"Two Martinis—dry," Marston said, unfolding his napkin. "Bring them right away."

"Not any for me," Stovebridge put in hastily. "I've got to run this afternoon."

"Oh, shucks! What's one cocktail?" expostulated the other. "Just put a little ginger into you."

But Stovebridge persisted in his refusal; already he had taken considerably more stimulant than he felt was wise. So when the cocktails came Marston drank them both.

While his friend was writing out the order, Stovebridge glanced idly about the well-filled room. He gave a slight start as his eyes met those of Dick Merriwell, who was seated with his party three or four tables away. The Yale man was looking at him with a certain steady scrutiny that was a little disconcerting. There was no gleam of friendliness in his dark eyes, but rather a cold, steely glitter. His fine mouth was set in a hard line, curving disdainfully at the corners, as though he were regarding something beneath his contempt. It was not a pleasant expression, and, despite his belief that the other could really prove nothing, Stovebridge could not help feeling a little uneasy.

"Who are you staring at?"

Marston's drawling voice roused Stovebridge, and, turning quickly, he looked at his friend.

"Merriwell," he breathed softly.

"Bah!" snapped the other. "He can't do anything. We'll put a spoke in his wheel. For goodness' sake, Brose, do brace up and forget it!"

Stovebridge made an effort to do so, but all the time he was eating lunch he had an uneasy feeling that those cold eyes were still fixed upon him, and it was only by the most determined exertion of will power that he kept himself from looking again toward the table where Roger Clingwood and his guests seemed to be enjoying themselves so thoroughly.

As they came out to the veranda after lunch, Roger Clingwood pulled out his watch impatiently.

"Almost two!" he exclaimed. "What in the world is the matter with Layton?"

He turned to a short, pleasant-faced, youngish-looking fellow who, also watch in hand, was looking anxiously down the drive.

"Heard anything of Charlie Layton, Niles?" he asked.

"Not a thing," the other answered petulantly. "I can't understand what's delayed him. He promised to be here soon after twelve, and the race was to be pulled off at three. People are beginning to come already."

"Sartoris is there to meet him, I believe," Clingwood remarked.

"Yes, and I tried just now to get him on the phone, but couldn't."

Jack Niles shut his watch with a snap and shoved it back in his pocket irritably. He was extremely homely. Every feature seemed to be either too large or too small, or not placed right on his face; but for all that there was something very attractive in his expression, and in the straightforward, honest directness of his brown eyes. His clothes were loud almost to eccentricity, and it was quite evident that he was a thorough-going, out-and-out sport.

As he started to walk away, Roger Clingwood caught his arm.

"Oh, by the way, Jack," he said suddenly, "I want you to meet my friend Merriwell. Dick, this is Jack Niles, to whose efforts is due the fact that we still occasionally have athletic events at the club."

As Niles turned quickly, his hand outstretched, the worried look on his face gave place to one of surprised interest.

"Not Dick Merriwell, of Yale?" he asked eagerly.

Dick smiled as he took the other's hand.

"I happen to be," he said quietly.

He felt a sudden liking for this homely young fellow with the honest eyes, who looked as though he was square down to the very bone.

"Well, say!" Niles exclaimed, as he gripped Dick's hand and worked it up and down like a pump handle. "If this isn't a little bit of all right. I've seen you play ball, and I've seen you run, but I never had a chance of shaking hands before. What are you doing away out here?"

"Touring with some friends of mine," Dick answered smiling. "I'd like you to meet them."

He introduced Buckhart, Tucker and Bigelow, and for a few minutes they stood talking together.

"I don't know what we'll do if Layton throws us down," Niles said anxiously. "We've made so much talk about the race, and there'll be an awful mob here to see it. Oh, there's Sartoris! Now we'll find out something. Excuse me, will you?"

Without waiting for a reply, he dashed down the steps toward a car that had just driven up. Its occupant, a tall, bare-headed fellow in tennis flannels, sprang out, waving a yellow envelope in his hand.

"He can't get here until to-morrow," he explained. "Held up by a wreck on the road."

Niles took the telegram in silence, and, as he read it, his face shadowed.

"Well, what do you think of that?" he muttered, as he crumpled it in his hand. "To-morrow! And look at the bunch that's here to-day, expecting to see something good. Coming thicker every minute, too."

He glanced down the drive where several cars were in sight, heading toward the clubhouse.

"Wouldn't that drive you to the batty house!" he went on. "I suppose it's up to yours truly to get busy and announce that there 'won't be no race.'"

His eyes, full of an expression of whimsical chagrin, roved slowly over the crowd which had hastily gathered at the approach of Sartoris, until they rested on Dick Merriwell's face.

The next moment a gleam of hope had leaped into them, and Niles sprang up the steps to the Yale man's side.

"Say, what's the matter with your taking Layton's place, old fellow, and saving my rap?" he asked eagerly.

Merriwell smiled a little.

"It would be rather difficult to take his place," he said slowly. "Layton is one of the best milers in the country, and it's a long time since I've done any running."

"Oh, that be hanged!" exploded Niles. "You're too blamed modest. You can do it if you want to. Come ahead, old fellow, and save me from making an ass of myself by disappointing this crowd."

"When you put it that way, Niles, I can scarcely refuse," Dick smiled. "I'll be very glad to do what you want, only you mustn't expect too much of me."

Jack Niles was overjoyed.

"That's bully!" he exclaimed. "You've helped me out of a deuce of a hole and saved the day. It's just my luck to find a substitute as good or better than the original."

Brose Stovebridge stood near, a slight sneer on his face.

"It's lucky I'm not the one who didn't show up," he drawled. "Merriwell seems to think such a lot of this fellow Layton that I don't suppose he could possibly have been induced to run against him, if our positions were reversed."

Apparently his words were intended for the man next to him, but they were quite loud enough for the Yale man to hear.

The latter turned and surveyed Stovebridge with a cool, disconcerting glance.

"I happen to have run against Layton several times, Mr. Stovebridge," he said quietly. "If he were here to-day, I should be very glad to do so again. I hesitated just now—for another reason."

To the guilty man, his meaning was obvious; and though Stovebridge shrugged his shoulders with affected indifference, his face flushed, and he made no reply.

"Come ahead, fellows, and get ready," Niles broke in briskly. "We've got just ten minutes to start on time."

He took Dick's arm and hustled him through to the dressing room, where he hunted up running trunks, shoes, and shirt; and in less than the allotted time, the Yale man was ready for the contest.

As they came out of the clubhouse and walked over to the track, Merriwell felt a thrill of the old enthusiasm. The well-kept track and the crowd of spectators thronging both sides made his blood course more swiftly and caused his eyes to sparkle.

They went directly to the starting point, where Stovebridge presently joined them. Niles, mounted on a stand, megaphone in hand, waved his arm for silence. When the hub-bub of talk and laughter had ceased he put the instrument to his lips.

"Gentlemen," he declaimed, "I have to announce that Mr. Layton has been detained by a wreck and cannot reach the club this afternoon."

A murmur of disappointment arose from the crowd, which was quickly stilled by another motion from Niles.

"I have, however," he went on, "secured an efficient substitute in the person of Dick Merriwell, of Yale, who has kindly consented to run in order that we shall not be disappointed."

As he jumped to the ground, the quick round of hearty applause, mingled with cheers, showed that Merriwell's name was not unknown. Then the buzz of talk started up again with renewed vigor, as the judges and timekeepers consulted with Niles and arranged the details of the race.

Dick stood a little to one side of the mark, talking to Buckhart, whose face was aglow with enthusiasm.

"Lick the stuffing out of the coyote, pard," urged Brad, in a low tone. "You can sure do it if you try."

"No question of my trying, old fellow," Merriwell smiled. "There's no use in going into a thing unless you do your best! But they seem to think this fellow is pretty good, and you know I'm out of practice."

"That don't worry me a whole lot," the Texan grinned.

"Say, Merriwell, come over here, will you?" Niles called, standing near Stovebridge.

"We'll have to toss for positions," he explained, as Dick walked over to him. "The track is just a mile in circumference, so that you'll have to make one complete circuit, and of course, the fellow on the inside has a little the advantage."

He took a coin out of his pocket and sent it spinning in the air.

"Heads, or tails?"

"Tails," Dick said quickly.

The other caught the coin deftly.

"Heads it is," he grinned. "You lose. Take your places, gentlemen— Stovebridge, inside; Merriwell, out."

Dick toed the mark, and his eyes wandered for an instant down the long line of eagerly watching men. As he did so, he caught sight of the dark, sullen face of Jim Hanlon glaring at him from behind two of the clubmen.

"Still thinks I'm it, by the looks of him," the Yale man said to himself. "I must have a talk with him when this is over."

Then he thrust the fellow out of his mind and crouched for the start. Stovebridge was beside him, vibrant and ready. The two timekeepers stood by the mark, stop watches in hand. Niles stepped back a pace and drew a small revolver from his pocket.

"Are you ready?" he called in a clear voice.

He raised the revolver above his head.

"Set!"

Both runners quivered slightly, as they waited with every muscle tense the moment when they could shoot forward down the track.

The sharp crack of the pistol split the silence, and like a flash both men leaped forward, to the accompaniment of a bellow from the watching crowd, and flew down the stretch of hard, dry cinders.

Merriwell had made the better start and was slightly ahead of the other man. Presently it was seen that this lead was slowly increasing, and the spectators cheered wildly as they observed it, for as a rule they were an impartial lot and believed in shouting for the best man. Besides they were grateful to the stranger for having made the race possible.

Almost imperceptibly this lead increased. In spite of his lack of practice, the Yale man was wonderfully speedy and ran in almost perfect form, and with amazing ease. His body was bent forward but slightly, with his head held up naturally. He threw his legs out well in front with a full easy stride, and brought his feet down squarely, his thighs and knees thrown a little forward. There was absolutely no lost motion. His arms swung easily beside his body, and, with every stride, seemed to help him along.

Stovebridge ran well, but he had a bad trick of swinging his arms back and forth across his body, which retarded him slightly, and moreover, in his haste to finish the stride, he bent his knee somewhat, thus losing a fraction of an inch each time, which would mount up considerably in the course of the mile.

The first quarter of a mile was made by Merriwell in a fraction over a minute—almost sprinting time. Stovebridge was barely two seconds longer. Then both men seemed to settle down to a slightly easier gait, for such speed could not be kept up for the entire distance, and the second quarter took several seconds longer.

The excitement was intense. Men shoved and jostled each other in their eagerness to get a good view; some even ran out onto the track behind the runners. There was no more talking and laughing. A tense silence had fallen upon the crowd as they watched breathlessly.

Suddenly the Yale man was seen to stumble and almost lose his footing. As he recovered his balance with a tremendous effort, Stovebridge shot by him, and a great sigh went up from the crowd.

"He's twisted his ankle!" gasped Jack Niles, his fingers closing on Buckhart's arm with unconscious strength.

The Texan made no reply. His face was set and a little pale.

The next instant Merriwell had recovered himself and flashed on down the track with almost his former speed. To most of the spectators there did not seem to be anything the matter with him, but those who were near enough to see his face, noticed the lines of pain in it, and the great beads of perspiration which stood out on his forehead.

"By Jove, that's plucky!" Niles muttered. "It's the nerviest thing I ever saw."

His keen eye had instantly taken in the situation. In some way the Yale man had strained his ankle, but, instead of giving up the race he was going to fight it out to the finish.

As Merriwell flashed over the three-quarter mile mark, Stovebridge had a good twelve feet lead, but was showing signs of exhaustion. His breath came in gasps, the sweat poured down his face, and his stride was perceptibly shorter.

The Yale man, on the contrary, was in much better condition, except for his left leg, which he seemed trying to favor at each step. It was apparent to everyone, by this time, that he was suffering tortures with every stride, but he showed no signs of giving up. Instead, to the amazement of all, he took a fresh spurt and actually began to gain on his opponent.

Slowly he crept up. Foot by foot the distance between the two was lessened, until at length it was reduced to a yard. But there was not enough time. Already the finish was in sight, and the eager watchers waited in strained silence the end of this amazing race. Could the gamey fellow from Yale possibly make up those three feet in the few seconds which remained? They feared not, for almost without exception, their sympathies were with the man who was now showing such extraordinary pluck.

There was a final spurt on the part of both men, and then, almost in the last stride, Stovebridge flung himself forward with uplifted arms, and breasted the tape a fraction in advance of Dick.

The Clover Club champion had won, but the resulting applause was strangely feeble. There was scarcely a man present who did not realize that Merriwell was the better of the two.

As Dick reeled across the line, he staggered and a spasm of pain flashed into his face.

Jack Niles caught him by the shoulder.

"Quick, Buckhart!" he ripped out in his sharp, decisive tones. "We must get him into the house and look after that ankle. Good nerve, my boy—good nerve!"

Merriwell smiled faintly.

"Well, I lost the race for you, Niles!" he said.

"Lost be hanged!" snapped the other. "You're the gamest piece of work that ever came down the pike. Why the deuce didn't you stop when you twisted your ankle that way?"

"I don't generally give up when I can still go ahead," Dick said quietly.

"Well, you've got that foot of yours into a beautiful condition," Niles went on. "It's beginning to swell already. Here, sit down, while we take you into the house."

He and Buckhart clasped hands and, lifting Merriwell up between them, started slowly back toward the clubhouse, the spectators straggling behind, discussing the result with much interest.

The two fellows carried Dick into the dressing room, where he rested on a chair while they bathed his ankle in cold water and then bandaged it as tightly as they could to keep down the swelling.

"How the mischief did you do it, pard?" Buckhart asked, while this was being done.

"I think I stepped on a small stone," Dick answered "At least it felt like that."

Niles looked up quickly.

"A stone!" he exclaimed. "That's impossible. I walked over the track an hour before the race and it was in perfect condition. It couldn't have been a stone."

"Well, it felt like one," Dick smiled. "I can't swear to it."

Niles turned to one of the men who had acted as timekeepers, and who was helping them with the bandage.

"Say, Johnson, just take a run out to the track and see if you can see anything of a stone, will you?" he asked. "I want to find out about this."

Johnson was back in a few minutes and reported that he could not find even a pebble on the track. He had questioned the dumb fellow, Hanlon, who was raking up near the clubhouse, and found that he had not yet touched anything on the track.

"I must have been mistaken, then," Dick said lightly. "It was just pure carelessness."

He took a shower and then dressed and limped into the reception hall with Buckhart and Niles, who had waited for him.

A group of men were talking in the centre of the room, and Niles stepped aside for a moment to speak to one of them, leaving Merriwell and the Texan standing close beside one of the big windows which opened on the veranda.

Brose Stovebridge was lounging in a wicker chair just outside, and as Dick noticed him he saw a look of eager interest flash into the fellow's eyes, which were turned toward the drive.

A moment later Fred Marston came in sight, walking rapidly along the veranda, and presently stopped beside his friend's chair.

"Well, did you get it?" the latter asked eagerly.

"Sure, I did," returned Marston with a smile.

He pulled a small parcel wrapped in brown paper out of his pocket and handed it to Stovebridge, who almost snatched it out of his hand.

"Ah," he breathed in a tone of relief. "I guess that will settle his hash. He can suspect all he wants——"

He broke off abruptly as he turned his head and looked into Dick Merriwell's cool, slightly smiling eyes. A sudden rush of color flamed into his face, and, with a quick drawn breath, he half rose from his chair.

"What's the matter?" asked Marston.

Then, following the direction of the other's fascinated gaze, he too, saw the Yale man, and scowled fiercely.

"Come in and let's get a drink," he said abruptly. "I need a bracer."

Stovebridge got up a little unsteadily, and the two vanished in the direction of the buffet.

Dick looked significantly at the Texan.

"What do you think of that, Brad?" he asked quietly.

"Huh!" grunted Buckhart contemptuously. "The onery varmit's sure a whole lot shy of you, pard. If he isn't the coyote you're looking for, I'll eat my hat. You hear me gently warble!"

Merriwell gazed thoughtfully out of the window.

"I wonder what was in that package," he mused. "And I wonder too, where this Marston comes in."

"I reckon he's in the same class as Stovebridge," the Texan said emphatically. "I wouldn't trust him as far as I could throw a yearling by the tail."

Jack Niles came up briskly at that moment.

"Well, fellows, let's make ourselves comfortable outdoors," he said. "You don't want to stand on that leg of yours more than you can help for a while, old chap."

"It's feeling pretty comfortable just now," Dick returned, with a smile. "Your bandages are all to the good."

At the same time he was not sorry to sit down in one of the big wicker chairs, soon becoming the centre of a laughing, joking crowd of men, all bent on showing their admiration for the Yale athlete who had given such an exhibition of nerve and pluck as few of them had ever seen.

Merriwell thoroughly enjoyed himself, and was so taken up with the discussion and talk that he had no time to give to the problem which he had set himself to solve. At length, as the afternoon wore on, the fellows began to drop away. One by one, or in parties of two or three, they left the club in motor cars, runabouts, or on horseback, and by six o'clock there were only about a dozen left on the veranda, who were either stopping at the club or taking dinner there.

Then Dick remembered Jim Hanlon, and turned to Buckhart who sat beside him.

"Say, Brad," he said in a low tone. "Do you think you could find that dumb fellow and bring him into the clubhouse? You know I wanted to straighten him out about who ran over the little girl. He seems to have an idea that I did it."

The Texan got up readily.

"Sure thing. He ought to be around somewheres—maybe in the kitchen."

It was ten minutes before he came back with the announcement that Hanlon was not to be found. They had told him in the kitchen that the fellow usually went home at six o'clock.

"Well, it doesn't matter much," Dick said. "I'll probably see him to-morrow."

Very soon afterward they went in to dinner. Niles and two other men joined them, and they made a jolly party around a big table in the middle of the room, which was not so empty after all, quite a number of people having driven out to the club especially to take dinner there. Stovebridge and Marston sat at the same table they had occupied at lunch, and Dick noticed that both seemed to be hitting it up pretty freely.

The evening being a little chilly, they did not return to the veranda after dinner, but made themselves comfortable in the reception hall, where a fire had been lit in the great stone fireplace.

Presently Merriwell remembered that he wanted to call up the Hanlon farm to find out about the little girl, and, on inquiring, found that the telephone was in a small room opening out of the hall.

He had no trouble in getting the number, and Mrs. Hanlon herself came to the telephone. She seemed very much worried and nervous, and told that the doctor had been there almost all the afternoon. The child's arm had been broken and her head badly cut, and, from the symptoms, the physician was afraid that there was some internal trouble.

"Poor little kid!" Dick muttered as he hung up the receiver. "I certainly shall do my best to show up the brute who is responsible for that. He ought to get the maximum penalty, and if she doesn't pull through I shouldn't like to be in his shoes."

He opened a door which led directly outside, and stepped out on the deserted veranda. It was a perfect night, still and rather cool for that time of year, and, as he looked up at the glittering stars, he drew a long breath of pure oxygen.

All at once he heard a stealthy footfall behind him, and, half turning, he caught a glimpse of a crouching figure close upon him.

As he leaped instinctively to one side he felt the impact of a spent blow on his back. Something sharp pricked his skin.

He whirled around swiftly, only to see a shadowy figure leap from the end of the veranda and disappear into the darkness.

# CHAPTER V.

## THE STRUGGLE IN THE DARK.

Like a flash Dick was after him, but as he reached the edge of the veranda, he realized the futility of pursuing the would-be assailant. The fellow, whoever he was, evidently knew the ground thoroughly, and, handicapped as the Yale man was with his bandaged ankle, it would be a waste of time to try and catch him.

He walked slowly back into the light that streamed out through one of the windows, and slipped off his coat.

Just between the shoulders was a clean cut about twelve or fourteen inches long, evidently made by an extremely sharp instrument.

The Yale man gave a low whistle.

"That fellow was out for blood," he murmured. "That's about as close a call as I've ever had. I wonder——"

Putting his hand up to his back, he found that both shirt and undershirt had been cut through, though not so badly, and that there was a tiny cut in the skin just between the shoulder blades.

Thoughtfully he slipped into his coat again.

"That couldn't have been Stovebridge," he mused. "Much as the fellow hates me, I don't believe he would deliberately attempt murder."

He glanced through the window into the reception-hall. Neither the tall athlete nor his friend Marston were in the room.

Dick shook his head slowly.

"Just the same, it wasn't him. It must have been that dumb fellow. He's been looking at me all day as though he would like to knife me, and now he's tried it. I wish I could get hold of him to convince him that he's on the wrong track."

Just now, however, the Yale man was more troubled as to how he could get up to his room and slip into his spare coat without attracting attention by passing through the reception hall. He saw nothing to be gained by letting the clubmen know what had happened. They could do no good now, and Roger Clingwood would be worried to death and tremendously mortified at the thought of such a thing happening to his guest.

He remembered having noticed a small stairway leading from the second floor straight down to an outside door which Clingwood told him opened on the drive at the other end of the house—a door that was occasionally used by members who wanted to go directly to their rooms.

This door might possibly be unlocked. At any rate it was worth trying.

Slipping around the house, he found to his relief that the door yielded to his touch. In a moment he was upstairs, and had taken the coat from his bag and slipped into it. Then he threw the other on a chair and went downstairs again.

No one made any comment on his rather long absence, and presently they all adjourned to the billiard room. Not wanting to tax his ankle, Dick did not play but sat watching the others, and by ten o'clock, he was so sleepy that he could scarcely keep his eyes open.

Niles noticed this as he stood beside the Yale man watching Buckhart run off a string.

"Say, old man, you look as if you were about ready for your downey," he grinned.

Dick smiled.

"I am," he confessed. "Sitting around this way, doing nothing, always sends me off."

"I don't feel any too wide awake myself," the other remarked. "As soon as we finish this game, we'll strap up that ankle of yours, and then all of us can hit the pillow."

The others being of the same mind, they presently put up the cues. The Yale man's ankle was treated with iodine, freshly bandaged, and everyone trouped upstairs.

The entire second floor of the clubhouse was divided into a series of small single rooms opening off a long hall. Most of the club members who stayed there regularly, had quarters on the third floor, where the rooms were larger and where there would be less need to shift around to accommodate a large number of guests.

The Yale men had been assigned four of these rooms nearest the stairs, and there were only two other rooms on that floor occupied, one by Roger Clingwood, who was spending the night there on account of his guests, and the other by a friend of Jack Niles.

Clingwood went before them, switching on the lights in each room, and, having seen that they were provided with everything, he bade them good night.

Bouncer Bigelow betrayed no interest in anything, save his overweening desire to get to bed, and, closing his door at once, he proceeded to disrobe in haste.

Tucker, however, wide awake and lively as usual, skipped into Buckhart's room where Dick had stopped for a minute's talk.

"Well, how does the sleuthing come on?" he chirped, as he dropped down on the bed. "What clues has the great Sherlock Holmes unearthed?"

"Not as many as I'd like, Thomas," Dick smiled. "While I'm morally certain that Stovebridge is the man we're looking for, I can't quite prove it."

Tucker's eyes widened.

"Whew!" he whistled softly. "Stovebridge, eh? The great and only distance runner. Keep it up, Richard. There isn't a man about these parts I'd rather see nailed. He thinks he's just about the warmest baby that ever chased over a cinder path. You ought to have heard him blowing around after the race this afternoon, when anybody with the brains of a hen could see that you were the better man. It made me sick."

Dick smiled. "He won fairly enough; but I would like to know how that stone got on the track—for it was a stone without any doubt."

"Maybe that flabby, rum-soaked friend of his put it there," suggested Tucker seriously. "He's another one I'd like to sock in the jaw."

Merriwell's eyes twinkled as he got up and moved slowly toward the door.

"What's the matter with you, Tommy?" he asked. "Seems to me you're awfully savage to-night."

"It's my nature," Tucker returned plaintively. "I really have the sweetest disposition you ever saw, but there are some men that rile me like a sour gooseberry."

He gave a sigh and dropped back on the bed at full length with the air of one who was comfortably settling himself for a long stay.

"Now, look ahere, little one," Buckhart said firmly, as he beheld these preparations, "you needn't think you're going to settle down there for one of your talk fests. I'm going to bed, and I reckon you'd better hike for your own bunk. You hear me!"

Tucker arose with an injured look on his freckled face.

"I'm thankful I haven't the inhospitable nature of some people," he remarked, as he edged toward the door. "I've heard much about the free, open-handed nature of Westerners, but the only one I ever had the misfortune to get real intimate with, has such a mean, envious, grudging——"

He dodged through the door just ahead of the Texan's shoe, and finished his sentence in the corridor:

"—— unaccommodating disposition, that he must be the exception that proves the rule."

"Go to bed, you little runt," Buckhart grinned. "You sure buzz around worse than a mosquito. Go to bed before I lay violent hands on you."

"Don't you dare put your hands on me," defied Tommy. "I'll chaw you up if you do. You hear me gently——"

The Westerner made a dash at him, and the little fellow skipped into his room and snapped the key.

Dick, who had been watching these proceedings with a smile, now walked down the hall to the room next to Buckhart's and, stepping in, closed the door mechanically behind him.

Then, as he groped for the electric light button, he suddenly remembered that, when he had stepped into Brad's room, he had left his own light turned on. In fact, it had been burning ever since Roger Clingwood had come upstairs with them.

This was rather peculiar. He remembered distinctly that there were two globes, one on each side of the dressing-table; it seemed impossible that they should both burn out at the same time. Some one must have turned the switch. And the annoying part of it was that he did not know where that switch was. He turned to open the hall door and let in a little light from outside, and as he did so he suddenly realized that there was some one else in the room.

Instantly he held his breath and listened. The sound of guarded breathing was unmistakable; some one was there, and, what was even more unpleasant, that some one was between him and the door.

For an instant Dick stood like a statue. Could this be Jack Niles, or one of the other members of the club playing a trick on him? It did not seem likely, and yet who else——

Jim Hanlon!

As the thought flashed suddenly into his brain, it must be confessed that his heart began to beat a little unevenly though the hand which reached out and began to grope along the wall for the switch was perfectly steady.

He must find that button. With the light on, he had not the slightest fear of his assailant, armed though he probably was. But in the pitch darkness of the room the other had an immense advantage of which, the Yale man's experience earlier in the evening warned him, the fellow would not hesitate to avail himself. His fingers searched the wall swiftly, but in vain.

Then a board creaked softly near the door. The man was coming toward him.

Merriwell at once abandoned his search for the switch and turned to face the intruder. His back was toward the wall, and he could not see his hand before his face. There was a little satisfaction in the thought that the other man was probably no better off.

Then the unpleasant recollection came to him of having heard that when a person has lost one or more senses the remaining ones become more keen and powerful. It was possible that this fellow could see in the dark, or at least, distinguish enough to give him a great advantage.

Very softly the stealthy sound came on; the other had apparently removed his shoes and was walking in his stocking feet. The Yale man pictured to himself the attitude the fellow would take. His head and shoulders would be bent in a crouching position, the right hand, holding the knife, extended a little, with the point out. With this in mind, he leaned forward a little himself, his feet braced, both arms outstretched before him, and waited.

It seemed an interminable time before his keen eye saw what seemed to be a shadow looming up not a foot away. Without an instant's hesitation, he plunged forward and made a beautiful flying tackle. As he had hoped, he caught the fellow fairly about the knees and, with a crash which shook the room, they went down together.

Like a flash, Dick twisted around and made a grab for the unknown's right wrist. In the darkness he missed it, but managed to get a grip on the arm just below the elbow.

Then followed a brief but desperate struggle. The fellow writhed and twisted and did his utmost to break away and free the hand which held the knife, but, having once closed with his enemy, Merriwell had little trouble in pinning him down.

He had scarcely done so when the hall door was flung open and Buckhart stood on the threshold, Tucker just behind him.

"Suffering coyotes!" the Texan exclaimed as his eyes fell upon the two men in close embrace on the floor.

Then he pushed the electric light button, which was close beside the door, and the room was flooded with brilliancy.

"Come in, Brad," Dick said quietly, "and close the door."

Buckhart and Tucker both stepped inside, the latter shutting the door after him.

"Kindly relieve this gentleman of his sticker, one of you," came again in Merriwell's even tones.

To hear him, one would never have supposed that he had just been engaged in a struggle for his life.

The fellow clung desperately to the long, keen knife, but the big Texan seized his wrist with a grip of iron, and the next moment the weapon clattered to the floor, being at once secured by Tucker.

Merriwell sprang lightly to his feet, and his assailant followed his example more slowly and stood sullenly eying the three men.

It was Jim Hanlon.

"The miserable snake in the grass!" roared the Texan, his great fists clenched and his eyes flashing fire. "He ought to be thrashed within an inch of his life, and I'm going to do it!"

Dick put a detaining hand on his friend's arm.

"Wait a minute, Brad," he said quietly. "Don't be in such a hurry. This fellow is only doing what he thinks is right. I want to talk to him."

He took a step forward and stood for an instant looking steadily at Hanlon.

"You can understand what I am saying, can't you?" he asked presently.

The other nodded sullenly.

"You came here to-night to kill me because you thought I was the one who ran over your sister?" Dick queried.

The deaf mute made an emphatic gesture of assent, and his black eyes flashed.

Merriwell continued to eye the other steadily.

"I did not do it," he said quietly.

A look of scornful disbelief lit up Hanlon's sombre eyes.

"Listen to me," said Dick slowly, "and I will tell you what happened this morning. My friends and I were driving to the club from Wilton. At the curve we saw something in the road, and stopped. When I got out I found that it was a little girl, unconscious and bleeding from a great gash in her forehead. I carried her into the farmhouse and found that she belonged there. She was not dead at the time, but badly hurt, and the doctor was sent for at once——"

He stopped abruptly. The dumb youth was searching frantically in his pocket for something; his mouth was trembling and his eyes filled with a wild eagerness.

Dick stepped over to a small desk and took out a sheet of paper, marked with the club letterhead, which he handed to Hanlon.

"Is that what you want?" he asked quietly.

The fellow snatched it from him and, turning to the dressing table, rested it on the polished surface while he scrawled a brief sentence. Then he thrust the paper into Dick's hands.

"Not killed—is that true?"

The Yale man looked up from the paper.

"Perfectly true," he said. "She is alive now. I telephoned to Mrs. Hanlon this evening and found that she was alive, though in a very critical condition."

The other took the paper and wrote again.

"Will she die?"

"I don't know," Merriwell said simply, as he read the question.

Jim Hanlon seemed to be in an agony of indecision. His hands clenched and unclenched and the slender, brown fingers twitching nervously. All the time his glittering black eyes were fixed fiercely on the Yale man's face as if he were trying to plumb the depths of the other's soul and read his very thoughts. Finally he reached out, took the paper from Merriwell's hand, scrawled a sentence and gave it back again.

"If you didn't run over her, who did?" was what Dick read.

As he raised his eyes again to Hanlon's face, the Yale man felt a thrill of pity go through him at the thought of what this fellow must be suffering. He had also a distinct feeling of admiration for the manner in which the mute was persevering in the face of all obstacles in his search for the man who had been responsible for his little sister's injuries.

Whether Dick approved of the other's primitive method of taking the law into his own hands was another matter. Though the Yale man's temper was under perfect control, it was still alive, and there had been a time when he might have done just what this dumb boy was trying to do. It was not strange, then, that there should be a certain bond of sympathy between the two.

"I am not sure," he said, handing the paper back to Hanlon. "I have been trying all day to find out."

The other wrote hastily and returned the scrawl.

"Who do you think it is?"

Merriwell hesitated. The ferocity had quite gone from the boy's face, and its place been taken by a look of intense pleading. The Yale man wondered whether it would be right for him to give voice to his suspicions. And yet, they were more than mere suspicions. In his mind there was no doubt whatever that Stovebridge was the guilty man, but the difficulty was to get absolute proof.

As he watched the play of emotions on the mobile face of the lad before him, a sudden thought leaped into Dick's brain which made his eyes sparkle and brought a half smile to his lips. What a solution that would be—to make this fellow whom Stovebridge had fooled and played with the means of bringing the clubman to justice!

"I think it is Stovebridge," he said aloud; "but I am not sure. I want you to find out the truth. Can you read the lip talk at a distance—say at fifty feet?"

Hanlon nodded emphatically.

"Good! Well, this is what I want you to do. Stovebridge and this Marston are great pals, and I believe Marston knows all about the accident. They are likely to talk it over to-morrow—probably on the veranda; for Marston always sits there. Of course, they would not talk loud enough for any one sitting near them to hear, but they would never suspect you, if you were out raking the drive. Yet you could read their lips and understand. You get my meaning?"

There was a look of admiration in the boy's eyes as he nodded.

"You've sure got a head on your shoulders, pard," the big Texan said enthusiastically. "That's a jim dandy scheme."

Dick only smiled and looked at Hanlon.

"I will fix it so that you will be put to work on the drive in the morning," he said. "And you know what to do. If they say enough to betray themselves, write it down and come to me with it. I'll do the rest."

The dumb fellow nodded emphatically. The dark eyes were full of a keen intelligence as he looked at the Yale man.

"Well, I think that's about all we've got to say to-night," the latter remarked, after a thoughtful pause. "It's pretty late, and you'd better be getting home."

Still the other hesitated, and a flush slowly mounted into his tanned face. Then he took the paper and wrote two words on it.

"I'm sorry."

Merriwell smiled a little.

"Oh, that's all right," he said quietly. "You thought you were doing the right thing."

He opened the door and stepped out into the hall, the fellow following him. They went down the narrow flight of stairs to the door which opened onto the drive—a door that Dick found had been left unlocked. With a brief gesture of farewell, the dumb man vanished into the darkness. Merriwell turned the key and came back to his room, a look of satisfaction on his face.

# CHAPTER VI.

## DICK MERRIWELL WINS.

About ten o'clock next morning Brose Stovebridge and his friend Marston were sitting together in the latter's favorite corner of the Clover Club veranda.

Considering the crowd of the day before, the place seemed deserted. One man, absorbed in the morning paper, lounged at the far end of the veranda, and a foursome was just teeing off on the links across the drive; but otherwise there was no one in sight.

Presently the deaf mute, shouldering a rake, came around the corner of the house and began to rake up the roadway.

Fred Marston yawned.

"Deuced dull this morning," he drawled.

"Little early yet for any one to be around," Stovebridge returned absently.

He was dressed much as he had been the day before, except that he wore a cloth cap of medium black and white check, obviously new.

"Cap worked to a charm, didn't it?" Marston remarked after a moment's pause. "I saw Merriwell taking it in when we drove up, and it stumped him, all right. He'd be surprised to learn that I bought it yesterday afternoon."

"Yes, it's got him guessing all right," the other answered. "He may suspect what he likes, but he can't prove anything on me now."

Despite the athlete's assumption of nonchalance, there was an underlying note of anxiety in his voice which Marston seemed to notice.

"What's the matter with you, anyway?" he asked in a peevish tone. "You ought to be chipper as a lark, and yet I swear you've got something on your mind."

Stovebridge glanced quickly around, but there was no one within hearing distance.

"I can't help worrying about the girl," he said in a low voice. "I heard this morning that the doctor was there all night. They're afraid of internal complications."

"That's too bad, of course," Marston remarked, without any particular feeling in his voice. "But I wouldn't lose any sleep over it. You're safe, no matter what happens."

"But if she should die, there'll be a rigid investigation," Stovebridge said slowly. "You can't tell what they might unearth. The idea makes me cursed nervous."

"For goodness' sake, don't borrow trouble!" the other said sharply. "If you keep on going around with that long face some one will begin to smell a rat. All you've got to do is to sit tight and say nothing. They can't prove anything on you if you only throw a good bluff."

Neither of them gave a thought to the dumb youth who was raking the drive some forty feet away. But had Stovebridge seen the ferocious glare in the dark eyes which were furtively watching him, he would have been more than disturbed—he would have been seriously alarmed.

Marston yawned again and stretched himself lazily.

"Wish somebody would come around so we could get up a little poker game," he remarked. "This sitting here doing nothing is deadly dull."

Stovebridge arose to his feet with sudden resolution.

"Get your clubs and let's go around the nine hole course," he suggested. "It will do you good."

"No thanks," Marston drawled. "I never by any chance enjoy doing the things that are good for me, and you know I hate golf. Toddle along, Brose, and I'll wait here until somebody comes around that has a sensible idea of amusement."

Stovebridge shrugged his shoulders resignedly.

"Well, I'll have to do it alone, then," he said as he started for the dressing room for his clubs.

When he returned, a few minutes later, Jim Hanlon had disappeared.

"Aren't you going to take a caddy?" Marston inquired as his friend crossed the drive to the first tee.

"No; I've only got a few clubs. I can manage without one."

Marston watched him drive off with a tolerant smile, and when Stovebridge had disappeared over a knoll, he got up and lounged through the reception hall to the buffet.

Stovebridge was not playing in good form at all. He drove wretchedly, his brassy shots were impossible, and even his putting worse than he had ever known it to be before. Consequently by the time he had holed in at the fifth green with a score greater by fourteen than ever before, he was in a furious rage and cursed the clubs, the balls, the course—everything but himself.

With an effort he pulled himself together and made a fair drive from the fifth tee. The course was rather winding and along one side was a thick wood, which had been left quite untouched when the links were laid out.

As he followed the ball he saw that the wind had taken it close to the trees, if not in amongst them, and he cursed fiercely again.

When he came up, however, he found that it lay about six feet from the edge of the wood, and, with an exclamation of satisfaction, he took his cleek out of the bag and swung it once or twice over his shoulder.

His back was toward the trees, and he did not see the figure which crept stealthily out of the underbrush.

The next instant there was a rush behind him, something struck him on the back, and, taken by surprise, the clubman lost his footing and fell, with Jim Hanlon on top of him, clutching his windpipe with all the strength in his slim, muscular fingers.

After the first, momentary shock of surprise, Stovebridge struggled desperately, finally succeeding in tearing the choking fingers from his throat and struggling to his feet. For a moment he stood silent, his breath coming in gasps and his eyes full of a great fear, as he faced the crouching figure before him.

Then, without warning, the clubman snatched up the iron-headed cleek and, springing forward, struck the other a terrific blow over the head.

Hanlon reeled and collapsed in a silent heap on the ground, blood smearing his forehead.

For a full minute Stovebridge stood as if turned to stone. His face was white as chalk, as he gazed in horror-stricken fascination at the silent thing before him.

Then he passed one shaking hand across his forehead in a dazed manner.

"What have I done?" he muttered in a strange voice. "What have I done?"

His eyes traveled slowly to the blood-stained cleek, and with a shudder he hurled it from him into the woods.

"I've killed him!" he gasped hoarsely. "What shall I do? Where shall I go?"

Suddenly he raised his head and listened intently. Was that the sound of voices coming from behind the hill yonder? They must not find him here. He must fly somewhere—anywhere to get away from that horror on the ground whose ghastly half-closed eyes seemed to be watching him.

In a panic of fear he snatched up his golf bag and, without a backward glance, sprang into the woods and disappeared.

Presently the crashing of the flying man through the undergrowth died away and all was still. A gray squirrel poked his head out of the bushes and, sighting the huddled heap, fled with chatterings of alarm. Then came the distant sound of talk and laughter from beyond the hill, and the next moment a small, white sphere came sailing through the air and landed with a thud on the turf close to the body of Jim Hanlon.

It was as though the thing had roused him, for with a low moan he stirred uneasily and opened his eyes.

Following the thud of running feet, some one knelt beside him and raised his head, and the half-conscious boy found himself gazing into Dick Merriwell's eyes, full of compassion and concern.

"Who did it, Jim?" he asked quickly.

Then he suddenly remembered.

"Was it Stovebridge?" he questioned eagerly.

Hanlon nodded weakly.

"Which way did he go?"

The dumb boy shook his head.

"You don't know?" Dick said disappointedly. "Did you find out anything? Is he the one who ran over Amy?"

Hanlon nodded, and his eyes took on a faint gleam of rage.

"What's happened?" asked Jack Niles as he hurried up.

Then he saw the boy's face.

"By Jove!" he exclaimed. "Somebody hit him! What cur would do a thing like that?"

The Yale man looked up at him, and his dark eyes were cold and icy.

"Our friend Stovebridge is the man," he said in a tense voice.

"What?" Niles cried in utter amazement. "Stovebridge! The cowardly hound! But what reason——"

"I rather think it was because Hanlon found that Stovebridge was the man who ran over his sister," Dick explained quietly. "They must have had an altercation, and this is the result."

Overcome with amazement, Jack Niles listened to Merriwell's brief explanation; and when the Yale man had finished the other's face was dark with rage. Roger Clingwood had come up with Buckhart and Tucker in time to hear it.

"The scoundrel!" he exclaimed. "I'll have him run out of the club for this."

"Out of the club and into jail!" supplemented Niles fiercely. "The child may die at any moment, I hear."

"The thing is to catch him," Clingwood said anxiously. "No doubt after this, he's run away."

Jim Hanlon staggered to his feet with Dick supporting him.

"I think I can catch him," the Yale man said quietly. "Look after Hanlon, will you, Brad."

Buckhart stepped over and took the dumb boy's arm, and without a word Merriwell turned and sprang into the woods, Niles following close at his heels.

Almost at once he found the bloody cleek and, a few feet farther on, came upon the bag of golf sticks, which Stovebridge had thrown aside in his haste. Then, with what seemed to Niles almost superhuman skill, the Yale man picked up the trail of the fleeing scoundrel, and followed it on a run. His lame ankle was forgotten; he betrayed not the slightest limp.

To one of Dick's training, trailing was a comparatively easy matter in the woods, where broken twigs, bruised leaves, and bent branches of the bushes marked the way clearly. But when they emerged from among the trees to the close cropped sward of the links again, he scarcely lessened his speed. It seemed as though he knew almost by intuition which way the man had gone.

Very soon Niles fell behind. For all of his condition he was beginning to be winded, while his companion showed no signs whatever of even hurried breathing.

Rapidly the distance between them increased as Merriwell forged ahead, and presently he vanished over a high knoll, leaving Niles to plod on alone, gasping and breathless, but determined not to give up.

At last he reached the summit and there he paused with an exclamation of satisfaction.

A perfectly straight stretch of green was spread out before him. It was over a mile in length, and by far the longest hole of the course. Though there were several slight undulations, it was for the most part quite level, being broken here and there with grassy bunkers placed to make the hole more difficult.

About half way down the stretch a party of golfers had stopped their play and were staring in astonishment at the strange sight of two young fellows tearing over the grass as hard as they could run. The one in advance was Stovebridge, who ran desperately as though his life depended on it. His face was white and set, his breathing labored, his eyes full of a great fear.

A hundred yards behind him Dick Merriwell was covering the ground at an amazing speed. Apparently unhampered by golfing clothes or bandaged ankle, he ran lightly and easily as though on the cinder track. It seemed to the excited Niles on the hill top that he almost skimmed over the ground like a bird.

"Jove, what running!" he cried aloud. "Oh, I wish I had a watch! I never saw anything like it on the track. There can't be eighty yards between them now; he's gained twenty in a couple of minutes. Stove must be getting winded. There! What a jump! He took that bunker like a bird. Stove had to climb over it. What a hurdler he must be! Another five yards gained."

For a moment he stood silent, shading his eyes with his hand.

"Another bunker!" he cried presently. "Merriwell is a perfect wonder. He's as fresh as when he started. Great Scott! I never saw anything like this in all my life."

Niles was fairly jumping up and down in his frenzied excitement.

"Go it! go it!" he cried. "Stove's all in. Only fifteen yards more. Why didn't I bring a watch? He's making a record! Go it, Dick! Ten yards more —eight! Oh, why isn't there somebody else here to see this! He's got him! He's got him!"

Fairly shrieking out the last words, Jack Niles plunged down the slope, his arms waving like an erratic windmill, and ran toward the two men who stood together at the far end of the course. One, cool and fresh, his breath coming a little unevenly, stood with his hand on the shoulder of the other, who was exhausted to the verge of collapse, breathing with great gulping gasps, unable to get enough air into his lungs. His whole frame trembled, and his guilty eyes, unwilling to meet the stern, accusing ones of the man before him, were fixed upon the ground.

# CHAPTER VII.

## THE BRAND OF FEAR.

It was not a lively party that approached the clubhouse half an hour later. Merriwell had turned his captive over to Roger Clingwood and Jack Niles, and was devoting his attention to the dumb boy, who had so far recovered as to be able to walk with very little assistance.

Brose Stovebridge looked like another man. With dragging feet and eyes fixed on the ground, he was the picture of guilt as he slouched along between the two other clubmen. Roger Clingwood's eyes, wearing a mingled expression of anger and humiliation, were set straight ahead, as though he could not bring himself to look at the fellow who had so disgraced his club. The homely, honest features of the other man, showed only a fierce contempt. Behind them straggled the curious party of golfers who had witnessed that extraordinary race.

As they approached the veranda, a tall, well-built fellow with bronzed face and pleasant gray eyes, stepped forward from the group assembled by the door.

"Hello, Niles," he said, holding out his hand. "Awfully sorry I disappointed you yesterday, but it couldn't be helped. I'm ready to run your champion to-day, though."

"Glad to see you, Layton," Niles said warmly. "I don't know——"

Roger Clingwood's cold, cutting voice interrupted him:

"We have no champion, Mr. Layton. Mr. Stovebridge will soon be no longer a member of the club."

A gasp of astonishment went up from the listening members, and a feeling of utter desolation and despair swept over Stovebridge, who turned his back swiftly on the veranda.

"And if he were a member," supplemented Niles, "he would no longer be champion. Dick Merriwell holds that honor at present. I have no doubt he will race you any time you wish."

A look of pleased surprise flashed into Layton's face as he caught sight of Dick for the first time, and, stepping forward quickly, he took the Yale man's hand.

"Awfully glad to see you, old fellow," he said warmly.

Then he turned to Niles.

"A race between us would be pretty much of a farce," he smiled. "Apparently you don't know him as well as I do. If there's one fellow I'll pull my colors to, it's Merriwell of Yale."

Roger Clingwood stepped forward and touched Niles' arm.

"Take him upstairs and lock him in the end bedroom while I telephone the police," he said in a low tone. "Much as I loathe the fellow, there's no reason why he should be put to needless humiliation."

With the disappearance of the two into the clubhouse, a perfect Bedlam of eager, breathless questions were flung at the other men of the party, and, as the story was briefly told, exclamations of amazement, contempt and scorn arose on every side. Some of the men were even incredulous. It did not seem possible that the dashing, debonair Stovebridge, one of the most popular of their number, and the best all-around athlete in the club, could have been guilty of such behavior; but they were at length convinced, and Roger Clingwood was urged to lose no time in summoning an officer to take him into custody.

As Brose Stovebridge crossed the threshold of the bedroom, his self-control snapped like a broken thread and he flung himself face downward on the bed, uttering a gasping cry of despair. Lying there, shaken with dry, racking sobs, he thought of the little child whose life had been the penalty of his recklessness. There was no doubt in his mind that she had died, and for the first time in his life the thought of his own troubles was swallowed up in the agony of that greater wrong he had done another.

Jack Niles gazed down at the man who had once been his friend, and his first feeling of infinite contempt gradually changed to pity. The man was suffering—suffering keenly; and Niles did not like to see any one suffer.

"Brace up, Stove," he said roughly, but with kindly intent. "Take your medicine like a man. There's no use crying over spilt milk."

A shiver went through the other's frame.

"It's spilt—blood—I'm thinking about," came in muffled gasps.

Suddenly he sprang to his feet and faced Niles. His eyes were full of unutterable despair; there were traces of tears on his cheeks, his hands clenched and unclenched ceaselessly.

"You won't believe me, Jack," he said in a strange, unnatural voice, "but I'm not thinking about myself, I don't care what they do to me. It's the idea of that little child, dead—killed by my own hand as surely as though I had shot her through the heart—that's driving me mad."

Niles opened his lips to speak and then closed them again. It was not up to him to tell Stovebridge that, so far as he knew, the child was not dead. She might have died that morning—they had been expecting it all night—and it would be cruel to raise any false hopes.

So he muttered a few rough words of sympathy and, closing the door, locked it on the outside.

His heart sank as he walked out on the veranda and saw the rugged face of little Amy's father. The child must be dead, and he was telling Clingwood the sad news. He pressed up to the two.

"An' so he says there ain't any more fear of her dyin'," the man was concluding. "She'll be all right as soon as thet arm o' hers gits well."

"Splendid!" exclaimed Clingwood, his eyes brightening. "I can't tell you how glad I am."

Niles had heard enough. The child was not likely to die, and he hurried over to Dick Merriwell.

"Say, Dick," he began hesitatingly, "Stove is pretty near crazy up there with the idea that he has killed the little girl. Now, Hanlon says she's going to get well after all. Don't you think you ought to tell Brose? He's given up thinking about himself and says he don't care what they do to him; but he's just about wild with remorse. I hate to think of a fellow suffering the way he is."

The Yale man hesitated for an instant, and then his face cleared.

"Why, yes, I'll tell him," he said readily. "If he were only thinking of the consequences to himself, it would serve him right to be kept guessing; but, as it is, that would only be needless cruelty."

He turned quickly and disappeared into the house.

Upstairs, Brose Stovebridge was pacing up and down the room in a frenzied manner. His eyes were wild and his brown hands trembled as he lifted them now and then in an aimless fashion to his ghastly, set face.

"A murderer!" he muttered, in a strained voice. "Twice a murderer! I never thought of it in that light the other time."

He stopped in front of the mirror and gazed fixedly at the reflection of his strangely altered face.

"What are you made of?" he whispered hoarsely—"what can you be made of to do the things you've done and not to care? Is there no soul, no conscience—nothing to make you care?"

He turned away from the glass, laughing harshly.

"Nothing there—nothing but a horrible face!"

Then fear seemed to grip him and drive remorse away.

"They've sent for the police!" he gasped wildly. "They'll be here soon and drag me away. The jail, a barred cell, the courtroom full of scornful, grinning faces that were once my friends! And then—and then—perhaps, the electric chair!"

His voice sank to a vibrant whisper, and at the last words he caught at his collar like one choking.

"I can't stand it!" he muttered. "I'm—afraid!"

Suddenly he stood erect and listened. Some one was coming upstairs. He crouched by the window, his white face turned breathlessly toward the door. Now they were coming down the hall. Another moment the key would turn, the door would open, and they would drag him away to prison. He shuddered.

"I can't stand it," he muttered—"I won't stand it!"

Summoning all his resolution, he slipped through the window and hung by both hands. As the key clicked in the lock, he dropped to the ground, staggered, regained his footing with an effort, and then ran across the drive toward the automobile sheds.

He did not see Dick Merriwell's head appear at the window and then quickly disappear. He did not know that he was flying from his own salvation. His one desperate thought was to get away.

He reached his car and, cranking the engine with feverish haste, sprang into the seat and swiftly backed her out. With a sharp turn, he went through the gears with a rush and started the car out of the club grounds at top speed.

As he dashed by the end of the veranda a yell arose:

"Stop him! Stop him!"

Several men ran out, waving their arms, but it was of no avail. He disappeared down the drive like a streak of light.

Merriwell, Niles and several others ran back for their cars to give chase; and as the fellow with the homely face and honest eyes bent to crank his engine, he shook his head seriously.

"He's crazy," he muttered to himself—"clean daffy. If something don't happen pretty quick, I miss my guess."

It was a long, long time before the jolly, happy-go-lucky Niles could thrust out of his mind the picture of that face—set, strained, and ghastly white, the eyes wide open and glittering with a strange light, the colorless lips parted over the clenched teeth. It was a face which bore the brand of fear; the face of one going to destruction.

Stovebridge whirled out of the club gates into the highroad, skidding, barely missing the ditch; but he did not pull down the speed a hair. Down the road he went, a blurred streak of red. He must get away. He would not be caught.

Presently he turned onto a narrower road which led over the hills into the more unsettled country. He knew they would follow him, and he meant to give them a long chase.

The road wound up hill and down dale, through farming country and wheat fields, with now and then a stretch of woods or meadow land. Once he flashed past a farmhouse where a woman stood drawing water from an old well, and as she caught a fleeting glimpse of his face, she gave a cry of horror and gazed after the thick cloud of dust, her hand lifted to her heart. The brand of fear was very plain.

On went the car like a flying monster. The man was pushing her to the utmost, and she responded nobly. They were nearing the river which he meant to cross by an old, unfrequented bridge close beside a deserted mill. He would fool them all, for few knew of the crossing which cut off several miles on the way to the wilder country beyond. He had not been that way himself in many months, but he knew it perfectly.

Up a steep hill he flew on the high, flashed over the level summit, and began the rough, winding descent. He was driving recklessly, but with splendid skill. A little grove of trees blurred past, and then he reached the river bank.

Too late he saw that he had blundered.

The bridge was gone!

Following a grinding shock of the emergency, the car shot through the frail protecting timbers at the brink, and, for one brief, awful instant, seemed to hover in the air above the river.

With a tremendous splash, it struck the water and sank beneath.

By some strange freak of chance, Stovebridge had been flung free of the entangling car, and presently, dazed by the shock, he struggled to the surface and strove to reach the shore.

But the current was very swift, and something seemed to drag him down. Still he struggled frantically. He must reach it. He did not want to drown. He was afraid to die, as he had been afraid of many things in life.

His arms grew numb and his legs seemed to have no feeling left. If he could only loosen the weight which dragged him down! It was as though hands were clutching him and pulling him slowly but inexorably below the surface.

Finally into his numbed brain came the thought that they were really hands—the hands of the child! Ah, well, it was only justice that the weak fingers of the little one he had murdered should have grown strong enough to draw him to his destruction.

He was tired. If he could only give up and cease to try. But he did not want to face the child down in the deep, cold river. The water washed over his face and he struggled weakly to raise his head, but could not. In his ears there was a distant roaring which grew louder and louder. The dragging hands were very heavy. Why not stop battling and let it go? Life was not worth the effort. His arms dropped feebly and a sense of infinite rest and peace stole over him.

The roaring ceased.

# CHAPTER VIII.

## THE YOUNG MAN IN TROUBLE.

When Dick and his friends left the Clover County Club, to continue their trip, Forest Hills was their next scheduled stopping place.

"Try the Burlington," said Roger Clingwood, as he bade the party good-by; "the restaurant is the best in the place."

Following Clingwood's advice Dick and his friends had gone at once to the Burlington, and after removing the stains of travel, sought the dining room.

As the head waiter spied them, he conducted them to a round table near one of the open windows and drew out the chairs with a flourish.

As soon as they were seated, Tucker reached for the menu.

"Well, let's get this struggle over with," he remarked, as he ran his eye down it. "I eat from a sense of duty. Hotels must be supported. Mere grub is repugnant to me, but I have to go through the motions."

Buckhart looked at Dick and lowered one eyelid.

"Catch on to his order, pard," he murmured.

At that moment the waiter approached with pad and pencil.

"What are you going to have, Tommy?" Dick asked. "Don't torture yourself too severely."

The little fellow's brows were knitted in deep thought.

"H'm! A little *consommé* to start with, I think. That ought to taste pretty good on a warm day like this. Then—let me see. A *filet mignon* sounds right. Potatoes come with it, I suppose?"

"Yes, sir," nodded the waiter.

"Lima beans and green corn will do for the other vegetables. Follow that with a lettuce salad; and, for dessert, sliced peaches with a portion of vanilla ice cream. That's about all, except that I want a pot of coffee with cream brought with the filet."

He sat back in his chair and unfolded his napkin with an air of much satisfaction.

"Looks like you got a rake off from the management," the Texan grinned.

"Aren't you the real clever thing to guess it," returned Tucker. "How else do you suppose I make expenses? These hotel proprietors are only too glad to give a little bonus to a good-looking chap like me. Gives tone to the establishment, you know."

Merriwell gave his order and then, sitting back, glanced casually around the room. It was well-filled with the usual crowd of business men, among whom were a few ladies in light summer dresses, and a pleasant air of refinement pervaded the establishment.

Presently Dick noticed a party of three young fellows who were lunching at a table in the centre of the room. One of them faced him—a pleasant-looking, well set up man of about twenty-two, with clean-cut features and curly, brown hair; and, as the Yale man glanced at him, he hastily averted his eyes as if he had been staring.

"I suppose there isn't any chance of going through the mine this afternoon," Dick remarked, turning back to his friends. "Clingwood said the morning was the best time. We can put in the rest of the day looking the town over, and after dinner I'll hunt up the superintendent, Orren Fairchilds, and give him that card of introduction."

"I think I'll take a rest," yawned Bigelow. "The roads were awful this morning. I'm black and blue all over from being jounced around."

"Hear him talk!" jeered Tucker. "He's so packed with blubber, you'd have to jab something into him a good two inches before he could feel it."

Dick glanced over at the other table again and met the curly haired fellow's eyes fixed squarely on him. One of his companions had half turned and was also regarding the Yale man intently.

"They're certainly going to know me the next time they see me," he thought. "I wonder if I have ever met them before."

He decided that he had not. Endowed with an extraordinary memory, he never forgot a face, and those two were totally strange.

The next moment he was surprised to see the brown-haired man rise from his table and come across the room toward him.

"I beg your pardon," he said, pausing beside Dick's chair; "but isn't your name Merriwell—Dick Merriwell?"

There was a slightly puzzled look on Dick's face.

"It is," he answered. "But I don't remember——"

"No, of course you don't," the other interrupted with an embarrassed smile. "You've never laid eyes on me before; but I've seen Merriwell pitch several times, and the minute you came into the room I was sure you were he."

He hesitated for an instant, and Dick waited quietly for him to continue.

"I'm the captain of the Field Club nine here in Forest Hills," the tall fellow went on presently. "Our big game—the game of the season—is scheduled for to-morrow, and our battery is beastly weak, especially Morrison, the pitcher. I thought—I wondered whether it would be possible for you to come out to the grounds this afternoon and give us a pointer or two. I—I know I've got nerve, but that game means a lot to us. My name is Gardiner —Glen Gardiner."

Merriwell's heart warmed to this frank, pleasant-voiced young fellow, who was so obviously embarrassed at the favor he had ventured to ask; and, as Gardiner finished speaking, the Yale man rose quickly to his feet and held out his hand.

"I'm very glad to meet you, Mr. Gardiner," he said heartily. "You're not nervy at all. I shall be delighted to help you in any way I can. We were just wondering how we could put in the afternoon. I'd like you to meet my friends, Brad Buckhart, Tommy Tucker, and Bouncer Bigelow."

Gardiner's face glowed with pleasure as he shook the Texan's hand.

"I've seen Mr. Buckhart before," he said quickly; "and I'm very happy to meet you all. You have no idea, Mr. Merriwell, how much I'll appreciate your coming out and coaching us."

"Better wait until you've seen how I can coach before you thank me," Dick smiled. "Won't you bring your friends over and lunch with us? There's room enough at this table, and we can get some more chairs."

"Thank you very much, but we've just finished," Gardiner said. "I know they'd be awfully pleased, though, to sit here while you eat yours."

He went back to his own table and returned with the two men, whom he introduced as Ralph Maxwell and Stanley Garrick. The former played short-stop on the nine and was short and wiry, with red hair and freckles. He was not unlike Tucker in looks and manner, and the two took to each other at once. Garrick, who played second, was tall and rather ungainly, with a no-ticeable deliberation of speech and manner. To the casual observer, he seemed slow and clumsy, but on the diamond he was anything but that.

They were both delighted to meet the Yale men, and, drawing up some chairs, made themselves comfortable while the latter began on the luncheon which had just appeared.

"Who is it you play to-morrow?" Dick asked, as he took up his knife and fork.

"The Mispah team—the mine boys," exclaimed Gardiner. "They've got a crackajack nine this year and have licked everything they've been up against, so far. We have a pretty good organization ourselves, and we've won every game we've played. So you can see that it will be a hard fight from start to finish. If we win, we'll hold the state championship."

Dick nodded.

"I see; but how does it come that these mine fellows are so good? They don't generally amount to much at scientific baseball."

"It's on account of Orren Fairchilds, one of the mine owners," Gardiner answered. "Perhaps you've heard of him?"

"Yes, I have. But I didn't know he was one of the owners. I thought he was the superintendent."

"He's both. He also happens to be one of the greatest baseball enthusiasts in the country. Before he went into mining, he played on one of the big-league teams, and he's still a crank over the game. He got together the most promising of the young fellows in the mine and practically taught them the game from start to finish—spent months coaching each man separately and the whole nine together. He hardly ate or slept during that time, and, as a result, he's got a crowd that he boasts can lick anything in the country outside the big leagues."

"He must be all to the good," Dick said, smiling. "He's a man after my own heart, and I shall be much interested in meeting him to-night."

"You have an appointment?" queried Gardiner.

"No; a card of introduction from a mutual friend," Merriwell returned. "We are anxious to go through the mine to-morrow, if possible."

"You'd better be at his house before seven to-night, then," Gardiner said. "He has dinner at half-past six, and the minute he's through he goes up to the diamond he's laid out near the mine, where the boys practice until dark."

"Much obliged for the advice," Dick smiled. "I'll be there on the dot; for our only reason for coming to Forest Hills was to see the mine."

# CHAPTER IX.

## A DISGRUNTLED PITCHER.

"What seems to be the matter with this pitcher of yours?" Merriwell asked a little later.

"Poor control," Gardiner answered briefly. "He's got excellent curves, but he's wild. Some days he is fine, especially if we have things our own way from the start. But let the other side get a few hits off him to begin with, and he seems to go all to pieces."

Dick took out his pocketbook, and selecting a bill, handed it to the waiter.

"That's a bad fault," he commented. "Curves are no earthly use unless a man can control them. Does he use his head?"

Gardiner hesitated a moment.

"Well—sometimes," he said slowly. "I hate to knock a man, especially a fellow I don't like, but you can't very well help us much unless you know all about him. Morrison's great trouble is a case of abnormally swelled head. Up to a month ago we had another pitcher we could fall back on. He didn't have many fancy stunts, but he was steady, and in the long run he made a better record than Morrison. But he had to leave town, and since then Edgar seems to have the idea that he's the whole team and that we can't get along without him. He's a great masher, and when he's on the slab he spends more time thinking how he can make a hit with the girls in the grand stand than in preventing the batters from making a hit in the box. We've had several run-ins on that account, but there's no reasoning with a fellow like that. I freely confess that, personally, I don't like him; but I hope that fact hasn't made me unfair."

He looked questioningly at Ralph Maxwell.

"It hasn't," the latter declared quickly. "You haven't been hard enough on him. The fellow doesn't make any pretense at training. There's hardly a night that he isn't to be found at Dolan's Café on Front Street. I don't mean that he gets jagged, but he certainly drinks and smokes a lot there; and you can't tell me that a fellow can play good ball when he spends his time that way."

Dick picked up his change from the silver tray the waiter had just laid in front of him, and they all arose and started for the door.

"You're up against a hard proposition," said Merriwell. "It's always difficult to do anything with a man like that. They usually resent advice and never by any chance follow it. How is your catcher?"

"Fine!" declared Gardiner enthusiastically. "Burgess is a great pal of Morrison, but he's all to the good. More than once he has pulled Edgar out of a hole and saved the day."

"A good catcher is worth his weight in gold," Merriwell said, with a side-long glance at Buckhart, who appeared deaf.

"Let's go out this way," he went on. "I thought we would use the car this afternoon, so I left it at the side entrance."

As they went down the steps, Maxwell and Garrick started to walk away.

"See you on the field," the former called back.

"Hold on," Dick said quickly. "Aren't you going right over there?"

"Yes; but——"

"Well, come along with us, then," the Yale man invited, as he slipped in the coil plug. "There's room enough for everybody, if you don't mind crowding."

The two fellows came back and squeezed into the tonneau with Tucker and Bigelow, who had given up his idea of taking a nap. Dick cranked the engine and took his seat at the wheel, Gardiner beside him. The Texan sat on the side of the car with his feet hanging out.

The Field Club was situated in the residential part of town and covered a good deal of ground. Besides the diamond, there was a good nine-hole golf course, excellent tennis courts, and a simple, attractive and well-arranged clubhouse. This last was built at one side of the diamond, so that the club members could enjoy the game from the wide veranda, which completely surrounded the house, quite as well as the spectators in the grand stand.

Under Gardiner's direction, Dick drove the *Wizard* through the entrance and up to the veranda, where a number of young fellows in baseball suits were congregated.

"Hello, Glen," one of them called out, as the party came up the steps. "We'd about given you up. Thought you were lost, or something."

"It's about time you showed up," another said rather sharply. "Practice ought to have begun half an hour ago. I've got a date at five o'clock, which I propose to keep."

He was a tall, dark, rather good-looking fellow, who was evidently quite aware of the fact, and as he spoke his full, red lips were curved in a slight sneer.

Gardiner flushed a little at the other's tone, but otherwise paid no attention to it.

"I know that, Morrison," he said pleasantly; "but I guess we can make up the lost time. Fellows, I want you to meet Dick Merriwell, the famous Yale pitcher, who has been so good as to say he'd coach us a little for the game to-morrow."

A suspicious gleam flashed into Morrison's eyes as he extended a languid hand.

"Glad to meet you," he drawled. "Merriwell, did you say? You go to Yale, do you?"

This assumption of ignorance was affectation, pure and simple. The Forest Hills pitcher knew perfectly well who Dick Merriwell was, but he thought it might irritate the Yale man if he pretended never to have heard of him.

It had, however, no such effect.

"Yes, I happen to," Dick said good-naturedly, as he shook the fellow's hand, and turned to meet the other men.

"You fellows go ahead and start practice," Gardiner said, when the introductions were complete. "I'll slip into my clothes and be with you in half a jiffy."

He disappeared into the clubhouse, and the others left the veranda and walked out to the diamond. Merriwell was chatting with the catcher, George Burgess, a short, stout heavily built fellow with a good-humored face and small, twinkling eyes.

"Gardiner tells me you're up against a hard proposition to-morrow," the Yale man remarked.

"Yes, the mine boys are a tough crowd to beat," Burgess returned. "But I guess we can do it."

He slipped his mask on and began to buckle his chest protector.

"Let's see how your wing is to-day, Edgar," he called. "One of you fellows stand up here and be struck out. You're all ready, Art. Come ahead."

Arthur Dean, a well-built, muscular fellow who played third, picked up a bat and walked over to the plate.

Morrison went into the pitcher's box, a sullen look on his face.

"I like that fellow Merriwell's nerve, butting in this way," he muttered. "I suppose that fresh Gardiner thinks I need coaching. Well, he won't show me very much."

He tried an outshoot, and was chagrined when it missed the pan by a good foot and Burgess had to stir himself to get it.

"Wild, Morrie—wild," the stout fellow said, as he tossed the ball back.

Morrison bit his lips. The next ball was high. It held no speed, but it passed so far above Dean's head that Burgess was forced to stretch his arms at full length in order to pull it down.

He shook his head as he snapped it back.

Then the pitcher sent a speedy one straight over the pan, and Dean cracked out a clean single toward right field.

Gardiner appeared in time to see this performance, and, though he said nothing, his face wore an anxious frown.

"I think I'll get out where I can see his delivery better," Dick said, as the captain approached.

"I wish you would," Gardiner returned in a low voice. "He's pretty wild, isn't he?"

Merriwell nodded and walked out on the diamond, taking a position behind Morrison, who had just received the ball from the field.

"Now, Reddy, get up to the plate and see what you can do," Gardiner directed. "See if you can't strike him out, Morrie."

"He can't do it," grinned Maxwell, taking a firm grip on his bat. "Bet you can't fan me, Edgar, old boy."

Morrison flushed a little as he toed the plate, his eyes fixed on Burgess.

The catcher signaled for an incurve, and the next moment Maxwell dodged back to avoid being hit by the ball.

"I don't want a present of the base, thank you," he laughed. "Try again, Morrie."

Morrison scowled and whipped a swift shoot, which was entirely too high. The following two balls were equally wild, and the red-headed chap tossed his bat to the ground with a grin.

"Told you that you couldn't," he said triumphantly.

The lanky Garrick took his place, and, after giving him three balls, the pitcher sent one straight over the pan, which Garrick promptly swung at and laced out a hot two-bagger.

"What's the matter with you, Morrison?" Gardiner said sharply. "What's the good of curves if you can't get them over? You've got to take a brace pretty soon, or we might as well make the Mispahs a present of the game."

The pitcher's face darkened and he controlled himself with an effort.

"There's no use killing yourself at practice," he said, with affected nonchalance. "I'll be all right in the game."

"I shouldn't like to bank on it," Gardiner retorted, with some heat. "I could mention a few games in which you were decidedly *not* all right. The trouble with you is that half the time your mind isn't on what you're doing. A fellow can't pitch and think about something else at the same time."

Morrison flushed hotly.

"You don't say so!" he sneered. "Perhaps you'd like your Yale friend to show me how it's done. That's what you brought him here for, isn't it?"

Gardiner's chin squared.

"I asked him here to coach us all," he said quietly. "So far, you seem to be the one to need it the most."

Morrison's eyes flashed and he wheeled suddenly and faced Dick, who was standing behind him.

"Perhaps you'll be so kind as to give us an exhibition of your skill," he said ironically, in a voice which trembled with suppressed anger. "You pitch, I believe?"

"Occasionally," Merriwell returned carelessly; "but I doubt whether I can be of any assistance to you. Your curves and speed seem to be all right. A man can only acquire good control by constant practice and unremitting attention to the game."

The ball came bounding across the diamond from the field, and leaning over, Morrison scooped it up and tossed it to the Yale man.

"Sounds good," he sneered. "Just show us a few."

He folded his arms, an ugly look on his face, and stepped back, while Dick took off his coat and rolled up his right sleeve, exposing an arm of such perfect development that even the man whose place he had taken could not suppress a feeling of envious admiration.

Gardiner picked up a bat and stepped to the plate; the catcher crouched and gave a signal, which Dick recognized as the call for a drop. As the ball left Merriwell's fingers, it seemed that it would pass above the first baseman's shoulders. Too late the latter saw it take a sudden downward shoot and plunk into the catcher's big mitt.

"Gee! that's a dandy," Gardiner exclaimed, as Burgess tossed the ball back.

The next one was a beautiful outcurve which cut the corner of the plate, though the batter had not thought it possible for the ball to pass over any part of the pan. He planted his feet firmly, a little frown on his face. Though he knew Merriwell was giving Morrison an object lesson, he did not propose to be fanned by the Yale man if he could help it.

Dick placed his feet and rose on his toes for a moment. Backward he swung, poised upon one pin, his left foot lifted high above the ground. Forward he threw his body with a broad, sharp swing of his arm, and the ball came sizzling over the inside corner of the rubber, Gardiner missing cleanly.

A murmur of astonishment and admiration went up from the little group which stood near the plate. To have their heaviest hitter struck out by the first three balls pitched was something the members of the Forest Hills nine had never expected to see. Gardiner threw down his bat with a little grimace of disgust.

"That's some pitching," he said. "I haven't had that happen to me in many moons. Now, Edgar, suppose you see what you can do."

But Morrison was walking rapidly toward him from the pitcher's box, his hands clenched and his face dark.

"You can't make a monkey out of me," he snarled. "I'm through."

Gardiner looked at him in amazement.

"Do you mean you won't pitch to-morrow?" he asked.

"Neither to-morrow nor any other day," snapped Morrison. "Nothing would hire me to pitch on this team after the dirty trick you've played bringing a fellow in to make a show of me. Think I'm a fool?"

Gardiner flushed hotly.

"Nobody could make a fool of you," he said, with sarcastic emphasis. "You seem to have been born that way."

The angry man disdained any reply.

"Any of my friends will have to choose now between Gardiner and me," he went on furiously. "If they prefer playing on his team, well and good; but at that moment they cease to be my friends. Understand?"

He cast a significant glance at George Burgess, and, turning on his heel, walked rapidly toward the clubhouse.

Burgess hesitated for an instant and, with a shrug of his shoulders, slowly unbuckled his chest protector and threw it on the ground, together with his mask and mitt. Then he followed Morrison.

The flush had died out of Gardiner's face, leaving it a little pale. His eyes traveled slowly over the faces of the remaining men.

"Well," he said quietly, "any more?"

Unconsciously, perhaps, he looked at Roland Hewett, the centre fielder, a slim, fastidious fellow with thin, blond hair and pale blue eyes, whom he knew was another friend of the deserting pitcher. There was a worried, undecided look on his weak face.

"I don't know——" he stammered. "I—I believe I'll go and see if he really meant what he said."

Then he, too, left the group on the diamond and presently disappeared into the clubhouse.

For a moment no one spoke. Then Reddy Maxwell broke the silence.

"Well, fellows," he said, with forced cheerfulness, "I should say that the team is better off without a bunch that will desert it at a time like this."

"But how the deuce are we going to fill their places?" Irving Renworth, the right fielder, asked apprehensively.

"By Jove, fellows. I'm sorry!" Gardiner broke in contritely. "It's all my fault. I shouldn't have talked that way to Morrison, knowing how touchy he is."

"Oh, cut that, Glen," Maxwell said quickly. "It would take a wooden man to stand Morrie's nasty, sneering way without answering back. I'm glad he's gone, though I am surprised at Burgess backing him up."

"Yes, don't worry, Glen," Garrick said in his deliberate manner. "It wasn't your fault. We'll have to make the best of it, and look around for some one else."

The captain ran his fingers despairingly through his thick brown hair.

"We can fill Hewett's place all right, and we might find a catcher," he groaned. "But how in the world do you expect to get hold of a pitcher in less than twenty-four hours, when I've tried in vain to do that very thing ever since Smith left us a month ago?"

A hand clapped him on the back, and the big Texan's hearty voice sounded in his ears.

"Brace up, bucko! You don't seem to be wise to the fact that you've got a battery complete right on the ground; and, in the field, Tucker can knock spots out of that quitter. You hear me gently warble!"

Gardiner turned swiftly as though he could scarcely believe his senses.

"What?" he exclaimed. "You mean that you would——"

"That's sure what I'm trying to express," Buckhart grinned. "Seeing as we're someways responsible for that bunch going on strike, it'll only square things up if we take their places. How about it, pard?"

"Of course, we'll play," Dick said quickly, "if they want us to."

A sudden smile flashed into the first baseman's face.

"Want you!" he cried. "Well, I guess yes! Only I should never have dared suggest such a thing. Talk about luck! Why, this is the best thing that could have happened. We'll give the mine boys the surprise of their lives, and a minute ago I was thinking of throwing up the game. Gee! I can hardly believe it's true."

Dick looked at his watch.

"We've got a couple of hours yet which we may as well put in practicing a little, don't you think?" he remarked. "That is, if you can supply us with togs."

"Sure thing," Gardiner returned. "Come in to the house and I'll fit you fellows out."

It was amazing how quickly the anxious, worried looks on the faces of the Forest Hills boys were replaced by grins of joy, as they realized their good luck. A few minutes later they were dashing about the field after flies, scooping up hot liners, or taking turns at the bat with an enthusiasm and vim which was a marked contrast to the demeanor they had displayed earlier in the afternoon.

Merriwell became so interested in the practice that he delayed longer than he had intended. The result was that he had barely time for a hasty shower in the dressing rooms of the club, which was followed by a dash back to the hotel where he swallowed his dinner at a speed which was ruinous to his digestion. Even at that, it lacked only five minutes of seven when the turned into the drive and stopped the *Wizard* at the entrance of Orren Fairchilds' costly and beautiful residence, in the most exclusive section of Forest Hills.

"Doesn't look much like the home of a man who cares for nothing but business and baseball," he thought, as he ran up the marble steps and pushed the electric button.

The door was promptly opened by an impressive butler, who ushered the Yale man into the drawing room.

"Mr. Fairchilds is at dinner," he announced, "but he will be through directly."

Dick took out the card on which Roger Clingwood had written simply, "Introducing Richard Merriwell, of Yale," and handed it to the man.

"Will you give this to him when he has finished," he requested.

"Very good, sir," returned the butler. "Will you be seated, sir."

He took the card and disappeared, while Merriwell dropped into a chair and glanced around the great room, which was furnished richly, but in perfect taste.

The next moment some curtains at the other end were thrust violently aside and a man entered hurriedly.

"Dick Merriwell, as I live!" he exclaimed, advancing with outstretched hand. "You haven't changed a particle since I saw you twirl years ago at New Haven. Jove, that was a game! My boy, I'm very glad to meet you."

He was short and slim, with a brisk manner and springy walk. His thin hair and heavier moustache were slightly tinged with gray; nevertheless he certainly was not much over thirty-seven or eight, and with his healthy brown skin and alert, twinkling brown eyes, he did not appear even that. Dick took an instant liking for him as he shook his hand heartily.

"I hope I haven't interrupted your dinner," he said. "They told me you had it early."

"Not at all, not at all," returned the mine owner briskly. "I do have it early. I always make a point of attending the evening practice of my team. Have you seen Clingwood lately? I haven't laid eyes on him in over a year. Does he still play golf?"

Merriwell smiled at the half-contemptuous tone in which he brought out the last word.

"Yes, he's an enthusiast. Says there is no game like it."

"Bah!" snorted Fairchilds. "An old woman's game. That's the only fault I have to find with Clingwood—he doesn't like baseball. How any sane, healthy man can stand up and say he isn't interested in the greatest game on earth—the only game, to my mind, that's worth the time and trouble that's spent on it—I can't understand."

"I hear you've got a great team up at the mine," Dick remarked.

The little man's eyes sparkled.

"We have—a dandy team," he said enthusiastically. "They've wiped up the diamond with everything they've met this year, and to-morrow I expect them to win the game of the season with the Field Club nine. Of course, you'll be on hand for that?"

Merriwell nodded with a smile. He expected to be very much on hand.

"Say, why can't you come up to the field with me now and watch the boys practice?" the mine owner said suddenly. "You'll see some work that will surprise you, considering that six months ago the boys knew very little about the game. Come along; my car's waiting outside now."

He rose quickly to his feet.

"I think I'd better not, Mr. Fairchilds," Dick returned quietly, as he faced him. "You see, I've promised to pitch for the Forest Hills team to-morrow."

The sharp little eyes of the older man fairly bulged out with surprise.

"You've what?" he exclaimed.

"I've promised to pitch for the Field Club fellows," the Yale man smiled. "Morrison, their pitcher, and his friend, George Burgess, left the team in a huff this afternoon. Gardiner asked me to come out and give Morrison a few points, and the fellow, getting mad at what he was pleased to call my interference, quit, taking the catcher with him. Naturally, having been, in a way, responsible, I volunteered to take his place, and my chum will catch."

The mine owner dropped back upon his chair.

"Well, I'll be jiggered!" he exclaimed.

"I hope you don't disapprove," Dick said quickly.

"Disapprove! No, of course not. It will make the game all the more interesting. I never did like that fellow, Morrison, and he can't pitch for sour apples. But I must get up and tell the boys about this. We'll have to get in all the practice we can to-night. I don't feel quite so cocksure of winning as I did a few moments ago."

He stood up quickly and started for the door, the Yale man at his side. In the hall he took his hat from the butler, and then stopped suddenly and looked at Dick.

"I reckon my wife must be right," he said, his eyes twinkling. "She says I haven't got an idea in my head but baseball. Here I'm running off without ever asking you what I could do for you. You must have had a reason for coming."

Merriwell smiled.

"I did have a favor to ask," he said. "I am very anxious to go through the mine with three friends, if it's possible."

"Why, certainly," the older man returned briskly. "Delighted to have you. Come up to the offices to-morrow about nine, and you'll find me there. Will that time suit you?"

"Perfectly," Dick answered. "And I'm sorry to have taken so much of your time to-night."

The mine owner laughed.

"I'm right glad you did," he said, as they went down the steps. "You've given me some valuable information."

He paused and looked at Dick shrewdly.

"I only wish I'd seen you pitch inside of two years. I expect you've developed a lot of new tricks in that time."

"Oh, I don't know," the Yale man smiled.

Orren Fairchilds sprang into a big gray car which stood near the steps, while Dick hurried forward to get the *Wizard* out of the way. He sprang into his seat and started the engine, which was still warm, and as he did so, he heard the voice of the older man behind him.

"Just the same, my boy, don't think you've got a cinch, to-morrow. Good night."

"Good night," Merriwell called back.

The *Wizard* shot down the drive and into the street, with the gray car close behind. Dick waved his hand in response to a salute from the other man, who turned in the opposite direction and quickly disappeared. Merriwell drove slowly back toward the hotel.

He was much taken with the enthusiastic mine owner, whose simple, straightforward manner was a pleasant contrast to the airs affected by some wealthy men he had met.

"You'd never imagine, to look at him, that he was burdened with over-much coin," the Yale man thought. "Yet Gardiner says that he and his brother are sole owners of the mine, and must have four or five million a piece. He certainly is a baseball crank, and yet I should think it would be great fun, if a fellow had plenty of money, to see how good a team you could make out of ordinary material."

The Fairchilds' place was situated at the extreme limits of the city, and, as Merriwell passed through the residential section, he drove slowly in order to observe some of the houses and well-kept grounds along the street.

Suddenly he heard a stifled cry from the sidewalk, causing him to swerve in toward the curb and slow down to a crawl. The next moment he saw a young girl trying to free herself from the grasp of a man, and instantly he jammed on the brake and sprang out of the car.

"Let me go!" cried the girl. "Take your hands off me!"

Her face was flushed and her eyes wide with fright as she strove to shake the fellow's hand from her arm. Then she caught sight of Dick.

"Oh!" she exclaimed quickly. "I'm so frightened. Won't you please make him go away."

Almost before the words were out of her mouth, the Yale man sprang forward and, catching the man's wrist in a grip of iron, tore it from the girl's arm and sent him reeling against the fence.

Then, to his amazement, he recognized the scowling face of Edgar Morrison, the Field Club pitcher.

"Curse you!" snarled the fellow, advancing with a threatening gesture. "Butting in again, are you? I'll teach you to mind your own business!"

Dick laughed lightly.

"Come right along." he said quietly. "I'm always ready to learn, even from a cur like you."

With a furious oath, Morrison lunged forward and attempted to hit Merriwell; but his blow was parried, and he received a return punch that sent him reeling.

Uttering a frightened cry, the girl turned and fled down the street.

Morrison was back at Dick in an instant, fairly foaming with rage. He had quite a reputation in Forest Hills as a fist-fighter, and when he kept his head he could put up a good, scientific scrap. The Yale man found no difficulty, however, in parrying his furious, savage lunges, and presently he got in a straight uppercut on the fellow's chin which sent him to the ground with a crash.

Dick stood over the man, waiting for him to rise.

"Anything more you'd like to teach me?" he asked quietly, as Morrison staggered to his feet and stood swaying, one hand lifted to his chin.

For a moment the other did not speak. Though his ardor for fighting seemed to have cooled considerably, his rage was apparently unabated, and mingled with it there was a look of unutterable hate in the fierce dark eyes, which were fixed on the contemptuous face of the Yale man.

"Not here—not now," he muttered. "But I'll teach you a lesson some day that you won't forget in a hurry, curse you! I'll get even with you yet."

With a shrug of his shoulder, Dick walked over to the car.

"You'll have to be quick about it," he said, as he took his seat at the wheel. "I don't propose spending much more time in this town of yours."

He started to let in the clutch, and then suddenly half turned in his seat, looking Morrison straight in the eyes.

"One thing more," he said in a low, cold tone, which held a decidedly threatening undercurrent. "If I catch you annoying that girl again, or any other woman, I'll take great pleasure handing you another bunch of fives. Understand?"

# CHAPTER X.

## IN DOLAN'S CAFÉ.

Morrison watched the car disappear down the street, and clenching his fist, shook it fiercely in the air.

"I'll get even with you yet, you meddling fool!" he rasped.

He took out his handkerchief and pressed it to his bleeding chin. It was not a bad cut, but the humiliation, of being knocked down in a public thoroughfare by almost the first blow struck, ate into his very soul and made him grind his teeth in a blind, bitter rage.

To have suffered at the hands of Dick Merriwell added fuel to the blaze of his resentment. The happenings of that afternoon had made him hate the Yale man almost as much as he did Gardiner, whom he had always disliked, but he had come out of that affair with flying colors. He had crippled the Forest Hills team so that they would stand no show whatever against the mine boys; likely they would have to forfeit the game for it would be impossible for them to find both pitcher and catcher at so short a notice and his heart rejoiced at having evened up his score with Gardiner at last.

But on the heels of that triumph came this new disgrace, the very thought of which made him clench his teeth and long fiercely to have that Yale upstart at his mercy, somewhere, somehow, so that he could pound the fellow until his arms were tired.

He had no desire to stand up against Merriwell in a fair fight. Wild with rage as he had been, Morrison realized that the Yale man had enough science to handle him with one hand. But he would give almost everything he possessed to get even with Merriwell in some perfectly safe way, which carried no risk with it. Of that sort of stuff was the former pitcher of the Forest Hills team.

He was aroused by the sound of footsteps and, glancing up, saw several men coming toward him. He did not linger, but hurrying to the near-by corner, dodged into a side street, and made his way swiftly to the car lines on Woodland Avenue.

Swinging himself on the rear end of an open car, he sat down in the shadow. He had intended going directly to Dolan's Café for a bracer, but just before the car reached that corner the colored lights of a drug store caught his eyes, and, leaping off, he went inside.

Here he got some court-plaster which he applied to the cut on his chin, explaining to the clerk that he had fallen and struck his face on the curbing. That done, he started for Dolan's.

Almost at the threshold he came face to face with George Burgess and Roland Hewett, who greeted him warmly.

"We've been looking all over for you, Morrie," the former said quickly. "Where the mischief have you been?"

"Oh, up street a ways," Morrison returned vaguely. "Let's go in."

They pushed through the swinging doors, passing the bar, and went on into a large room beyond, which was the distinguishing feature of Dolan's.

The place was long and lofty, with walls and floor of marble, and was filled with little tables, set around with heavy mission chairs. It was brightly lit with many electric clusters which brought out in their full crudity the gaudy decorations and flashy pictures.

But to the cheap sport of Forest Hills, there was nothing gaudy about it. It represented to him the very acme of luxury, and night after night he would spend the evening there, with others of his kind, in talk and loud-mouthed bragging, smoking cigarettes and stretching to the utmost limit the time allowance of a five-cent glass of beer.

For some vague, inscrutable reason he thought that this was manly. He never seemed to realize what a poor fool he was to waste his short leisure hours in that foul atmosphere, poisoning his lungs, his stomach, and his mind at the same time. He never seemed to know that a man is not valued for his ability to smoke and drink, but for what he is—for what he has done that is worth while and uplifting in this world.

The three fellows sat down at one of the tables, and Morrison touched the bell.

"What's the matter with your chin, Morrie?" Hewett asked curiously, as he settled himself in his chair.

The dark-haired fellow raised his hand carelessly to the court-plaster.

"Oh, that, you mean?" he asked nonchalantly. "I cut myself shaving."

The waiter appeared.

"What'll you have, fellows?" Morrison went on. "I'm going to take a rye high ball."

"Beer for me."

The other two spoke together.

Burgess took a box of cigarettes from his pocket and passed them around. They all lit up, and presently the drinks were brought and set down before them.

"Have you heard the latest?" Burgess inquired, exhaling a cloud of smoke.

"What latest?" asked Morrison.

"Why, about the team. It didn't take Gardiner long to fill out places."

As Morrison put his glass down on the table, his hand trembled a little.

"What do you mean?" he asked slowly.

Burgess gave a short laugh.

"He's got Merriwell to pitch, and that fellow Buckhart to catch."

"What?" exploded Morrison.

His face had paled a little and he looked as if he could not believe his senses.

"Yes, that's straight goods," Burgess assured. "He's even filled Hewett's place with Tucker, another of that crowd, who, I understand, has played short on the varsity nine. Not bad for a pick-up, is it?"

For a moment the former pitcher of the Forest Hills seemed unable to utter a word. His face purpled and his eyes flashed with rage. The veins on his forehead stood out like cords.

Suddenly he burst out in such a frenzied volley of cursing that his two companions looked at him in astonishment.

"Say, Morrie, ease up a bit," cautioned Burgess. "Pretty quick we'll be thrown out of here."

"Yes, what's the use of losing your temper that way," put in Hewett nervously. "The thing's done, and it can't be helped now."

Morrison glared at him.

"Who wouldn't lose his temper?" he frothed. "You would, if you had a little more red blood in your veins. It's enough to drive a man crazy to have this upstart from Yale step in and get all the credit after I've pitched the whole season and done all the hard work."

"Now, look here, Morrie," George Burgess said sharply, "there's no sense in cussing Merriwell that way. He's no more to blame than I am. After you had stepped out it was only decent for him to volunteer to take your place, especially when Gardiner's bringing him out to the field started the whole row."

Morrison took a gulp from his high ball and set down the glass with such violence that some of the liquid slopped over on the table.

"Oh, so you're going back on me, are you?" he sneered. "Maybe you'd like to boot-lick Gardiner and get back on the team."

The stout fellow flushed a little and a dangerous look came into his small eyes.

"That will about do for you," he said in a tone of suppressed anger. "You know I'm no quitter."

Several men entered the room at that moment, and, as Morrison's eyes fell on one of them, he calmed down suddenly.

"There's Bill McDonough," he said in a low tone.

Burgess nodded.

"So I see. I wonder what he's doing here. Old Fairchilds is daffy about close training."

The man to whom they referred seated himself at a table near them and ordered vichy. Apparently one of his companions joked him about the drink, for he grinned broadly, showing a gaping hole in his upper jaw where two front teeth were missing.

"You betcher life it won't be that ter-morrow night," he said loudly. "After we've wiped up the ground with them dudes, training is broke, and it's me for the beer can. Gee! I wisht I could have a schooner ter-night. I got a thirst a yard long."

He was a big, burly, rough-looking fellow, with a bull neck and amazingly long arms. A jagged scar, running from the edge of his close-cropped, stubby hair almost to the corner of his hard mouth, gave a sinister expression to his unattractive face. It was not the face of a man one would care about encountering in a lonely place on a dark night.

While McDonough did not exactly live up to his tough appearance, there were yet vague stories afloat concerning him which were not the most creditable. Nothing had ever been proved against him, but where there's smoke, there is usually some fire; and there was a general impression in Forest Hills that Bill McDonough would allow few things to stand between him and the accomplishment of a purpose.

He was one of the foremen at the Mispah Mine, the acknowledged leader of the mine boys, and the star pitcher on Orren Fairchilds' baseball team.

There was a speculative look in Morrison's dark eyes as he watched the fellow drink his vichy at a gulp and then call for more.

Then a sudden idea flashed into his mind, and he leaned toward his two companions.

"Say, fellows," he whispered, "I've a good mind to call Bill over and tell him about this business of Merriwell's pitching to-morrow."

Burgess frowned a bit.

"What good will that do?" he asked.

Morrison hesitated for an instant.

"Well," he said significantly, "you know Bill's reputation. If he should pick a fight with Merriwell, or do something equally effective, Gardiner would be minus a pitcher."

The stout fellow leaned back in his chair and surveyed his friend curiously.

"Sometimes you're one too many for me, Morrie," he said slowly. "Where do you get these ideas, anyhow? Would you really think of doing a thing like that?"

Morrison looked a little annoyed.

"You're too finicky altogether, George," he returned. "I shouldn't be doing anything out of the way by simply telling McDonough that this Merriwell is going to take my place in the box to-morrow."

"Oh, you know well enough what I mean," Burgess retorted. "What's your object in telling him? Because you hope Bill will do something dirty to prevent Merriwell's playing."

"I don't see anything out of the way about it," put in Hewett. "It would be an easy way of getting even."

The stout chap looked at him contemptuously through narrowed lids.

"Quite your style, isn't it?" he inquired.

Then he turned to Morrison.

"Go ahead and tell him if you're set on it," he said shortly. "But I wash my hands of the business. I refuse to be mixed up in it."

He got up from the table, and, without further words, walked to the door and disappeared.

"George is amusing when he throws one of those virtuous bluffs," he said sarcastically.

He glanced over at the other table.

"Say, Bill—McDonough," he called.

The big fellow looked around quickly.

"Oh, hello, Morrison," he bellowed. "How's things?"

"Come over here a minute, will you? I want to talk to you."

"Sure, Mike."

McDonough arose and, stepping over to the chair Burgess had just vacated, plumped himself down.

"Well, what's up?" he inquired, with a grin.

"What'll you have—vichy?"

"Sure. I could drink gallons of the stuff without quenching my thirst."

Morrison beckoned to a waiter and ordered a siphon of vichy, then he leaned forward with his elbows on the table and surveyed the hulking giant before him.

"I just wanted to give you a little point about the game to-morrow," he said significantly. "Do you know who's going to pitch?"

"Sure," grinned McDonough. "Some guy from Yale College."

Morrison's jaw dropped.

"Who told you?" he gasped in astonishment.

"Why, the old man. Who else do you s'pose would?"

"The old man!" Morrison exclaimed in bewilderment. "Fairchilds, you mean? How the deuce did he find out?"

"Give it up. Told us to-night when he come up for practice."

Morrison was silent for a moment.

"You take it pretty calmly," he said presently, a morose scowl on his face.

"Why shouldn't I?" demanded McDonough. "The old man said he was a crackajack, but I guess he won't get much on yours truly."

Morrison threw back his head and laughed, long and loud.

"Say, you're pretty cocky, Bill, aren't you?" he inquired. "I suppose you think there isn't a man living that can strike you out. Did you know that this Merriwell is the best amateur pitcher and all-around baseball player in the country. The managers of the big-league teams have had their eyes on him ever since he entered Yale. He could get any price he wanted this minute, if he'd go into professional ball. Why, you'll be easy fruit. He'll make pie of you and your whole team. There won't be any pieces left to pick up. He'll make a holy show of you to-morrow unless——"

He hesitated, his eyes fixed curiously on the big man's face, which during that short speech had mirrored a variety of emotions that were passing through the man's mind. Incredulity, surprise, amazement, uneasiness, and consternation flitted rapidly across it and finally gave place to a sinister look of rage which was not prepossessing.

"Say, what yer giving us?" he said hoarsely.

"The truth," Morrison returned simply. "He's all I said he was, and more."

Taking out his cigarette case, he selected a cigarette, passing the case to Hewett. Lighting up, he leaned back in his chair, his eyes fixed keenly on McDonough's face.

The big man was staring absently at the table, his heavy brows drawn together in a black scowl. With one square, callous forefinger he traced a pattern with some vichy which had spilled on the polished surface. All at once he raised his head and looked fixedly at Morrison, who gave a slight start at the expression he saw in those sullen orbs.

"Unless—what?" demanded McDonough in a suppressed tone.

Morrison hesitated.

"Unless—well, there're plenty of ways to stop a man from playing baseball," he finished lightly.

For a full minute the two looked at each other in silence. It seemed that something was passing from one mind to the other. Then the big fellow arose slowly to his feet.

"Much obliged," he said shortly.

Without another word he returned to his table, and a moment later Morrison and Hewett passed out through the bar and into the street.

"I—think—I'll go home," stammered the latter. "It's getting late."

His weak face was a little pale and his hands shook nervously.

"Well, so-long, Hew," his companion said carelessly. "See you at the game to-morrow."

Left alone, he strolled aimlessly down the street until he came to the entrance of the Burlington Hotel. There he hesitated for a few moments and finally went up the steps and into the lobby.

As he did so he gave a sudden start. Across the room, seated sidewise on a big leather sofa, was Dick Merriwell. His back was toward the entrance and he was deep in conversation with some one whose face Morrison could not distinguish.

The sofa was one of those large double ones with a high back between the two seats, and, almost without realizing why he did it, Morrison walked softly across the lobby, and sat down on the other side with an air of affected carelessness.

Merriwell was talking, and Morrison could distinguish the words quite plainly.

"You never saw such a baseball crank in your life. I don't believe he thinks of anything else out of business hours. He says if we come up to the mine at nine to-morrow he'll have us shown all around."

Morrison gave a start and his dark eyes gleamed.

"The mine!" he muttered to himself. "They're going through the mine to-morrow, and McDonough's foreman on the lower level. What a chance!"

Without stopping to hear more, he sprang up and went hurriedly into the writing room, where he sat down at a small table and drew a sheet of the hotel paper from the rack.

First carefully tearing off the heading, he picked up a pen and wrote rapidly. Then he looked around for a blotter, but there was none in sight.

"Where the deuce do they keep the things?" he muttered angrily.

Finally he jerked open a drawer and found a stack of new ones inside. He snatched up one of them and carefully blotted the scrawl. Then he folded the note and put it in his pocket.

"I must get a plain envelope at the stationer's," he murmured, "and then find a boy to take it to Dolan's before Bill gets away. I rather think you may have an interesting time at the mine to-morrow, my friend."

As Morrison peered out into the lobby, he was dismayed to find that Merriwell and his friend Buckhart had left the sofa and were talking to the clerk at the desk. His first instinctive impulse was to dodge back into the writing room. Then he gave a muttered exclamation.

"Pshaw! What a loon I am! I've got as much right in this hotel as he has, and he'll never know what I came here for."

Squaring his shoulders, he stalked toward the entrance, with eyes averted from the desk, and disappeared into the darkness.

"There goes your friend, the pitcher, pard," Buckhart grinned. "Wonder what that varmint's doing here."

Dick shrugged his shoulders as he turned away from the desk.

"Give it up, Brad," he said carelessly. "I don't know that I care very much. I want to write a letter to Frank. Will you wait for me, or join Tommy and Bouncer upstairs?"

The big Texan yawned.

"Sure, I'll wait," he said. "Might as well scrawl off a note myself, since I've got the chance."

They went into the writing room, and each sat down at a small table. Taking a sheet of paper from the rack, Dick wrote rapidly for several minutes. He was telling Frank what they had been doing for the past few days, and, when he had finished that, he stopped to think out their itinerary for the next week.

"Let's see," he murmured meditatively. "We'll stay here over Sunday, and start Monday morning. By Monday night we ought to be in——"

He stopped, his eyes fixed curiously on the oblong, white blotter which lay before him.

"That's funny," he said slowly.

The Texan looked up from his letter.

"What is?"

Dick did not answer at once. He picked up the blotter and scrutinized it closely. It was a fresh one and apparently had been used but once. Evidently some one had written a short note in a heavy, scrawly hand with a stub pen, and blotted it in haste. What had attracted the Yale man's attention was his own name reversed, which appeared almost at the top of the blotter.

"This is very interesting," he said at length. "Somebody seems to have been taking my name in vain, and I'm a little curious to see what the connection is."

He pushed back his chair and stood up, the blotter in one hand. Over the mantel at the other end of the room was a long mirror, and walking across to it, Dick held the blotter up to the glass. Buckhart had also risen and was looking at the reflection over his friend's shoulder.

"Merriwell," deciphered Dick slowly; "mine—to-morrow—your chance—miss—want to put—business—pitch."

The Yale pitcher turned and eyed his friend quizzically.

"This is decidedly interesting," he remarked. "Even more so than I expected. There's some more words in between the others that are not very clear, but perhaps we can make something out of them. Get a sheet of paper and a pencil, will you, Brad?"

The Texan made haste to bring paper and pencil, and, laying the former on the mantel shelf, Dick studied the blotter carefully again. Presently he wrote something on the paper and turned again to the blotter.

He kept this up for ten or fifteen minutes in silence, and at the end of that time he picked up the paper and carried it back to one of the desks.

"That's about all I can make out," he said, as he sat down and spread the sheet out before him. "Draw up a chair and let's see how it reads."

The Texan pulled a chair up, and they bent their heads over the desk.

What they saw was fairly clear. A few letters were missing, but not enough to destroy the sense of the letter.

"Merriwell wi—be—mine to-morrow—ni— —— ock. —his—s your chance. —nt miss it—yo— want to put hi— —ut of business so—e —an — pitch —— nst —ou."

"That's as plain as daylight," Dick said, with satisfaction. "Put in the few letters which are missing, and it will read like this:

"'Merriwell will be at the mine to-morrow at nine o'clock. This is your chance. Don't miss it, if you want to put him out of business so he cannot pitch against you.'

"That's really the most interesting epistle I've read in a long time, old fellow," Merriwell went on. "Short, and to the point. No address, no signature. The plot thickens, Bradley, my boy."

"It sure does, pard—a-plenty," growled the Westerner. "I'd like to know the onery varmint that wrote it. I'd make him a whole lot shy about repeating the performance. You hear me softly warble!"

"I'd rather know who it was written to," Dick said meditatively. "Then I'd know who to look out for."

He looked at Buckhart with a sudden gleam in his eyes.

"Did you notice where Morrison came from when he went through the lobby a little while ago?" he asked slowly.

The Texan brought his clenched fist down on the desk with a crash that made the pens and inkwells bounce.

"By the great horn spoon!" he exploded. "He came out of this very room. The miserable snake in the grass! He ought to be tarred and feathered, only that's a heap too good for the coyote."

Dick smiled quietly.

"I rather thought he might be the one," he remarked. "It's the sort of trick you'd expect from a fellow like that. He's evidently found out that we're going to play to-morrow, and he's so dead sore that he's willing to do anything to prevent it."

He glanced at the letter again.

"Written to some one in the mine, that's plain," he murmured. "Also some one who plays on their nine. Notice where he says, 'so he cannot pitch against you.' Well, I don't know that we can glean any more information by poring over this thing. We'll have to keep our eyes open to-morrow at the mine and look out for snags. I'll just keep this blotter; we may have use for it sometime."

He tucked it carefully away in his pocket, together with the transcription he had made, and resumed his letter. When this was finished he addressed and stamped it, and, after posting it in the lobby, the two chums stepped into the elevator and were carried up to their rooms, where Tucker and Bouncer had retired more than an hour before.

# CHAPTER XI.

## THE EXPLOSION.

The Mispah Mining Company of Forest Hills had the reputation of being one of the best managed, as well as one of the most paying, propositions of its kind in the State.

Though technically a stock company, it was practically owned by the two brothers, John and Orren Fairchilds, who were thoroughly up to date in their methods and believed in giving their employees the benefit of every possible convenience and comfort.

The natural result was that the men gave them willingly more real work and good results than they could possibly have secured by the grasping, driving methods of some more shortsighted business men; labor troubles were practically eliminated, and everything worked smoothly and in perfect harmony.

The mine was located in the mountains to the north of Forest Hills. In fact, that portion of the town, occupied mainly by the miners, with its rows upon rows of comfortable frame cottages, closely abutted on the land owned by the company along the level ground at the foot of the rocky slope, where was situated the large brick office building, which was used by the officers of the company, their clerks, surveyors, draftsmen, and civil engineers.

Here were also storehouses, railroad sidings, and a number of other buildings, which looked almost like a little town in itself, while behind the office building was the baseball diamond, laid out by the enthusiastic Orren Fairchilds, with its grand stand, bleachers, and high board fencing, complete.

Halfway up the side of the mountain, perhaps a thousand feet above the level, was the main shaft of the mine, with its shaft house, pumping station and all the infinite details which go to the proper equipment of a mine. Made of timber cased in sheet iron, well painted, they seemed to be poised on the side of the mountain like a fly on a wall, and the stranger always expressed wonderment as to how they had been built in that apparently inaccessible spot.

Connecting the two levels curved the inclined track, down which shot cars, filled with ore destined for the smelter, to be carried back empty, or filled with supplies, shifts of laborers, or any one else who wanted to go up to the mine. For this was the only way of reaching the mouth of the shaft.

At five minutes before nine the *Wizard*, with Dick Merriwell at the wheel, whirled through the open gates which marked the entrance to the property of the Mispah Mining Company, and drew up before the handsome office building.

The four Yale men alighted and walked into the main office, where Dick sent his card in to the mine owner. The office boy returned with a message that Mr. Fairchilds would be out in a few moments, so they made themselves comfortable on a heavy oak bench that stood near the door.

In less than ten minutes Dick's friend of the night before appeared from his private office, and advanced with outstretched hand.

"Well, well, my boy, how are you this morning?" he said briskly. "I hope you're ready for a good sweat. It's pretty warm down on the lower level."

Then his eye fell on Buckhart.

"Bless my soul!" he exclaimed. "The Yale catcher, or I'll eat my hat! I don't know your name, but I never forget a face."

"Buckhart," Dick put in, as the Texan shook the older man's hand. "Bradley Buckhart from Texas."

"Glad to meet you—very glad," the mine owner said in his sharp, incisive manner. "Have you brought any more of your team with you, Merriwell? I foresee that my boys will have to stir themselves to lick you this afternoon."

Dick smiled.

"Tommy Tucker, here, sometimes plays short," he explained. "He's going to hold down centre field to-day."

There was a whimsical look of mock consternation on Orren Fairchilds' face as he shook hands with Tucker and Bigelow.

"I wish you'd brought the other six along," he said. "There'd be some honor in beating the Yale varsity."

Without waiting for a reply, he ushered them into an adjoining room, which was fitted up with a number of lockers, and opening one of them he began to toss out a variety of garments.

"We'll have to change here," he explained. "There'd be very little left of your regular clothes if you went down in them."

In the course of five minutes all five were arrayed in rough woolen trousers, flannel shirt, heavy shoes, and felt hats. The transformation was astonishing. But for the healthy tan on their faces, they might easily have been taken for a party of laborers, ready for their daily descent into the mine.

The mine owner then led the way through the office and across the yard to a platform outside the smelter. Here they climbed into one of the short, dumpy little ore cars and were borne swiftly up the incline.

It took but a minute to reach the top, where they found, to their surprise, that there was a good deal more space than they had supposed.

Jumping out of the car, they followed their guide into the pump house where they gazed in surprise at the huge engines which worked night and day pumping air into the underground workings, and drawing out through the ventilation shafts the hot, poisonous vapors from below.

From thence they passed quickly to the shaft house, where two mammoth hoisting engines of a thousand horse power each operated the cages, of which there were four, the main shaft being divided into that number of compartments.

The engineer and his assistant nodded as the chief entered.

"Be one along in a minute, Mr. Fairchilds," the former said, as he glanced at the dial before him.

In less than that time, a cage shot up from the shaft and two miners stepped out. One of them was a big, burly fellow with a long scar on one side of his face.

"Hello, Bill," the mine owner called. "After anything important? I want you to show us around down below."

The fellow grinned, displaying a void on his upper jaw where two front teeth were missing.

"Need a little powder, that's all," he said. "I'll be with you in a jiffy."

He strode out of the door, and Orren Fairchilds turned to Dick.

"That's my prize pitcher," he explained. "Six months ago he knew as much about baseball as a two-year-old, and I thought he'd never be able to get a ball over the plate. But he was anxious to learn, and we kept at it. I'm proud of him now."

The fellow came back on the run, a package of dynamite sticks swinging carelessly from one hand. At the sight of them, Bigelow's fat face turned pale and he edged away a little.

"My goodness!" he whispered hoarsely to Tucker. "Look at the way he carries them. What if they should drop."

"Don't worry, Bouncer," Tommy returned, with a nonchalance he was far from feeling. "It needs a spark combined with the concussion to set it off."

"Still, I don't like it," complained the fat chap.

The mine owner had paused at the cage door.

"Merriwell, shake hands with my pitcher, McDonough," he said briskly. "You two boys will be up against each other good and hard this afternoon."

Dick put out his hand promptly, and the miner's great paw closed over it with a grip which gave a hint of amazing strength. He looked the Yale man straight in the eyes, and for a brief instant Merriwell seemed to read something like a threat which flashed into those dark orbs and was gone.

"Glad to know you," McDonough said quietly. "I reckon we'll try to give the grand standers the worth of their money."

He followed Dick into the cage and dropped the dynamite on the floor with a thump which made Bouncer jump nervously. Then the descent began.

In an instant the floor of the shaft house had vanished and they were dropping noiselessly into the darkness, lit only by the flickering rays of the lantern which hung from the top of the cage, showing the timbers that lined the shaft seemingly leaping upward.

Bigelow caught his breath in a sudden gasp and clutched Tucker's wrist convulsively.

Presently the cage passed a large, irregular, well-lighted room opening back into the rock from the side of the shaft. Men were busy there, and they could hear the throbbing of machinery at work.

"That's one of the stations," explained Fairchilds. "It's the opening to one of the intermediate levels, but we won't stop. I want you to see the lowest level."

Down they went. Other stations flashed past at regular intervals until they had counted seven or eight of them. Presently the cable supporting the car began to take on a peculiarly disagreeable bobbing motion, which gave the novices an odd sensation, as though they were hung over an abyss by a rubber strap, and caused Bouncer to clutch Tucker again and gasp anew. Then the car stopped and they stepped out onto the floor.

The station of the lowest lift was like all those they had passed—well-lighted, walled, floored and roofed with heavy planking, and filled with all sorts of mining supplies. A narrow-gauge track led from the shaft back into the drift, or tunnel beyond, which was fairly well lighted by electric globes at intervals along the walls.

McDonough took the lead, and they at once plunged into the tunnel, which had a barely perceptible upward grade.

"Follows the course of the vein, you understand," the mine owner explained, as he pointed out where the ore had been taken out along one side of the drift. "We'll get to where they're working in a few minutes, and then you can see how it's done."

"Look out!" yelled McDonough warningly.

He caught Dick's arm and drew him back against the wall, the others following suit, and a moment later a laden ore car flashed past in the direction of the shaft, and disappeared.

Presently they turned into a crosscut, and a few minutes later they began to pass small groups of men working at the rock with picks and bars. Almost without exception they were stripped to the waist, for the heat had become oppressive, and was growing greater as they advanced.

They crossed the openings of innumerable small drifts which led out of the main tunnel, some of which were short, blind tunnels, while others extended for a long distance, sometimes curving around and returning to the drift from which they started. It was a veritable labyrinth.

At length they reached a spot where a number of men were loading the ore cars, and the mine owner stopped.

"This will show you the working as well as any place," he said, taking off his hat and mopping his forehead. "You notice that the tunnel runs along one side of the vein? That's to prevent caving. The ore is much softer than the rock through which it runs. You can see for yourselves how it is taken out with pick and bar. Sometimes we help it along with a blast."

While he was talking Dick stepped up to the side of the drift and looked closely at the vein. It did not look in the least like one's preconceived notion of gold ore, but the Yale man had had enough experience to see that it was good stuff.

"It ain't as rich here as we struck it a ways back," said a voice.

And turning, Dick saw McDonough standing at his side.

"Still, I shouldn't mind having a couple of thousand tons of this ore," Merriwell said, smiling.

The big fellow grinned.

"Me neither," he returned. "But if you'll step into this here crosscut, I'll show you something that's about three times as good."

For an instant the Yale man hesitated, thinking of the sinister note on the blotter. But here in this lighted spot, with men on every side, there was nothing McDonough could do, even if he was the man to whom that note was written. Certainly he didn't propose to let the fellow think he was afraid.

"Why, yes," he said quietly; "I'd like very much to see it."

The rest of the party were busy watching the miners and paid no attention when Dick turned and followed the brawny foreman about twenty feet back along the passage and then into a drift which ran at right angles.

This drift curved so sharply that they had not gone more than a dozen steps before the entrance was lost to sight. Presently McDonough stopped and held his candle close to the wall.

"That's some to the good, I tell you," he said enthusiastically; "and it's better yet further on. We——"

He broke off abruptly and listened.

"Gee! There's the old man calling!" he exclaimed. "Hold this, will you? I'll be back in a jiffy."

He thrust the candle into Merriwell's hand and darted back along the passage. Dick examined the ore with much interest. It certainly was rich and averaged much more to the ton than that in the outer drift. A footstep sounded, and looking up, he saw a figure advancing toward him from the opposite end of the passage. For a moment he thought it was McDonough, and wondered how he had managed to get around so soon; for he comprehended at once that the tunnel must have another entrance. Then the man spoke, and he realized that it was Orren Fairchilds.

"Taking a look at my prize vein, are you?" the mine owner said briskly. "How did you find——"

A sudden, muffled roar drowned his voice. A cloud of smoke belched from the wall, and the next instant a huge section of the rock crashed down into the tunnel, filling it to nearly half its height, and totally obliterating every sign of the unfortunate man who had stood there.

The cry of horror which Dick Merriwell uttered as he sprang forward, changed to one of joy when he saw that, instead of being utterly crushed, Fairchilds had escaped the heaviest part of the fall by a swift, forward plunge, and was only pinned down by the weight of some large chunks of rock which had dropped on his legs.

He saw something else, too, which sent a thrill through him and turned his tanned face a shade less brown.

Directly above the mine owner, a great mass of loosened rock hung as if suspended by a thread, and as the Yale man glanced up, it quivered a little. The slightest movement—the vibration of a voice, perhaps—would send it crashing down on those two beneath. Yet Dick did not hesitate an instant.

Swiftly sticking the candle upright in a crevice, he bent over the fallen man and, with infinite caution, began to lift the pieces of ore from his legs.

Despite the shock he had experienced, Orren Fairchilds was quite conscious. Lying on his back, his eyes fixed on the tottering mass which was poised above him, he knew well that death was staring him in the face, and he appreciated to the full the heroism of the man who was deliberately risking his own life in what seemed a futile attempt to save another's.

He moistened his dry lips.

"You can't do it," he whispered. "Leave me. Get back—quickly! Another moment and it will fall!"

He dared not raise his voice; his eyes never left the trembling rock above him.

Dick Merriwell made no answer; apparently he did not consider one necessary. One by one the heavy chunks of rock were lifted up and put aside.

"Go, I tell you," repeated the mine owner in that same suppressed tone. "Why don't you go? Do you want to be crushed to death?"

The Yale man dashed the sweat from his eyes.

"Do you really think I will?" was all he said.

"No," breathed the older man. "No, I don't; but I wish——"

He stopped suddenly, his eyes widening with horror. The rock was moving. Slowly, slowly, it crept forward, sending rattling showers of dust and small stones in its wake.

"It's coming!" gasped Fairchilds. "It's moving! For God's sake save yourself!"

Abandoning all caution, Dick rolled the last piece of rock from the fallen man and, catching him in his arms, staggered backward.

There was another crash, louder than the first, as the great mass plunged downward into the tunnel. Something struck Merriwell on the right shoulder, hurling him against the wall, and thence to his knees.

Then came the flash of light along the passage, the sound of hurrying feet, the quick, staccato note of many voices raised in excitement, and the next instant Dick felt himself caught up in a powerful grasp and literally carried out of the drift into the main tunnel.

Wrenching himself free, he turned and looked into the face of Brad Buckhart, drawn, white and horror-stricken, great beads of perspiration standing out on his forehead.

"You?" Merriwell exclaimed. "I thought—— Thank you, old fellow."

The Texan drew one sleeve across his forehead.

"By George, pard!" he grunted; "I sure thought you were done for that time."

"Where's Mr. Fairchilds?" Dick asked anxiously. "Did he get out all right?"

"He did, thanks to you, my boy."

The mine owner's voice sounded from the tunnel's mouth, and the next instant he appeared, supported by Bill McDonough and another miner. There were cuts on his head and face, one hand was bruised, and he could not stand alone; but his eyes were bright and his voice firm.

"By gorry!" he exclaimed. "That was the closest thing I ever saw. I shall never forget this, Merriwell. Are you hurt?"

Dick smiled.

"None to speak of," he returned. "Shoulder a little numb, that's all."

"Good."

The monosyllable was snapped out like a pistol shot, and into Orren Fairchilds' face came a look which seldom appeared there, and which those who knew him dreaded. His eyes grew cold and hard and piercing, and, as he turned slowly from one to another, men dropped their heads, and with nervously shuffling feet and crimsoned faces awaited in awe-struck silence the inevitable explosion.

It came.

"Who set off that blast?"

There was a steely menace to the words as they issued from the mine owner's set lips.

Not a man spoke. Not one in the circle lifted his eyes. Fear and embarrassment made them all look equally guilty.

"McDonough!"

Fairchilds withdrew his hand from the foreman's arm, and the big fellow took a step forward.

"McDonough, you're in charge of this level," snapped the mine owner. "Who set off that blast?"

The man with the scar moistened his lips with his tongue. His face was a little pale, but he met his chief's eyes squarely.

"I don't know," he said in a level tone—"so help me, I don't."

There was a momentary silence as the bright, steely eyes of the smaller man seemed to bore into the foreman's very soul.

"You don't know?" he rasped. "You must know! A blast can't be planted without your knowing."

The burly giant never hesitated.

"I didn't know it was planted," he said in a low tone—"I swear I didn't. That's what I brought the powder down for. If you want to know what I think, I bet it was meant for me. There's a lot of fellows here's got a grudge agin' me 'cause they think I drive 'em hard; and I bet one of 'em put that blast there while I was up above, thinking to let it off the first time I went in there. When they seen me go in with Mr. Merriwell, they done the trick."

"Humph!" snapped Fairchilds. "What made you leave Mr. Merriwell there?"

"I thought I heard you calling me."

The mine owner looked a little doubtful.

"I did call you," he said slowly.

He tried to take a step forward, and a twinge of pain crossed his face.

"Get an empty," he said shortly. "I can't stand here any longer. I've got to go up."

His stern eyes left McDonough's face and traveled swiftly over the other men.

"But this thing is not going to drop," he rasped. "I'll find out who set off that blast if I have to grill every man in the shift. I'm going to get at the truth somehow."

An empty ore car was brought up and the mine owner helped into it. He was followed by the other members of the party. As McDonough stepped forward to help Dick into the car, the Yale man looked at him keenly, searchingly, with narrowed lids. It was the briefest sort of a glance, but there was something in Merriwell's eyes which caused the burly giant to move uneasily and turn away his head.

Dick sprang into the car without assistance. They moved slowly down the crosscut to the main drift, and were soon back at the station again.

By the time the mine owner's office was reached, Fairchilds was able to hobble along without assistance, though he still suffered considerable pain. He led the Yale men into his private office, where he insisted on Dick's taking off his shirt so that his shoulder could be attended to.

Though Merriwell made light of it, there was an ugly bruise where the piece of rock had struck him, and his whole arm pained him, as if it had been badly hurt. Fairchilds' secretary, who was experienced in looking after such things, painted it well with iodine, after he had assured himself that there were no bones broken, and cautioned Dick about taking care of it for a few days, so as not to strain it further.

"Swell chance I'll have of taking care of it, with a game on this afternoon," Dick remarked, as they were changing their clothes in the small room off the main office.

"Great Scott, pard!" Buckhart exclaimed in dismay. "I'd clean forgot the game. How in thunder are you going to pitch?"

Dick smiled.

"Be a south paw, I reckon, if I find the other wing won't stand the racket."

"But can you swing a bat?" Tucker put in anxiously.

"I hope so," Merriwell said quietly. "It's not so bad as all that, and it will be much easier this afternoon. Don't worry, Tommy; we'll get through somehow. I've got to pitch, you know. There isn't anybody else."

They had already said good-by to the mine owner, so when they finished dressing they went out to the car. Dick took his seat at the wheel while the Texan turned the engine over.

As they went through the gates, Tucker leaned forward from the tonneau.

"Where are you going?" he asked curiously.

Merriwell's eyebrows went up a little.

"Why, to the Field Club, of course," he returned. "Have you forgotten that we promised Gardiner to come there directly from the mine? We didn't get half enough practice yesterday."

# CHAPTER XII.

## THE GAME BEGINS.

A steady stream of baseball fans poured into the Field Club grounds. It was Saturday; there was not a cloud in the sky, and it seemed as though every man and boy, as well as the greater part of the women, of Forest Hills had made up their minds to witness the great game.

In perfect equality clerks rubbed elbows with their "bosses." Newsboys, with bare feet and dirty faces, shouted witticisms over the shoulders of bankers and merchants. Miners, in their rough working clothes, thronged the field in great numbers and kept up a continuous roar for their team. Automobiles had been barred from the grounds that afternoon, but an endless string of them lined the street outside.

The game was scheduled for three-thirty. At two the grand stand was crowded and the bleachers filled to overflowing. An hour later there was not a seat to be had for love or money; men were scattered all around the diamond, wherever they could find a place to stand, and a solid mass of humanity lined the fence back of the field. The wide veranda of the clubhouse was jammed to the very rail with wives and daughters of the members, in their bright summer dresses, whose gay chatter added a lighter note to ceaseless hum of many voices.

As the hour struck the mine boys took the field for fifteen minutes of short, snappy practice. As they did so a great roar went up from the bleachers, which continued long and loud until stilled by the upraised hand of Orren Fairchilds, who, despite his injury of that morning, seemed to be as active as any man on the field.

There was an anxious look on Gardiner's face as he came over to where Dick was warming up.

"How's the arm, old fellow?" he asked.

"Left's all right, but I'm afraid there's nothing doing with the other," Merriwell answered. "I can toss a couple with it, but that's the limit. Begins to pain right away."

"Think you can pitch nine innings with your left?" Gardiner inquired.

The Yale man smiled.

"I'll have to," he said quietly. "What troubles me more is swinging a bat. I can't put any strength into it. Guess I won't be much use to you in the hitting line."

"Don't worry about that," the curly haired fellow said quickly. "If you can only pitch through the game the rest of us will try and look after the batting. I reckon it's time for us to take the field."

As the Field Club team took the places of their opponents in the field, there was a good deal of cheering and stamping from the grand stand, but a noticeable silence from the occupants of the bleachers. Evidently the miners did not propose to waste their breath on the opposing nine.

With the hand on the big clock in the clubhouse tower creeping toward the half hour, the fans began to grow impatient. There was much shuffling of feet, catcalls and shrill whistles arose and mingled with them, cries of:

"Get a move on!"

"Get busy!"

"Play ball!"

At exactly three-thirty, the fellows raced in from the field, and the two captains got together with the umpires for the toss. The Field Club men won, and promptly took the field again amidst a roar of approval from the crowd.

The first man up was Jimmy Rooney, the Mispah catcher, a short, stocky, muscular fellow, with reddish hair and a mass of freckles. As he walked to the plate a cheer went up from the bleachers, which was quickly stilled as the umpire tore off the wrappings from a ball and tossed it to Dick.

"Play ball!" he called.

The Yale man caught it in his left hand and toed the rubber. Buckhart crouched and gave the signal for an outcurve, and the next moment the ball left Merriwell's hand.

"Ball one!" yelled the umpire.

The next one was also wild.

"Don't let him fool you, Jim," advised the mine owner. "Make him put it over."

A moment later Merriwell got the inside corner of the plate, and Rooney failed to swing.

"Strike!" barked the umpire, with an upward motion of his right hand.

The red-headed catcher squared himself and dug his toes into the ground. He wouldn't let another good one get by.

Merriwell took the signal for a drop. He started the ball high, but it dropped sharply and swiftly and Rooney decided to strike. Lunging at it, he hit it on the upper side of his bat and popped it high above the infield.

It was an easy fly and Reddy Maxwell got under it confidently. Perhaps he was too confident. At all events, he caught it and—dropped it.

Despite the fact that it seemed a sure out, Rooney was racing toward first as hard as he could go, and by the time Maxwell snatched up the ball and lined it to Gardiner, the miner had touched the bag.

Maxwell's face was crimson as he trotted back to position.

"Hard luck, old fellow," Dick said quietly.

"Blamed rotten, you mean," Reddy retorted. "I ought to be kicked all over the place."

Herman Glathe, a tall, blond German, came to the bat; and, at the first delivery, Rooney, who had taken a good lead off the cushion, went down the line toward second like a race horse.

It almost seemed as though Buckhart, having caught the ball, waited an instant for Maxwell to cover the sack. Then he sent the horsehide sphere whistling straight as a bullet into the hands of the red-haired shortstop, who bent a little forward to receive it and jabbed it on to Rooney as the latter slid.

"Out at second!" announced the umpire.

But his decision was almost drowned in the excited shriek which went up from the clubhouse veranda.

"Good boy!" Dick murmured, as he caught the ball.

The next moment Glathe had lined out a clean single into the outfield, and he reached the initial sack amidst a roar of applause from the bleachers.

As though to atone for this, Dick teased Sam Allen, the Mispah second baseman, into striking at the first two balls pitched. Then followed a couple of wide ones, but Sam refused to be further beguiled. At last he landed on what he thought was a good one, and lifted a high foul back of the pan, away near the grand stand.

Like a flash Buckhart snapped off his cage and perked his head up to get its bearings. Then he spread himself and just managed to smother the ball within five feet of the front line of spectators, who shrieked a frenzied approval.

"Two gone, pard," he grinned, as he lined the ball out to Dick. "See if you can't fan this Adonis."

Bill McDonough was swaggering to the plate with a smile of confidence on his ugly face, and, as Merriwell watched him through narrowed lids, he made up his mind to strike him out if he could.

He began on the miner with a jump ball. It shot upward and McDonough, who had felt certain of hitting it, missed cleanly, nearly throwing himself down with the violence of his swing.

"That's pitching, pard," laughed the Texan, as the sphere buried itself in the pocket of his mitt. "That's the kind."

The burly giant scowled a little as he stamped his spikes into the ground and squared himself, crouching and leaning a bit backward, with his weight on his right foot.

Merriwell shifted the ball in his fingers and took plenty of time. Suddenly he pitched, and the sphere came humming over with speed that almost made the air smoke.

Again McDonough missed.

A cheer went up from the crowd.

Dick felt that the batter would expect him to try a coaxer, for, with no balls called, most pitchers would feel that they could afford to waste one or two.

He glanced around at his backers, his foot on the slab. When he turned, he pitched without the slightest preliminary swing, sending over a high, straight, speedy ball. It had been his object, if possible, to catch the miner unprepared, and he succeeded. The batter struck a second too late, and the ball spanked into Buckhart's glove.

"Out!" shouted the umpire.

But the word was not heard in the tremendous roar which went up from the grand stand.

"Bully work, old fellow!" Glen Gardiner said enthusiastically, as they trotted in from the field. "You shut them out beautifully. Shoulder all right?"

"Fine!" Dick returned.

"Well, we'll see if we can't get a run or two," the curly haired captain went on, as he selected a bat. "Nothing like getting a good start."

But his hopes were soon shattered.

McDonough proved something of a surprise to the Yale men as they watched his work from the bench. He was not at all the type of man of which good pitchers are usually made. Huge almost to unwieldiness, with muscles sticking out like great cords, at first sight he seemed to lack the supple, flexible, swiftness so necessary to good work in the box. Neither did his rough, brutal face give any indication of mental agility and well-developed brain power, without which no twirler can succeed.

In spite of all this, however, he did astonishingly well. His chief reliance was a swift straight ball which started high and ended with a sharp drop. Besides this he was the master of a few good curves. But what surprised Merriwell was his amazing headwork. He seemed almost to read the mind of the man at the bat, and, by some marvelous intuition, to give him just the sort of ball he was not expecting.

Two strikes were called on Gardiner, who then popped an easy fly to the infield and was caught out.

Reddy Maxwell promptly fanned, to the tumultuous enjoyment of the mine crowd on the bleachers.

Tucker managed to bang a hot liner past second and got to first by the skin of his teeth. Urged by Gardiner, who was coaching, he danced off the cushion and, with the first ball pitched to Arthur Dean, he scudded down the line like a streak of greased lightning. Rooney made a perfect throw to second; but Allen dropped the ball, and Tommy, sliding, was safe.

It was a wasted effort, for Dean fanned, and the Forest Hills boys took the field again.

"That's the biggest surprise I ever had," Dick said, as he sprang up from the bench. "I didn't think he had it in him."

"Wouldn't have given ten cents for him that many minutes ago," growled Buckhart, buckling his chest protector with a jerk. "He's sure been well trained."

Max Unger, right field, started the inning with a high fly between short and third, which Garland misjudged, giving Unger plenty of time to jog to first. He was followed by Foy, the miner's third baseman, who lined a red hot single into the outfield.

Hodgson, shortstop, knocked a foul back of first, which Gardiner gathered in; and Hall, the Mispah first baseman, fanned in short order.

At second, Unger had been inclined at first to lead off pretty well, but two or three sudden throws from Merriwell, prompted by Buckhart's signals warned him to stick close to the hassock.

With two men out and two on bases, Mike Slavinsky, a stalwart Pole, came to the bat.

"Now, Slavvy, take it easy," admonished the mine owner. "Don't try to knock the cover off the ball. Just a nice little single. Rooney comes next, you know."

The big fellow grinned a little as he squared himself at the plate. But in spite of this warning, he swung at the first ball with such force that he turned halfway around.

"Easy now," cautioned Fairchilds—"take it easy."

Then Slavvy calmed down, let two coaxers go by, and hit the next ball a smash which sent it across the infield. Stan Garrick forked at it, but the sphere was too hot to hold, and he dropped it. While he was seeking to recover it, Unger made third, Foy landed on second, and Slavvy was too well down to first to be caught.

As Rooney advanced to the bat the Forest Hills infielders crept up into the diamond. If the miner played the game he would certainly try for a bunt, and they balanced themselves on their toes, ready to go after it if the fellow succeeded in laying one down.

For some unknown reason he did not try. Instead, he duplicated his high fly of the inning before, except that this time there was more muscle behind it and the ball went sailing into the outfield.

Buck Garland got under it easily and waited confidently for it to drop. To his intense dismay and everlasting shame, he repeated Reddy Maxwell's error, but with far graver results.

The men on bases were off like streaks of greased lightning, and, by the time Garland had secured the ball and lined it to third, Unger had crossed the plate and Foy was halfway down from third.

To cap the climax he made a high throw which Dean had to jump for. He succeeded in stopping the ball, but ere it reached Buckhart's eager, outstretched hands, the Irish boy had made a beautiful slide and his finger tips touched the plate.

A deafening roar went up from the bleachers, augmented by the enthusiasm of the men in the grand stand, and for five minutes the field echoed with the frantic cheering.

Glen Gardiner was sick at heart at this display of errors and the thought that their opponents had secured a lead of two runs. He looked desperately at Merriwell, who stood calmly waiting for the next batter to face him. With two men on bases, there was no telling where the mine boys would stop unless the Yale man checked them at once.

Dick seemed to be of the same mind, for he proceeded to fan Glathe in very short order.

"By Jove, this is fierce!" Gardiner exclaimed, as his men gathered around the bench. "We've got to brace up. What in the world got into you, Buck, to do a thing like that?"

Garland shook his head in despair.

"I don't know, Glen," he said, with a sickly grin. "It was awful. I ought to be kicked off the nine. I expect I've lost the game."

"Nonsense!" Merriwell said quickly, before the Forest Hills' captain could reply. "Don't say a game is lost before the third man is out in the last inning. Don't even think it, for just as sure as you do, you begin to lose heart and, whether you realize it or not, you slump. You don't make the effort—it doesn't seem worth while. A game was never lost for a certainty in the second inning, boys. What if they have a lead of two runs? That's nothing. Two runs are easily made up—and more. Make up your minds that we're going to win this game. We must win it, and we shall."

There was something magnetic in the Yale man's manner—something inspiring in his quiet, calm assurance, which seemed to put heart into the discouraged fellows, causing their eyes to brighten and their shoulders to square instinctively. The usually deliberate Stan Garrick snatched up a bat and advanced to the plate with the determination to start off with a hit.

"I must hit it!" he whispered to himself. "I must, and I will."

He was altogether too anxious to hit, and somehow, McDonough seemed to divine this, for the miner pulled him with the first two balls handed up, neither of which Stan touched.

"You've got him, Bill," chirped Orren Fairchilds, who stood a little to one side of the plate. "Keep it up."

"Look out for those wide ones, Stan," cautioned Gardiner.

Garrick knew he had been fooled into striking at what must have been balls, and he resolved to use better judgment. It seemed likely that, having deceived him in such a manner, McDonough would still seek to lure him into biting at the bad ones, and he resolved not to repeat the error.

The burly Mispah pitcher took his time. Dick was standing beside the mine owner, for it was his turn next at the bat, and suddenly he caught the flash of McDonough's eye as it was turned in his direction.

It was the briefest possible glance, for the next instant the miner whipped one over the inside corner of the plate with all the speed he could command.

Too late Garrick saw that the ball might be good. He could not get his bat around to meet it, and therefore let it pass, hoping the umpire would call it a ball.

"You're out!" came sharply from the umpire.

Garrick stepped back and tossed his bat on the ground.

"Too bad, Stan," Dick said, as he came forward to take his place.

"Take it easy, Merriwell," Gardiner advised, in a low tone. "It's better to let him fan you than to strain your arm."

Dick nodded comprehendingly. All the same he did not intend to strike out if he could help it.

He squared himself at the plate and faced the pitcher. McDonough turned the ball in his hands, and once more the Yale man caught that brief, almost imperceptible flash of the miner's eyes toward the right.

Then he toed the plate and sent in a swift one with a sharp outcurve.

Merriwell did not move his bat.

"Ball one!" cried the umpire.

Again McDonough tried a coaxer, but the Yale man refused to bite, nor did he budge when the ball came whistling over the plate a little too high and cut the pan almost on a level with Dick's neck.

"You've got him in a hole," laughed Gardiner. "He's going to make you a present of the base."

McDonough grinned sourly and then put one straight over the centre of the plate.

Dick played the game and let it pass.

"Strike one!" declared the umpire.

The miner reached for the inside corner on his next delivery and caught it. "Strike two!"

Then the Mispah man sought to send over a high one across Merriwell's chest.

Dick lifted his bat, holding it loosely, and dropped the ball on the ground with a skillful bunt. It rolled slowly along the base line, and both Mc-Donough and Rooney dashed after it, while the Yale man flew toward the base as though endowed with wings. Ten feet from the sack he launched himself through the air, feet first, and touched the hassock a second before the ball plunked into the baseman's glove.

"Safe!" yelled the umpire.

As Buckhart came to the plate, Dick took a good lead off the cushion, and, with the first ball pitched, he was away toward second running like a fiend.

"There's nothing the matter with his legs," chuckled Gardiner, as the Yale man picked himself up and dusted off the front of his shirt, one foot on the bag. "I only hope he don't jolt that lame wing of his too much."

This was just what Merriwell was taking particular pains not to do. He slid either feet first, or on his left side, and, though the shoulder gave a painful twinge now and then, he hoped it would hold out.

Meanwhile the big Texan, assured and smiling, squared himself at the plate. He refused to be fooled by the first ball, which went a little wide; but he presently picked out one of McDonough's benders which seemed to suit him, hitting it fair and square with a sharp, snappy swing which sent it out on a line.

It was a clean drive to the outfield, and two fielders chased the ball while Brad tore over first and managed to reach second a moment after Dick crossed the plate to the accompaniment of shrieks from the crowd, who billowed to their feet in the excitement of the moment, wildly waving hats and arms and shouting themselves hoarse.

The Field Club team had made a run.

# CHAPTER XIII.

## AGAINST HEAVY ODDS.

Gardiner was jubilant. With a run already, a man on second, and only one out, things were picking up.

"Take it easy, Irv," he said, as Renworth picked out a bat and advanced to the plate. "All we want is a nice single."

Then he hurried down to the coaching line at first.

Renworth was not a particularly strong batter. He was apt to lose his head and misjudge the balls, and, in spite of his determination to make a clean single or at least a bunt, he had two strikes called on him almost before he knew it. Then he popped a high fly over toward centre field, and, but for an error on the part of Glathe, he would have been done for. Luckily the big German muffed the ball, and Renworth cantered across the initial sack, while Buckhart reached third.

"Now, Buck, it's up to you," Gardiner cried. "You know what to do. Say, Tucker, come out and coach, will you? I'm up next."

As Garland came to the plate, Dick kept his eyes fixed on the burly pitcher. He was very curious to learn the reason for that momentary sidelong glance which he gave almost before every delivery. He thought he had solved the problem, but he was not quite sure. There it was again! A swift, glinting flash of his dark eyes, and then he pitched.

"Strike one!" called the umpire.

"I thought that was it," murmured the Yale man with much satisfaction. "He's getting his signals from Fairchilds. That's pretty clever."

Since his attention had been attracted to the pitcher's odd trick of hesitating almost imperceptibly before he delivered the ball Merriwell had been looking about for the reason. Soon he saw that the mine owner never left his position a little back of the base line some twenty feet to the left of the plate. He noticed, moreover, that Fairchilds was strangely silent while his own team was in the field, whereas, with them at the bat, he took to advising, coaching, and encouraging.

Dick, therefore, came to the conclusion that his first impression of the burly miner had been correct. It was not his brain which was doing such good work, but that of Orren Fairchilds. The mine owner had been able to teach the man curves and speed and good control, but he could not teach him judgment. Instead, he had done the next best thing, and by means of a clever system of signals, he himself practically did the thinking and directed every move made by the burly giant in the box.

At first, Renworth was inclined to stick much too close to the base to suit the vivacious Tucker.

"Get off! get off!" yapped Tommy. "Stir your stumps! Get to going! Drift away from that sack, Irv! Stop hugging it! It isn't a girl. Get a divorce from that cushion!"

Thus admonished, Renworth danced away from the hassock as McDonough received the ball from Rooney. Dick noticed the quick flash of his eyes, and the next instant the burly pitcher whirled without a warning and lined the sphere to Hall, who covered the base.

"Slide! Slide!" shrieked Tucker frantically.

Renworth did his best, but was caught almost by a hair's breadth, the umpire declaring him out.

Then McDonough wound up the inning by striking out Buck Garland.

"Never mind, boys," Gardiner said cheerfully, as they jogged into the field. "They're only one run ahead. We'll make that up."

But inning after inning came and went, and the score remained unchanged.

As the game wore on McDonough seemed to improve. His speed grew greater, his control more perfect, his curves more difficult; but more surprising than anything else was the wonderful headwork he displayed. He seemed to divine a batter's weak points with marvelous intuitiveness, varying his delivery with a cleverness which was almost uncanny. In addition to all that, he made so many brilliant put-outs on bases that the Forest Hills boys dared not take any chances. It was as though he had eyes in the back of his head.

To the great crowd in the grand stand and on the bleachers, even to the Forest Hills men in the field, it was an extraordinary exhibition of almost perfect pitching. Only one among them seemed to realize that the hulking miner in the box, whose name resounded almost continually from the mouths of the roaring thousands, was a mere machine, and that the real credit belonged to the quiet little man, standing silently near the home plate, his bright eyes taking in every inch of the field—a man who had once held a high place on one of the big leagues, but who was doing his playing now by proxy.

Dick Merriwell was fighting desperately against tremendous odds. As the game progressed his shoulder grew constantly worse. From the first occasional twinges it had advanced by leaps and bounds, to a constant, steady, almost intolerable pain, which caused him to catch his breath at every throw, and made each turn at the bat an agony.

But nothing of this appeared to the men on the field, much less to the spectators. With splendid grit and unflagging cheerfulness he kept at the work without a murmur, using every cure at his command and every possible wile on the man at the bat, though not sparing himself when speed was necessary. And, thanks to Buckhart's signals, the mine boys soon discovered to their cost that they could steal no bases on the Yale pitcher.

Off the field Merriwell's cheery voice, on the coaching lines or at the plate, put new life into the Forest Hills fellows and kept them from growing disheartened as the fierce battle waged without further tangible results on either side.

One man on the field saw more than did the others. The big Texan seemed to realize something of what his friend was suffering, and the knowledge spurred him to do more than his best. There were no errors in the Westerner's brilliant playing. There were no passed balls; his throws into the field were swift, accurate, and perfect; his eyes seemed to take in every foot of the diamond; and, time and time again, his rapid signals caused an unexpected put-out on bases.

At each turn at the bat he made a clean hit; one was a two-bagger, which the rapid fielding and steady play of the mine boys made ineffective.

But, in spite of all this, the seventh inning ended without either side having added to their score.

Before Dick went into the box he had Gardiner put his right arm into a sling. It seemed to him that if he could have it tied firmly so that it wouldn't swing he could get along better.

"If it's as bad as that you ought to stop," protested the curly haired captain.

Dick shook his head decidedly.

"At the beginning of the eighth!" he exclaimed lightly. "Never! It's a pity if I can't hold out for two innings. We've got to get at least a couple of runs, you know, old fellow."

Among the spectators the excitement was intense. Such a game had never before been seen in Forest Hills, and every man sat forward on the edge of his seat, his eyes glued on the field. Something must happen soon.

As Dick appeared with his arm in a sling, a voice from the bleachers roared:

"His wing is on the bum, boys! Now's the time to pile up the runs! Hammer the life out of him!"

But they did not.

Merriwell had resolved to hold them down. More runs at this stage of the game would be fatal, and, summoning every effort, he put forth all the skill that was in him. Grimly he kept at the work, pitching with his left hand, and striking out some of the heaviest hitters who faced him; and in little more than ten minutes the Mispah boys were back in the field.

Tucker now started the ball rolling by lining out a red hot one past shortstop. Dean fanned and Tommy stole second, making the cushion by a hair's breadth amid a cloud of dust. Then Garrick popped a fly out to left field, and, shrieking with joy, Tucker saw Slavvy muff it. Tommy scooted to third, while Stan made first by a close margin.

Fortune was certainly smiling on the Forest Hills boys.

Merriwell slipped the sling from his arm and, picking up a bat, walked over to the plate.

He allowed two strikes to be called and then bunted, sending the ball rolling and squirming toward first. He was out, but he had accomplished his purpose, for Tucker slid home and Garrick reached second safely.

The score was tied, and the crowd in the grand stand and about the field shrieked itself hoarse. There was a sullen silence from the bleachers.

Gardiner was delighted.

"That's going some!" he cried. "Now, Brad, see if you can bring in another."

The Texan refused to be tempted by McDonough's coaxers. He forced him to put one straight over and then fell on it with violent delight. It was a frightful smash, and the sphere went sailing on a line into the field to the right of centre.

There was nothing slow about Garrick as he dashed across third like a race horse and, in response to Dean's frantic urging, kept on toward home. He made the plate easily, and Buckhart got to second with a splendid slide.

"Got 'em going, boys," Brad shouted—"got 'em going!"

The crowd went wild and nearly stamped down the grand stand.

Renworth quickly fanned, but the Forest Hills boys did not care, for they were one run to the good.

As Merriwell resumed his sling and walked out to the box he was greeted with a sudden round of applause. Though they did not know the circumstances, the crowd seemed suddenly to realize how much of the success of the game was due to the grit of this cool, smiling stranger, who, in spite of his injured arm, was doing such splendid work.

Herman Glathe, the big German fielder, was the first to face the Yale twirler.

Dick took no chances. If he could hold them down for this inning the game would be won. He pitched skillfully and with care, and the German fanned.

"One down, pard," grinned Buckhart through the wire meshes of his cage. "Let the good work go on."

Sam Allen, the chipper little second baseman, picked up his war club and squared himself at the pan.

Merriwell was not hurrying, nor wasting his time. Perfectly calm and deliberate in his movements, he continued his work in the box, and Allen presently got a high drop which he decided to strike at when he saw it coming over in a manner that indicated that it would be good.

The ball hit the upper side of Allen's bat and went into the air.

Like a flash of lightning, Buckhart tore off his mask, whirled, looked upward, located the ball, and went after it.

A gust of wind carried the ball farther and farther away, but the Texan stretched himself amazingly and reached it as it came down. It stuck fast in the pocket of Brad's big glove; and the miner's exasperation was expressed by the manner in which he fiercely flung his bat toward the bench.

Two men were out, and Bill McDonough strode forward with a look of fierce determination on his face. He had made up his mind to line out the sphere or die in the attempt.

The Yale man was equally determined that he should not. He was pitching as if life and fortune depended on his performance. The torturing pain in his shoulder was forgotten as he grimly faced the hulking scoundrel at the plate.

His first ball looked fine to McDonough. Nevertheless, it shot upward with a little jump, rising over the miner's bat as he struck.

"Strike!" snapped the umpire.

"Get him, Dick—get him!" implored Tucker. "It will settle everything! Cook his goose!"

McDonough set his teeth with a snarl; his eyes gleamed fiercely.

He was ready with every nerve tense, hoping and desiring to meet Merriwell's speed fairly. But now, at this critical point, Dick, after using a delivery which seemed to prophesy a swift one, handed up the slowest sort of a slow ball. It came with such exasperating slowness from the Yale man's hand, that something actually seemed holding it back. In spite of everything he could do, McDonough struck too soon.

A snarl broke from his lips in a sound which was the height of rage expressed without words. His face turned purple and he gripped the handle of his bat with all the strength in his great hands. As he glared ferociously at the cool, half smiling face before him, something like a haze seemed to gather before his eyes. Before it had passed, Merriwell whistled over a high, swift ball which cut the plate in halves.

McDonough seemed to see something flit past, but it was the spank of the ball into Buckhart's glove that told him that Dick had pitched.

"Out!" cried the umpire.

With a roar like thunder, the crowd poured down onto the field in a human cataract from the stand, and, before he could escape, Merriwell was seized and lifted up on some one's shoulders. For a moment he struggled to get away; then, seeing it would be useless, he resigned himself to the inevitable and waited calmly until their enthusiasm should cool.

After marching about the field for a few minutes, they came back to the clubhouse and allowed him to slip to the ground. As he did so, Orren Fairchilds hurried up.

"Wonderful work, my boy," he exclaimed—"wonderful! By Jove! I never saw anything like it. It was a fair, square beat; and every bit of it was due to you—you and that catcher of yours. How did the arm hold out?"

Dick made a wry face.

"It's not as comfortable as it might be," he confessed.

"Well, I won't keep you," the mine owner said quickly. "You ought to get something on it at once. Come around to the club and take dinner with me to-night about seven—bring your friends with you. The Reform Club, on Locust Street, you know. Good-by."

With a wave of his hand, he disappeared into the crowd; and Dick hastened into the dressing room of the club.

A few minutes before seven o'clock that evening Dick drove the *Wizard* up to the entrance of the Reform Club, and slipping the plug into his pocket, alighted with his three friends.

In the reception hall an attendant came forward.

"Is Mr. Fairchilds here," Dick inquired—"Mr. Orren Fairchilds?"

The man looked at him rather curiously.

"Are you Mr. Merriwell?" he asked.

Dick nodded.

"Kindly take the elevator to the third floor," the attendant said quickly. "He asked that you be sent up directly you came. James!"

A page came forward, and the man said something to him in a low tone. Then he waved them toward the elevator, and in a moment they were whisked upstairs.

The page stepped out first and, going down the hall a few steps, opened a door and announced clearly:

"Mr. Merriwell!"

Dick stopped aghast on the threshold. The room was a private dining room and not small, yet it seemed to his startled senses to be full of people.

"There's some mistake," he gasped. "I——"

The mine owner suddenly appeared and seized his hand.

"Come in, my boy—come in," he said briskly. "What are you afraid of? Just a few people I wanted you to meet."

There was a smile on his face, and he winked at Buckhart over Merriwell's shoulder.

As in a daze, Dick followed his host into the room. He had a vague recollection of being presented to an amazing number of men, who smiled at him and shook his hand warmly. They were of all ages, from gray-haired, stout, substantial bankers and merchants, down to clean-cut, good-looking fellows of his own age, among whom he recognized smiling Glen Gardiner and most of the other members of the team.

One, a tall, handsome man of middle age, with a close-cropped beard and brilliant, kindly eyes, he heard spoken of as the mayor.

At length he found himself at one end of a very long table. Orren Fairchilds was on his left; he had quite lost sight of Brad and the others.

Presently the mine owner arose, and, as he did so, the talk and laughter ceased and silence fell.

"Gentlemen," he began slowly. "I have asked you here to-night to meet a young friend of mine. To many of you his name is well known as that of the best amateur pitcher in the country. Most of you had a chance of seeing his work this afternoon, when he pitched nine hard innings with as perfect form and most wonderful display of headwork that I have ever seen—and entirely with his left arm. His right was injured, and I should like to tell you how."

He paused. The smile had left his face and his eyes were deep with feeling.

"In the mine this morning there was a premature explosion of a blast," he went on. "I was caught by the falling rock and pinned to the ground, unable to stir. As I lay there on my back, I saw a great mass poised above me, loosened from the top of the tunnel, ready to fall at a breath and crush the life out of me. My friend, here, saw it too, and knew that he was risking almost certain death when he sprang to my assistance and began to drag the rocks off me.

"I begged him to go and leave me. It seemed useless for us both to perish. Of course, he refused. The rock began to move. I shrieked to him to go back, but he did not answer. The next instant he caught me up and dragged me back just as the mass fell. There had not been a second to spare. He had saved me at the risk of his own life."

The mine owner paused again, and one hand rested affectionately on the Yale man's shoulder. Then he leaned forward and took up a brimming wine glass.

"Gentlemen," he said slowly, as he held it up, "I drink to Dick Merriwell, the gamest pitcher, the truest sport, the bravest man I know."

Like one man, the company rose, holding their glasses high. As with one voice the shout of "Merriwell—Dick Merriwell!" made the rafters ring; and they drank the toast standing. Then they subsided into their chairs, and in the silence which followed, Dick pushed back his chair and stood up slowly.

His face was flushed, his eyes bright and, as he looked down that long line of friendly faces, something clutched his throat. For a moment he could not utter a word.

"Thank you," he stammered huskily. "I—I cannot say—another word, but just—thank you."

He dropped back upon his chair; a thunderous clapping broke forth, and something like a mist flashed across the Yale man's eyes and blurred his sight.

# CHAPTER XIV.

## THREE MEN OF MILLIONS.

Marcus Meyer, head of the wealthy firm of jewelers who did business under the name of the Meyer Diamond Company, was pacing restlessly up and down his luxuriously fitted up private office on the third floor of the Commercial Building in Denver.

He was a smooth-shaven, alert Hebrew of about thirty-nine or forty, well groomed and clothed with a fastidious taste, which was almost foppish, in garments of the very latest cut and material. In reality, however, there was nothing of the fop or fool about Marcus Meyer. He was a keen, quick-witted business man of extraordinary cleverness, and had the reputation of knowing more about the inside conditions of the diamond industry than any other individual west of the Alleghenys, save only the great Herman Spreckles, of Chicago.

As he walked restlessly from end to end of the long room, his troubled eyes sought the ornate clock which slowly ticked away the minutes on a mantel of carved marble, and every now and then his slim, well-manicured fingers strayed to his smooth, black hair in an unconscious gesture of impatience.

Presently he stopped at one end of the long mahogany table, which was set around with heavy leather-cushioned chairs, and occupied the centre of the room. Seated in one of these chairs was a man of about fifty-five. Short, stout, and comfortable of build, round-faced and rosy-cheeked, with light-blue eyes in which was a look of almost infantile innocence, one would never have guessed him to be the Philander Morgan who held a controlling interest in so many corporations on the Pacific Coast, and who was reputed to be the wealthiest man in San Francisco.

"I can't understand why he doesn't come," complained Meyer, in his quick, nervous manner. "The train was due at nine-fifteen, and here it is nearly ten."

He took out a handkerchief and passed it over his moist forehead.

Philander Morgan eyed him quizzically, with a slight pursing of his lips.

"Ah, you young men!" he said placidly. "How much vital energy you waste in worry! You prance about, tear your hair, and get hot and unpleasantly moist; and what do you gain by making yourself uncomfortable? Nothing. Spreckles will come because he said he would, and I have never

107

known him to break his word. There are such an infinite number of reasons why he should be late that it is useless to speculate. Take my advice and make yourself comfortable until he appears."

He folded his plump hands and gazed meditatively at the ceiling.

"I know it's absurd," Meyer replied, with a harassed smile; "but I can't help it. Besides, I have so much more at stake than you. In comparison to all the other irons you have in the fire, your interest in the diamond trade is insignificant. But should this monstrous, incredible thing prove true, I shall be ruined—totally ruined."

Philander Morgan withdrew his eyes from the ceiling and puffed out his fat cheeks.

"Tut! tut!" he protested. "Don't speak of it. Surely you have not allowed yourself to credit for an instant this wild rumor. It's absurd—impossible."

The Hebrew tapped nervously with his finger nail on the polished surface of the table.

"That's what I told myself at first," he said slowly. "I snapped my fingers at them—I laughed. It was inconceivable, beyond the bounds of reason. But later, every evidence seemed to point——"

A loud knock sounded at the door and he broke off abruptly.

"Come in!" he cried, springing to his feet.

The door slowly opened and an old man appeared on the threshold. He was very tall and very thin, with narrow, drooping shoulders and a slow, almost shambling step. His clothes were mussed and almost threadbare; but, in spite of that, it needed no more than a glance at the wrinkled face, the great mane of snow white hair brushed straight back from a high, broad forehead, the piercing eyes, bright as live coals, gleaming through big spectacles with rims of tortoise shell, to tell that he was somebody.

Such a man was Herman Spreckles, of Chicago. Rumor had it that, besides his many other interests, he was the moving spirit of a gigantic secret combination of jewelers which ruled the diamond market of the United States with a rod of iron.

Marcus Meyer hurried forward with both hands outstretched.

"My dear Mr. Spreckles!" he cried joyfully. "I am very glad to see you. We were beginning to fear that you had missed your train."

The tall man sniffed scornfully as he took one of the Hebrew's hands.

"Huh! Did you ever know me to miss a train, Meyer?" he inquired.

Then he looked out in the hall.

"Come in, Pickering—come in!" he said sharply. "Don't dawdle out there."

He moved away from the door, and a slim, alert-looking man of about forty appeared, at the sight of whom Marcus Meyer's eyes sparkled.

"Ah—Pickering!" he exclaimed with satisfaction. "I'm glad you're here. We shall need the skill of the best diamond expert in the country before we're through, or I'm very much mistaken."

Meanwhile Herman Spreckles had advanced to the table, where Philander Morgan arose ponderously to greet him.

"Ha! You here, too?" inquired the older man, peering through his spectacles. "This begins to look serious."

He shook hands with the stout man and dropped into a chair.

"Well, Meyer, let us get to business at once," he said briskly. "I must take the early afternoon train back. What's this cock-and-bull yarn you've been writing me about. Begin at the beginning and let us get through with it. Sit down, man—sit down! You make me nervous stamping up and down that way."

The Hebrew dropped upon a chair and passed his hand over his hair with a nervous gesture.

"You both had my letters in cipher," he began quickly. "You know about the mysterious diamonds which have been coming in to me for the past few months with such amazing regularity."

Spreckles nodded.

"Exactly," he said impatiently. "You purchased them on my instructions at the prevailing price, and I wired you to ascertain where they came from. Have you done so?"

Marcus Meyer made a gesture with his hands.

"I have, so far as has been in my power. There was no difficulty in finding out who they came from. Their original source remains as much a mystery as it was in the beginning. Perhaps, in order that we may have all the facts clearly, I had better tell the whole story briefly."

He looked questioningly at the white-haired Spreckles, who nodded silently.

"On the third of March," Meyer began, "a man came to me and asked whether I wished to buy some diamonds. I told him, of course, that I should have to examine them first, whereupon he promptly pulled out of his pocket an oblong package wrapped in white tissue paper. Imagine my astonishment when I unrolled it and found within, twenty perfect stones ranging from one to five carats in weight. They were flawless and of that exquisite blue-white color which, as you both know, is so sought after and so rare. I have sold no better stones than those for five hundred dollars a carat."

"And the man?" Herman Spreckles asked quickly. "Where did he say they came from?"

"He would not say," Meyer answered. "He would tell me nothing. He said that if I did not care to buy them he would go elsewhere. I finally paid him three hundred and fifty dollars a carat—a great bargain. As soon as he had gone, I sent for a detective and had inquiries made. The fellow was one Johnson, a native of Denver, who had been in a variety of enterprises, none of which were very successful. For the past year he had apparently done nothing at all, though the report had it that he lived very well, in a comfortable place on the outskirts of the city, where he kept an expensive motor car, among other luxuries. His only intimate was an eccentric fellow named Randolph, who came here from the East some seven years ago, built an extraordinary fortified dwelling in the mountains, and has lived there a recluse ever since, supposedly dabbling in chemical experiments of some sort."

"Ha!" exclaimed Spreckles. "You had this fellow Randolph looked up?"

"Not at once," returned Meyer. "At the time it seemed to me that he could have no connection with the diamonds. It was much more probable that Johnson had stolen or smuggled them; but as the weeks passed no stones of that description were reported missing, and inquiry at Washington revealed the fact that there had been no suspicious purchasing abroad. The day after I received that letter, Johnson appeared with another packet, which, on opening, I found to be in every way identical with the first. There were twenty stones of the same blue-white color, and they weighed, to a fraction of a carat, exactly what the first had weighed.

"I was dumfounded. It seemed incredible that such stones as those could have been brought into the country without my knowing it. I was positive they had not been stolen. Johnson persisted in his absolute silence regarding the source from which they came, he was even loath to let them remain in my hands for three days while my experts made an exhaustive examination of them. It was then that I wrote to you. I had already paid out nearly twenty-five thousand dollars for the first lot, and dared not sink any more money without your sanction."

"Quite so," nodded Spreckles. "You sent on one of the stones, and I wired you to purchase as many of them as you could, and to find out their source."

"Exactly," returned Marcus Meyer. "I paid the man and at once set the detectives on the trail of Randolph, for the thing was becoming too serious to neglect any clue, however slight. The report they turned in was singularly complete in some respects, and disappointingly lacking in others. Scott Randolph is a man of about thirty-two or three. He comes from a good New England family, and, while he was still in college, his father died and left him about seventy-five thousand dollars. He appears not to have any near relatives and but few friends. He graduated from Yale, and then spent three years at the Sheffield school of science, where he paid particular attention to chemistry and mechanics. After leaving New Haven he came directly to Denver, bought a tract in the mountains and built there a stone house which is absolutely impregnable. The windows are guarded with iron bars and steel

110

shutters, the door is of steel like a safe, and, so far as I could discover, no human being but this Johnson has ever been inside. His provisions are brought to the door and left there; apparently he does his own cooking, for there are no servants around."

Herman Spreckles lifted a thin, wrinkled hand.

"Wait," he said quickly. "What about the men who built the house?"

"All brought from a distance," Meyer answered. "None of them could be located. I did, however, examine a teamster who carted his belongings from the freight office. This fellow saw a few rooms in the lower part of the house and confirms the general impression that the place is as difficult to get into as a fort. Randolph's belongings were all carefully crated, but the teamster remembered that many of the crates were extraordinarily heavy; several, he knew, contained machinery."

"At regular intervals Randolph disappears. At first it was supposed that he had left the house, since no amount of knocking or pounding could rouse him. After my detectives got on the trail, they kept a strict watch of the place day and night to catch him when he came forth or returned, in order to find out where he went. They finally came to the conclusion that he did not leave the house. He did not issue from any of the doors or windows. His motor car remained unused in a small shed to one side of the larger building. It was apparent, therefore, that he shut himself up alone for some purpose."

He paused and looked from one to the other of the two men before him. They were both intensely interested in his recital. Philander Morgan's fat face had lost the look of baby innocence, and had taken on a keen, alert expression, which quite transformed the man. Spreckles' shaggy head was bent slightly forward and from beneath beetling brows his eyes gleamed like coals as he surveyed the Hebrew.

"Well," he said sharply—"well, what was that purpose?"

Marcus Meyer hesitated, his slim hand straying again to the smooth head.

"I can think of but one solution," he said slowly at length. "Wild, absurd, incredible as it may sound, I think the man has discovered the secret for which so many scientists have toiled in vain. I believe—he has found a way —of manufacturing diamonds!"

The stillness which followed the Hebrew's amazing statement was so intense that the slow ticking of the clock on the mantel beat on the tense nerves of the waiting men like the strokes of a hammer. Suddenly Philander Morgan snorted incredulously.

"Ridiculous!" he cried in a shrill voice. "The thing's impossible!"

Herman Spreckles made no reply, for several moments his piercing eyes remained fixed on Meyer's pale face. Then he turned swiftly toward the man he had brought with him.

111

"Pickering!"

The name came snapping from his thin, straight lips like the shot of a pistol, and the young man sprang up from where he had been sitting at the far end of the table and came forward.

"Yes, sir."

"Is such a thing possible—manufacturing diamonds, I mean."

James Pickering hesitated an instant.

"It has been done," he said slowly. "Both Edouard Fournier, of Paris, and Professor Hedwig, of Berlin University, have produced pure diamonds; but the process was so costly and the resulting stones so small, that their methods were not commercially practicable."

Again silence fell. Spreckles was thinking, while Philander Morgan sat aghast, with pendulous cheeks and popping eyes. His expression of dismay would have been ludicrous had the situation not been so serious.

Marcus Meyer passed a crumpled handkerchief over his moist forehead; then he began again.

"I can think of no other explanation," he said in a low, strained voice. "The man never leaves his house. His only known accomplice never leaves Denver. Yet, a few days after these regular periods of retirement, twenty-five thousand dollars' worth of exquisite diamonds are brought to me with the precision of clockwork. They are all of the same perfect quality and the carat weight of each package is identical. I could make out my check beforehand and it would be correct."

"You have the stones?" Spreckles asked quickly.

Meyer nodded.

"All except those in the first lot, which I have sold."

"Get them."

The Hebrew arose from the table and went over to a great safe in the corner. Opening this, he took out a small drawer, which he carried back and placed before the other two men. The contents of the drawer were hidden by a folded square of black velvet, and when this was removed and spread out on the polished mahogany, five small, insignificant-looking packets of white tissue paper were revealed.

With fingers that trembled a little, Meyer took up one of these packets, and, unfolding the paper, poured the contents out on the velvet square.

There was a glittering cascade of light as they streamed down onto the velvet and lay against the black surface, a blazing mass, catching the light from a thousand facets, gleaming with a wonderful fire, until even Herman Spreckles could not suppress an exclamation of admiration, as he leaned forward and plucked one between thumb and forefinger.

112

"A diamond of the first water," he said slowly, examining it intently. "And you tell me that has been made by the hand of man? I won't believe it."

He turned to Pickering, who stood behind his chair.

"Look it over, James," he said, "and let us know what you think of it."

The expert's face was slightly pale and his eyes very bright, but otherwise he betrayed no signs of emotion as he took the stone from the old man's hand and carried it over to one of the windows. Here he fixed a glass in one eye and began a thorough inspection of the diamond.

Philander Morgan clasped his chubby hands together nervously.

"But what are we going to do?" he asked plaintively. "If this man can make diamonds, the bottom will fall out of the market in no time. We'll be ruined. Our stock will be worthless. What are we going to do?"

Herman Spreckles surveyed him with a cynical gleam in his black eyes.

"Don't cry before you're hurt, Morgan," he said sarcastically. "Even if you lose your diamond stock, I hardly think you'll be a candidate for the poor house. Besides the stock has not depreciated yet, and it is our business to see that it does not."

He glanced up from under his shaggy brows at the expert, who was coming back from the window.

"Well, Pickering, what's the verdict?"

"It's a diamond, all right, Mr. Spreckles," the man said decidedly. "I'll stake my reputation on that. It has all the fire and color of the best products of the Kimberly mines, and is absolutely flawless. It's worth easily five hundred dollars a carat. Whether it is a natural or manufactured product I cannot tell. Had I not heard the story Mr. Meyer has just told, I would have sworn that this came from South Africa. As it is, I frankly confess I am puzzled. If this Randolph has discovered a process whereby diamonds like this can be made, he has done something which will cause a world-wide stir, and very probably world-wide ruin to a vast industry."

Philander Morgan moaned a little and wiped his fat face with a large handkerchief. Marcus Meyer was biting his finger nails nervously. Only the grim Chicago magnate remained apparently unmoved.

"Select some from the other packets," he said tersely, "and examine them carefully. We must be sure of the facts before we act."

The expert selected two stones at random from each of the four unopened packages, and retired with them to the window.

Spreckles leaned back in his chair and put the tips of his skinny fingers together.

"This Randolph," he began slowly, "receives mail, I suppose—parcels by express and by freight?"

"Very little mail," the Hebrew answered. "Most of it is apparently from chemical supply houses and other dealers. He seems to have no personal correspondence. It is also rare that anything comes to him by express; but he has a good many pieces of freight, which are invariably delivered by Johnson. So far as I have been able to discover, they also come from supply houses and seem to contain chemicals of some sort."

"We must make sure," Spreckles said significantly. "From this moment Randolph must receive nothing into that house which we do not know of. Above all, his letters must be examined carefully."

Marcus Meyer's face paled a little.

"But the government——" he protested.

"Tut, tut, my dear Meyer!" Spreckles said calmly. "You are a sensible man, and a clever one. Don't let us have any foolish qualms when a matter of such moment is at stake. There are plenty of ways in which this can be done quietly and safely by a man of your ability. I leave the details to you, who are on the ground. But I repeat that neither Randolph nor this man Johnson must receive anything which you have not previously read or examined. Well, Pickering?"

The diamond expert returned the stones to their original packets and faced his employer.

"They are identical with the first one," he said quietly. "Perfect, flawless, and of equal value. I think there can be no question that their source is the same."

"I expected as much," Spreckles said quietly. "Though I am not an expert like Pickering, my eyes are still pretty fair, and I have examined a goodly number of diamonds in my life. That will be all for the present, James. Be good enough to wait for me downstairs. I will be through directly and we can take lunch and return on the early train."

As the door closed behind the diamond expert, Herman Spreckles bent forward a little and fixed his eyes keenly on Marcus Meyer.

"In addition to the precautions I have suggested," he said quietly, "it is absolutely necessary for us to obtain an entrance to this house of Randolph's and make a thorough examination. That is the most important step of all. It would be more satisfactory if you yourself could be present, but I doubt whether that is possible. However, pick your detectives intelligently, tell them exactly what you want to know, and the result should be adequate."

The Hebrew's face turned pale and he twisted his fingers nervously together.

"But think of the risk," he objected. "That's a criminal proceeding. It's breaking and entering."

The older man waved away his objection impatiently.

"Don't be a child, Meyer," he snapped. "Everything, in this world is a risk. Do you realize that your very existence is at stake? If we don't get at the bottom of this business and stop it, you will be ruined, and Morgan and I will be severely crippled. Let us have no more of this foolish squeamishness. Do as I tell you, and do it at once."

As he arose, his gaunt height towered above his companions.

"One more thing," he went on. "Don't let the man suspect. Buy all the diamonds which are offered, and above all keep silent about them. Should a whisper of this get abroad, a tremendous slump in our stocks will follow. Keep me advised daily as to your progress. I am taking the two-fifteen train back. Don't hesitate to draw on me for money if you need it. Good-by."

He stepped into the hall and closed the door behind him, leaving Philander Morgan and Marcus staring at one another with expressions of the deepest anxiety and concern.

# CHAPTER XV.

## THE MYSTERIOUS MR. RANDOLPH.

Rather less than twenty-four hours later Dick Merriwell entered the lobby of the Brown Palace Hotel and walked directly to the desk.

"Anything for me on that last mail, Fred?" he asked.

The clerk turned to the rack behind him.

"I believe there is, Mr. Merriwell," he answered. "Yes, here it is. Only one, though."

"That's all I was expecting," he returned.

He walked slowly from the desk, tearing open the envelope as he went. Close by the door he stopped to glance through the several sheets it contained.

"He's well and flourishing, that's one good thing," he murmured. "It's so long since the last letter that I was beginning—— By Jove, what a peculiar coincidence!"

Without pausing to read further, he folded the letter hastily and hurried out of the door and down the steps. Waiting at the curb stood the *Wizard* in the front seat of which was Brad Buckhart. Letter in hand, Merriwell sprang up beside him.

"Say, Brad," he began eagerly, "talking about coincidences, I've got one here that beats the Dutch. Do you remember that interesting scrap of conversation we couldn't help hearing last night in the dining room?"

"I sure do," the Texan returned promptly. "The one between the dressy little Jew and the pudgy gent with the china-blue eyes, you mean?"

Dick nodded emphatically.

"That's it," he returned quickly. "They were talking about somebody by the name of Randolph—Scott Randolph, who evidently had something to do with diamonds."

"If I got their lingo straight, he had quite some to do with them," Buckhart put in. "Unless I'm a whole lot wrong, those same two gents were saying that this Randolph manufactured 'em."

"It did sound that way," Merriwell returned; "but of course, that's impossible. We must have misunderstood them. At any rate, they were very secretive about it, for the minute the little fellow noticed us, he nudged the big man and they shut up like clams."

He paused and unfolded the letter he had just received from his brother.

"Here's a letter which just came from Frank," he went on. "He's well and very busy and all that. Glad we're having a nice trip and a lot more that won't interest you. Then comes the coincidence. I just want you to listen to this:

"'This will reach you while you are in Denver,'" Dick read. "'I wish, if you have time, you would look up an old friend of mine who is located somewhere near there. He's a rather retiring chap and doesn't care at all for company; but we got to be pretty good friends at Yale, and afterward kept up a more or less regular correspondence for some time. I haven't heard from him in over two years, and several letters of mine have been unanswered. I'd like to know whether he is still in the land of the living; and, if so, what he is doing and why he doesn't write occasionally. He was a great fellow for experimenting with chemicals and had the most extraordinary inventive ability and talent for mechanics that I have ever seen. I fancy he is doing a lot of experimenting, though he never told me just what he was after. His name is Scott Randolph. If you find him, tell him I should very much like to hear from him again.'"

Dick folded the letter and restored it to the envelope. As he did so, a card dropped out of the latter and he stooped over to pick it up.

"Scott Randolph!" the big Texan exclaimed. "Now what do you think of that? This is a sure enough interesting gent. Mebbe he's got the receipt of making diamonds out of these chemicals he experiments with."

Dick secured the card from the bottom of the car and tucked it into his pocket.

"Just one of Frank's cards introducing me to his friend," he said. "I think I shall do my best to present it. From the way Frank writes about him, Randolph must be a good sort of a chap, and I'd like to meet him for other reasons."

Buckhart laughed.

"A chap that can make diamonds must be a very good sort," he observed. "I'd sure like to put my blinkers on him. Mebbe he'd present us with a bushel or two. You hear me softly warble!"

"That's all nonsense, of course," Dick smiled. "We must have misunderstood those men last night. You know we only heard a few words. But, all the same, I'd like to meet this Randolph. Now we've seen Tucker and Bigelow off for Colorado Springs, we haven't a thing on hand for the rest of the day, and we might as well start on a still hunt for this friend of Frank's. I'll run in and see if Fred knows anything about where he can be found."

He stepped out of the car and reëntered the hotel lobby, walking up to the desk. The clerk was not busy and turned to him at once.

"Say, Fred," Merriwell began, "I'm looking for a man by the name of Scott Randolph, who is supposed to live in or around Denver. Ever heard of him? That's a pretty big order, I know, but you seem to be wise to the life history of about every one in town."

The hotel clerk laughed.

"You've got me this time," he said. "Scott Randolph? I don't think I ever heard of him. What does he do? In business here at all?"

"I don't think so," Dick answered. "I believe he spends most of his time experimenting with chemicals, or something like that."

There was a puzzled look on the clerk's face as he looked meditatively across the lobby. All at once his eyes brightened.

"Say, there's old Captain Winters sitting over there," he said. "He's the boy that can tell you what you want if anybody can. He's a regular old man gossip, and there isn't much that gets away from him, I can tell you. If he ever wrote a book and put in it all he knows about people in this town, you bet your life there'd be things doing. Come over and I'll introduce you."

He slipped from behind the desk and walked across the lobby, with Dick at his side, approaching a little, weazened-up old man who was reading a paper in an armchair close by one of the big windows.

"Captain Winters," he said, "I'd like you to meet Mr. Merriwell, who is looking for some information about a party in town. I told him you'd be able to give it to him if anybody could."

The old man peered at Dick over the tops of his spectacles, extending a palsied hand.

"Pleased to meet you, young man," he piped in a shrill voice. "Pleased to meet you. Fred's a great boy to talk. Mebbe I know a thing or two about folks, but I ain't telling it all. He, he! I wouldn't dast. What was it you was wanting to find out?"

"I'm looking for a man named Scott Randolph, Captain Winters," Dick smiled. "I think he lives somewhere on the outskirts of town."

"Scott Randolph!" the old man said sharply. "Why, I'm surprised at ye, Fred. You'd oughter know who that is. He's the one that come here seven or eight years ago an' built that crazy house like a fort in the mountains off Bonnet Trail a piece."

"Oh, is that the man?" the clerk exclaimed. "I didn't know his name was Randolph. Well, I guess you can tell Mr. Merriwell how to get out there. I must go back to the desk."

He left them and Dick dropped into a chair beside the captain.

"Folks call it 'The Folly,'" resumed the old man with the peculiar zest and relish of a born gossip. "It's built like a fort, with bars to the winders and a door like a safe. Nobody knows what he does there, but they do say he invents things. Folks going by has heard enjines going fit to kill, an' onct Jake Pettigrew, that keeps the store in Duncan, seen a great flame o' fire shoot out o' the roof. Whatever he's doing, he ain't up to no good, you can depend. It's agin' nater an' the Bible to fool with the powers o' darkness."

"Did you ever see him, Captain Winters?" Dick asked curiously.

"Not more'n a couple o' times, my boy. He don't come around often. Sometimes folks don't set eyes on him for weeks at a time; then again, he'll come down to town in his autermobile. He's a smallish, bald man, not much to look at. Some say he's cracked, but I ain't comitten' myself."

The captain pursed up his lips and shook his head slowly with the air of one who could tell a good deal more if he only would. In reality, he had already exhausted his small store of wisdom regarding Scott Randolph, who remained a perplexing mystery that the old gossip had never been able to solve.

"Can you tell me how I can find this place?" Dick asked.

"I kin," answered the captain, "but it ain't likely to do you much good, cause he never lets anybody inside the door. Howsomever, you kin try, if you have a mind to. You know where Bonnet Trail is, I s'pose?"

"Runs out to the mountains a little south of Georgetown, doesn't it?" Dick asked.

"Yep. About twenty miles out is Duncan. It ain't much of a place; jest a few houses an' Jake Pettigrew's store. Randolph's place is some four miles from there, as I recollect. You'd better ask Jake, though, an' he'll tell you right."

Dick arose from the chair.

"Thank you very much, Captain Winters," he said, holding out his hand. "I'm very glad to have met you, and shall see you again while I'm here."

"Don't mention it," returned the old man. "Let me know if you get inter Randolph's. I'm kinder curious."

"I will," Dick laughed, turning toward the door.

Buckhart yawned openly as his friend appeared beside the car.

"Say, pard," he drawled, "why didn't you stay a couple of minutes longer and clean up the hour. I reckoned you were plumb lost and was just thinking of organizing a searching party of one to locate you."

Cranking the engine, Dick squeezed past the Texan and took his seat at the wheel.

"I couldn't break away from the old party who was telling me about our friend Randolph," he explained. "He seems to be something of a mystery to the people around here. In fact, it is quite doubtful whether we shall be let into his place, once we've found it."

"Say you so?" Brad inquired interestedly. "Let's hear about it."

Threading his way through the streets, Merriwell narrated for Buckhart's benefit the curious story, or rather fragment of a story, he had just heard from Captain Winters; and by the time they reached the outskirts of the city and wheeled into Bonnet Trail, the Westerner had all the particulars and was as much interested as his chum.

"Looks like there was something queer about this gent, pard," he remarked. "My curiosity has sure riz up on its hind legs."

The road was extremely bad, being full of ruts and bumps and apparently not much traveled, so that it took them a good two hours to reach Duncan, where Dick drew up in front of the one store the small place boasted. A tall, lank individual in shirt sleeves and cowhide boots lounged in the doorway, chewing a straw.

"Are you Mr. Pettigrew?" Dick asked, stopping the engine.

"I are," was the laconic reply.

"Can you tell me how I can get to Mr. Randolph's place?"

Jake Pettigrew nearly swallowed the straw in his surprise, and was some time recovering it. When he had done so, his face was rather flushed and in his eyes there was a look of unmistakable interest.

"Randolph's place?" he exclaimed. "The Folly, you mean?"

"That's what they call it, I believe," Merriwell answered.

"Take the footpath just beyond Injun Head Rock," the lanky man directed, resuming with an evident effort his air of indifference. "It's about four miles along the trail. You can't miss it, 'cause the rock looks like the head of an Injun. 'Tain't of'en Randolph has callers."

"So I understand," Dick said. "Is he at home, do you know?"

"So help me, no," the man answered hastily. "He may be, or he mayn't. I don't know nothin' about him."

The Yale man thanked him, and with the engine started, the car continued up the hilly trail on second speed. They passed the rocky peak which, strange to say, really did bear some resemblance to an Indian's head, and a few hundred yards beyond came to a clearly defined track leading from Bonnet Trail up into the foothills.

Dick turned the car in to one side of the road well out of the way. Pocketing the coil plug, he followed Buckhart out of the machine, and they started up the narrow, rocky track on foot.

It wound straight up into the mountains, hugging the steep wall on one side, while on the other the ground fell away abruptly into a multitude of gorges and ravines. Sometimes the descent was precipitous and the track seemed almost to be hung in mid-air over an abyss, while at other places the slope was more gradual and covered with great boulders, mingled with a heavy growth of pine and bushes.

At length they rounded a sharp turn and came out on a fairly level plateau, perhaps a hundred yards in diameter, completely hemmed in on three sides by high cliffs, while on the fourth it fell away abruptly into a deep ravine.

Facing them, and built against the highest cliff, was a stone house, which they at once made certain was the one they sought.

It was large and square, and composed entirely of the same dark, somber rock of which the surrounding mountains were made. Hugging, as it did, the cliff, it was somewhat hard to distinguish just where the natural rock ended and the house began. This difficulty was increased by the fact that the dwelling was in reality built into a sort of depression in the side of the cliff, the jagged top of which overhung the roof.

In the middle of the front side was a large door that seemed to be closed by a single sheet of iron or steel, while the windows, even on the upper floors, were protected by stout iron bars and some sort of inside shutters.

Taken all in all, it was a most dreary, desolate, prison-like structure, to which the surrounding barriers of jagged, gray cliffs, hard, bare, with no re-lieving touch of green, added an almost sinister grimness.

"By George, pard, what a place to live in!" Buckhart said in a low tone. "I'd as soon bunk up in a prison."

The depressing influence of the surroundings was so great that, uncon-sciously, the Texan had lowered his voice almost to a whisper.

His companion did not answer. His head was bent slightly forward and there was look of keen intentness in his eyes. The next moment he spoke.

"Listen!" he said softly. "What's that noise?"

In the silence which followed, a faint, regular, scraping sound came from their right. It was so slight that for a minute or two neither of them could place it. At length they decided that it came from around the corner of the building, a spot which they could not see from their present position at the entrance of the plateau.

Scrape, scrape, scrape. Scratch, scratch, scratch. It sounded, with the reg-ularity of clockwork.

Buckhart eyed his chum with a puzzled expression on his face.

"What the deuce is it?" he whispered.

"I'm not sure," Dick returned, "but it sounds like filing—as though some-body was filing an iron bar. I'm going to find out."

He dropped down on his hands and knees and commenced to creep slowly through the scattered boulders to the right. Brad promptly followed him, and in less than five minutes they were ensconced behind a great rock, from which a very good view of that side of the house could be obtained.

There was a momentary pause, and then they both peered cautiously around the corner of the boulder.

The next moment the Texan caught his breath with a sudden, swift intake, his eyes widened with astonishment. Dick, crouching beside him, pressed his chum's arm warningly, without for an instant averting his own gaze from the surprising sight before them.

# CHAPTER XVI.

## THE MYSTERIOUS HOUSE.

On the ground floor of this side of the house were two windows, barred and shuttered like the rest, and, crouching in a group about the one nearest the cliff, were four men.

They were roughly dressed in dark clothes and slouch hats, and their faces were completely covered with black masks. One of them was on his knees cutting methodically at the bottom of an iron bar, while a companion stood by his side, a bottle of oil in his hand, from which he occasionally poured a few drops on the saw. The other two men stood a little to one side, taking no part in the work, but watching its progress with every sign of intense interest.

When they had fully taken in what was going on, the two chums drew back into the shelter of the boulder and Dick eyed his companion significantly.

"Looks as though some one was even more interested in Randolph than we are," he murmured.

"That's what," Buckhart returned softly. "Did you ever see anything like their nerve, breaking into a man's house in broad daylight?"

At that moment the filing ceased and the watchers looked out just in time to scc two of the masked men take the bar in their hands and slowly bend it upward. That done, the fellow promptly commenced work on the next bar.

He had scarcely done so when the sound of some one carelessly whistling a tune, came faintly from a distance.

The effect was magical. The man at the bar sprang to his feet with an oath and dropped his file. The other three looked around in a startled manner, and there was a brief, hurried consultation between all four.

The whistle grew louder and more distinct. To Dick it seemed that the sound came from the ravine to the left of the house, but he was too much interested in the proceedings of the masked men, to pay particular attention to it.

After a swift interchange of words, the group split up and, hugging the wall of the house, stole noiselessly in single file toward the front corner.

The situation was growing more and more interesting. By squirming forward a little, Merriwell managed to reach a spot where he had a good view of both the front and side of the house. The next moment, to his amazement, he saw the head and shoulders of a man appear at the edge of the ravine and step up on the plateau.

Short and slim, he was dressed in a suit of khaki with leggings, as though he had been riding or taking a long walk. As he sauntered toward the door with a springy step, his cheery whistle sounded out of place in the gloomy desolation of the silent spot.

Dick caught his breath and his heart beat a trifle unevenly. The foremost of the masked men had almost reached the corner of the house when the whistling stopped and the slim unknown slipped his hand into his pocket and pulled out what was apparently a key.

Something was going to happen, and that very soon. Merriwell felt it instinctively and waited, muscles taut and nerves quivering, for the first move to be made. The Texan crouched behind him, also ready for business. Though he could not see the man at the door, Dick's eyes were riveted on the four masked ruffians, who betrayed by their actions that they were up to no good.

The slim man fitted the key into a lock; and then, with the resulting click, there was a rush of feet from the corner of the house as the masked men came at him in a bunch.

Though taken by surprise, the fellow at the door was quick as a cat. Whirling around, his back to the opening, he met the first comer with a straight blow from the shoulder which sent him reeling back against one of his companions. But the odds were too great, and almost instantly the man in khaki was borne to the ground by the sheer weight of his opponents, though he still continued to struggle desperately.

It was then that the two Yale men took a hand in the game. A swift rush carried them across the plateau, where they landed on the masked men with the demoralizing suddenness of a thunderbolt.

In grim silence each one seized a collar and jerked a man to his feet, at the same time administering a swift jab on the jaw which sent the fellows sprawling a dozen feet away. This performance was repeated with the other two, and, as the ruffians landed on the ground with a thud, the unknown sprang up with the elasticity of a rubber ball.

"Thank you, gentlemen," he said in a quick, incisive voice.

One hand slid to his hip pocket and he drew a serviceable-looking revolver, which he leveled at the masked men, who apparently about to resume their attack.

"Get!" he ripped out tersely, his eyes gleaming. "Beat it! Vamoose! If you're not out of sight in three minutes I'll drill you full of holes."

The tallest of the four—the one who had done the filing—seemed inclined to disregard the warning, but one of his companions plucked him by the arm and whispered a few words into his ear.

"Skip!" repeated the slim man. "I mean what I say. The next time I catch you around here I'll shoot first and you can explain afterward—if you're able."

Without further delay, the men turned and hurried toward the trail. The unknown watched them until they were out of sight, and then he wheeled quickly around.

"I seem to have an unexpected influx of callers to-day," he remarked. "Might I ask your business?"

His tone was cool and self-possessed, but he shoved the revolver back into his pocket as he spoke.

"You are Mr. Randolph," Dick inquired—"Mr. Scott Randolph?"

The stranger nodded and his eyes narrowed.

"I am," he said tersely. "And you?"

The Yale man took a card from his pocket and handed it to the other.

"My name is Merriwell," he said, quietly. "My brother asked me to give you this."

As his eyes fell on Frank Merriwell's card with the brief written words, "Introducing my brother Dick," the cold, questioning, almost skeptical expression, instantly left Scott Randolph's face, and his keen, gray eyes softened with a look of friendliness, mingled with regret.

"I'm awfully glad to meet Frank's brother," he said warmly, as he extended his hand. "The more so since you came just in time to help me out of a tight place. I hope you don't think I'm ungrateful because I didn't enthuse at first. The truth is, I've got so I look at every one with more or less suspicion, and, even though you did knock those ruffians around some, I couldn't understand what you were doing here."

Dick shook his hand heartily.

"Don't mention it," he smiled. "I think I understand a little of what you mean. It was rather startling to have four masked men pile onto you and then be assisted by two others who were total strangers. This is my friend Brad Buckhart, Mr. Randolph."

Randolph gripped the Texan's hand warmly and then looked at Dick again.

"How is Frank?" he asked quickly. "Though I don't deserve to know, after the beastly way I've neglected him lately. He was my friend at Yale—almost the only fellow I could really call a friend; but so much has happened in the past few years——"

He broke off abruptly and his face sobered.

"Perhaps some day you'll understand," he finished slowly. "Tell me about Frank."

"He's well and happy, and absorbed in his work," Dick returned. "He wanted me to look you up and see what you were doing and why you hadn't written."

Scott Randolph suddenly pulled out his watch and looked at it with a worried expression.

"By Jove, I'm sorry!" he exclaimed, his face clouding. "I'd forgotten. I can't stay here another minute—can't even ask you in. I have a most important—engagement. It's frightfully inhospitable, but I can't very well explain. Say, won't you both come back and take dinner with me at six o'clock? You can spend the evening, and we'll have a good talk. I can't tell you how beastly sorry I am."

Though Dick was rather surprised, nothing of it appeared in his manner.

"Why, I think we can," he said slowly. "We've nothing on for to-night and we might come."

"That's splendid!" Randolph exclaimed, in a tone of relief. "Come at six, and I'll be ready for you."

He had already picked up the key from where it had dropped to the ground and was fitting it into the lock with feverish haste. The two Yale men started away, when Dick suddenly remembered something.

"Those fellows were filing a bar in one of your windows," he called back.

Randolph did not turn his head.

"Thanks," he said hurriedly. "I'll look after it presently."

The next instant he had disappeared inside the house, and the steel door closed with a clang which resounded through the rocky gorge. As the two friends hesitated at the entrance to the plateau, they heard the click of the key and the sound of a bolt being shot home. Then silence fell.

Neither of the two chums spoke a word until they were well along the narrow track and the stone house was out of sight. Then Buckhart stopped suddenly.

"Well, of all the wild, woolly, mysterious goings on," he burst out, "this has sure got any I ever bumped up against skinned a mile. Say, pard, tell me honest what you think of a gent who is piled on by four bad men with masks, and as soon as we politely rescue him, he looks at us like we were bunco steerers, and asks our business. Furthermore, when he's found out we're fairly respectable he gives us the glad hand, and the next minute tells us to run away and play, and come back to dinner. I tell you there's something a whole lot queer about this here Randolph. You hear me talk!"

"He certainly seems to be a trifle odd in his behavior," Dick returned. "But, all the same, I rather like his looks. Wait until after to-night before we pass final judgment on him. He may have a pretty good reason for everything he's done. Come on, Brad, don't waste time here. It evidently hasn't occurred to you that the gentlemen with masks may have taken a fancy to the *Wizard* and made a quick getaway in her."

"Great Scott, no!" the Texan gasped. "I never thought of that."

Almost at a run, they covered the rest of the narrow path, and both gave an exclamation of relief as they reached Bonnet Trail and found the car safe and sound where they had left it.

"Gee, what a relief!" Dick said, as he gave the crank a flip and stepped into his seat. "I hadn't the slightest desire to hoof it back to Denver; and in these parts a stolen car is a mighty hard thing to get track of."

Turning the *Wizard* deftly, he started her back toward the city. An animated discussion at once arose concerning the mysterious Scott Randolph, his personality, his peculiar dwelling, and above all, his probable occupation, which continued until the hotel was reached; without, it must be confessed, arriving at any very satisfactory solution on any of the points.

Promptly at a quarter before six that night the *Wizard* again passed Jake Pettigrew's store, causing that worthy to gasp in surprise and instantly to be assailed with the awful pangs of ungratified curiosity.

The car did not stop. Disappearing up the hill in a cloud of dust, it was guided to the spot where it had rested earlier in the day, and the two fellows stepped out and walked briskly up the narrow path.

As they reached the plateau both men hesitated instinctively, their eyes traveling curiously over the front of the strange building. The sun was low in the west, and the frowning, battlemented cliffs cast weird, purpling shadows over the desolate spot. Out of these shadows rose the grim, gray, silent walls of the house. No cheerful ray of light penetrated through the steel shutters of the barred windows to welcome the expected guests. They were like the eye sockets in a skull—gaunt, dark, expressionless. A thousand things might happen behind those walls of which they would never give a hint.

With a shrug of his shoulders, the Texan likened the place to a tomb, and they walked forward and beat a resounding blow upon the door.

It was opened almost instantly, and Scott Randolph stood smiling on the threshold, his slim figure silhouetted against the blaze of light which streamed from the hall behind him.

"You're on time to the minute," he said briskly. "Come in and make yourselves at home."

Blinking in the glare of light, which was as grateful as it was unexpected, Dick and Brad stepped into the hall. Randolph swiftly clanged the door to behind them and shot the bolt.

"Where did you leave your car?" he asked, turning to them. "I assume that you came in one."

"Out on the trail," Dick answered. "I reckon it's safe, isn't it?"

The older man laughed.

"Sure thing," he said. "There's hardly any one uses the trail after dark. I have a little car which I keep in a shed a couple of miles this side of Duncan, but it's no pleasure to use it on Bonnet Trail, so I don't often take the trip in to Denver. Well, what do you think of my castle? Want to look around before dinner?"

The Yale men gave an instant eager assent. The glimpse they had already had of the broad, comfortably furnished hall, with its rugs and pictures and easy-chairs scattered about, all brilliantly lighted by the clusters of electric globes suspended from the ceiling, had amazed them and stimulated their curiosity. Somehow, it was so totally different from what they had expected, that Dick could not help commenting on it.

Scott Randolph laughed heartily.

"Did you expect to see bare prison walls and a stone floor?" he asked, when he had recovered his breath. "I don't know that I blame you, though. The outside of the place does look pretty fierce, but I had special reasons for wanting it that way, and I tried to make up for it as well as possible inside."

He opened a door to the left of the hall and stood aside for them to enter.

"This is my library and general lounging room," he explained. "It takes up this whole side of the house."

The room, a good fifty feet long and half as wide, was lined with bookshelves crowded to overflowing. A great stone fireplace occupied the centre of the outside wall, a piano stood in one corner, and all about were scattered comfortable chairs and couches, together with several tables on which were shaded electric lamps. The floor was covered with rugs and skins of various sorts.

"What a dandy room!" Dick exclaimed enthusiastically. "I don't know when I've seen one more homelike or attractive."

"It's where I rest from my labors and enjoy myself," Randolph said lightly. "We'll settle down here after dinner and have a good talk."

He led the way to the hall again and started upstairs. Then he seemed to change his mind.

"Let's have dinner first and do that afterward," he said. "Aren't you fellows hungry?"

Confessing that they might be induced to partake of food, they followed him through the door opposite the one leading into the library. Though not quite two-thirds the size of the big room, the dining room was still spacious. The furniture was of dark oak, simple but substantially made, the table being spread with a spotless linen cloth and lighted with shaded candles in silver candlesticks. There were places laid for three; a large, oblong chafing dish stood at one end, while in the middle of the table were several covered dishes.

Randolph motioned them to their places, taking his seat in front of the chafing dish.

"You fellows will have to be charitable to-night," he remarked, as he took off the cover and laid it aside. "My work is of such a nature that it is impossible for me to have servants of any kind about, and, as a result, I have grown accustomed to looking after things myself."

Dick looked at him in surprise.

"Do you mean to say that you never have any one here to cook or clean up?" he asked.

Scott Randolph hesitated.

"Well, not exactly that," he said slowly. "I have a fri—a man who comes in and helps me occasionally; but as a rule I look after myself. It isn't hard when you've grown used to it, and the chafing dish is a great help. Of course, when I'm alone, as I generally am, I don't do things elaborately."

His apology for the meal was quite unnecessary, for it was delicious and cooked to perfection. The two fellows enjoyed every mouthful of it, marveling how a man could live so well in a place that was so out of the way as to be almost in a wilderness.

Scott Randolph was an ideal host. Bright, witty, and entertaining in his conversation, he had, when he chose to exert himself, an extraordinary charm of manner. By the time they arose from the table and returned to the library, both Merriwell and Buckhart had made up their minds that he was a very good sort indeed, and were not surprised that he had been a friend of Frank.

They settled down comfortably on a couch, and for nearly an hour Dick regaled his host with everything he could think of that would interest him regarding Frank's doings, even giving him the latter's letter to read.

"I shall write to him to-morrow," Randolph said contritely, when the Yale man had finished. "I'm afraid, living in seclusion as I do, with scarcely any relaxation from an absorbing and interesting work, I've grown selfish. I don't want Frank to think I've forgotten him, for I haven't. One makes few enough real friends in this world, and a fellow is lucky to have one like your brother."

Dick hesitated for an instant.

"Would it be impertinent if I asked what your work is?" he asked slowly. "Frank was very much interested in it."

Randolph cast a swift glance at Buckhart, who was examining the bookshelves at the other end of the room.

"Shall you see Frank soon?" he asked, lowering his voice.

"Probably within a few weeks," Dick returned. "I'll drop in on him on my way back to New Haven."

"Then I will tell you, but you must not write it to him. You must tell it to him only by word of mouth, and then when he is alone. I shall have to ask for your word of honor that you will say nothing to any other living soul of what I am about to confide in you. Will you pledge me this?"

The Yale man did not reply at once. What could be the nature of a work which required such secrecy as this?

"I assure you it is necessary," Randolph went on in the same low tone. "If the slightest hint of my discovery should leak out, it would precipitate the greatest panic this country—nay, the world—has ever seen."

Dick gave a slight start. A sudden thought had flashed into his brain. Could it be possible that—— He recovered himself quickly.

"I give you my word, of course," he said gravely. "I shall say nothing to any one but Frank of what you have to tell me."

Randolph breathed a sigh of relief as he bent closer to the Yale man. His voice was so low that the latter had to strain his ears to hear.

"Listen," he murmured. "I have discovered the process of making diamonds. Not tiny pinheads such as Fournier of Paris has produced, but stones of any size I wish, which the greatest experts in the country cannot distinguish from the natural gems. By the merest chance in my experimenting, I have stumbled upon the secret for which men have sought since the world began; and wealth beyond the dreams of avarice is in my grasp."

# CHAPTER XVII.

## IN THE SHADOW OF THE CLIFFS.

For a moment Merriwell sat dazed and bewildered. It was true, then! Those few muttered words, overheard by chance the night before in the dining room of the Brown Palace, were true, and not wild figments of the imagination as he had supposed them. Somehow it did not occur to him for an instant to doubt Scott Randolph. Perhaps, had he not heard that stifled scrap of conversation, he might not have believed so readily this amazing, incredible statement. But it seemed to fit in so well with what Randolph had just told him—to confirm it, in a way—that he felt no doubt.

"Then what they said is true," he murmured, his eyes fixed in wonder on the face of the slim man beside him.

Randolph suddenly stiffened as though an electric current had passed through his body.

"Who said?" he rasped. "What did they say? Quick, tell me!"

Dick repeated the scrap of conversation he and Brad had heard in the hotel dining room, and as he listened Randolph's face paled.

"Who were they?" he asked in a strained voice, "What did they look like?"

Dick shook his head.

"I don't know who they were. One was a medium-sized Jew, very carefully dressed; the other a stout man with a fat face and small blue eyes. The expression on his face was like that of a peevish baby. They both looked like men of importance."

"Marcus Meyer!" Randolph exclaimed, with a sigh of relief. "I don't know the other one, but Meyer controls the diamond trade in the Middle West. They don't really know; they only guess. But even if they were sure, they would keep it quiet for their own sakes."

Buckhart strolled toward them at that moment.

"You folks must have Frank talked to death," he drawled.

"We've just finished," the older man said, with a smile, as he rose from the couch. "Would you boys like to look about upstairs?"

In one breath the Yale men expressed their readiness, following their host out into the hall and up the broad stairs. Randolph touched a button at the top of the flight which flooded the upper hall with light. The next instant

Dick thought he heard him draw a sudden, quick breath. Buckhart heard nothing, for he had dived promptly into an open door close to the head of the stairs.

"Any light in here?" he called.

Scott Randolph hesitated for the fraction of a second and then pressed a button on the wall.

"By George!" the Texan exclaimed. "This is sure a funny room. What's it for, anyhow?"

Stepping to the door, Dick looked in. The room was a small one, not more than twelve feet square, and had neither doors nor windows, nor any other opening save the entrance. It was absolutely bare of furnishings, with not even a shelf on the wall nor a scrap of paper on the floor. There was nothing but the four walls of gray stone.

"Looks like a vault," Buckhart remarked.

"It does, doesn't it?" Randolph said slowly. "But the only treasures I have kept there are expensive chemicals which cannot be exposed to light or air or dampness. If I should shut this door on you, I venture to say that in two hours at the latest, you would have exhausted every bit of oxygen in the place; and since it is absolutely air tight——"

"Say, don't!" the Westerner exclaimed, with an expression of mock dismay. "Let me amble out, quick!"

Scott Randolph laughed as Buckhart came out of the room, but his eyes narrowed a little when the Texan caught sight of the peculiar construction of the door. Instead of being of wood, it was of sheet steel. On one side were cemented slabs of stone so that, when closed, it would be absolutely impossible for a person inside to locate that door. On the outer side it was covered with the same oak paneling with which the hall was lined, and there were no signs of lock or catch, not even so much as a doorknob or latch.

"That's certain sure a neat job," Brad commented. "When it's shut nobody can tell where it is. Regular secret room, isn't it?"

"That was one of my hobbies," the man of mystery explained. "When it is shut, I can push a secret spring which slides a powerful bolt and holds the door so that it would be easier to tear down the wall than to open it."

He switched off the light and closed the door. Both Dick and Brad examined the wall closely, but neither of them could tell between which panels the joint came.

The remainder of the second floor was divided up into five bedrooms and a bathroom, the water for which was pumped into a tank on the roof by a windmill on the cliff above. Passing by a door at the end of the hall, which, as their host mentioned casually, opened into a store closet, they mounted to the next floor, which was given over entirely to the laboratory and experimenting rooms.

They were all filled with a multitude of machines and pieces of apparatus, many being of strange shapes and unknown uses. Randolph stepped forward to explain one of these to the Texan, giving Dick a significant glance, and at the same moment pulling open a drawer in a cabinet which stood against the wall.

Merriwell had difficulty in restraining an exclamation of amazement, for the drawer was half full of the most beautiful diamonds he had ever seen. They were of varying sizes from a pea to a small hickory nut, and Dick gave a stifled gasp as he looked at the shimmering, glittering blaze of light.

The man closed the drawer with a snap and turned to the visitors, his face a trifle pale. The drawer contained a king's ransom. It seemed beyond the bounds of reason that they could have been actually manufactured by this slim, quiet man.

"But how do you get away from this place without anybody seeing you?" the Texan was asking. "People say you're away for weeks at a time, but no one sees you go or come."

Scott Randolph threw back his head and laughed heartily.

"That's very simple," he said. "I don't go away. When a passion for work comes over me I shut myself up and absolutely refuse to open the door to any one. It's the only way I can accomplish anything. They may hammer and pound all they like, but I pay no attention to it. That's one of the reasons why I had this house built like a fortified castle. I can shut myself up in it and work undisturbed.

"Of course, I have to lay in a big supply of eatables, and so forth. For instance, this very afternoon I got in a big order from Jake Pettigrew's store; and, when you have gone to-night and the door is locked behind you, I shall begin one of these periods of retirement in order to complete some very important work. Nothing short of blowing the house down would induce me to open the door again."

As he finished he cast a significant glance at Dick, who thought he understood what that important work would be.

After looking about a little longer, they descended to the lower hall.

Glancing at his watch, Dick saw that it was almost ten o'clock.

"It's about time we were wandering," he said. "I can't tell you how much I have enjoyed myself, Mr. Randolph. It is very good of you to have us up here, and I shall be careful in delivering your message to Frank."

"The pleasure has been mine, I assure you," Randolph returned, as he shook hands with the Yale men. "It is not often that I have such a relaxation. I am only sorry that the pressure of work will not allow me to see you again.

However, we shall meet somewhere, some time. The world is very small, after all. Good-by, fellows, and good luck."

As he spoke, he swung open the great steel door, and, with a cordial good-by, Merriwell and Buckhart went out into the night. For a brief instant they stood in the brilliant square of light which poured out of the doorway. Then it was suddenly blotted out as the door clanged and the bolt was shot.

"He's sure not running any chances," Buckhart remarked, as they stumbled forward through the darkness. "I reckon his work must be mighty important when he has to shut himself up in a prison to do it."

Dick made no answer. He could scarcely say anything on that score without committing himself, so they felt their way along in silence until they struck the road. Their eyes becoming accustomed to the darkness, they made much better time to Bonnet Trail, where they found the *Wizard* safe and sound as they had left her.

Merriwell turned on the prestolite and lit the lamps, before cranking her. Then, circling around, he started slowly down the road toward the city.

As they passed Pettigrew's store a voice suddenly hailed them from the dark piazza:

"Hey, there, you fellows!"

Dick stopped the car and looked back.

"You want us?" he asked.

Pettigrew's lank figure loomed up out of the darkness as he hurried to the side of the *Wizard*. His lively curiosity had made it impossible for him to sleep, and he had been sitting alone on the piazza for some time waiting for the return of the Yale men.

"I jest wondered how you made out up to The Folly?" he remarked, with an attempt at casualness.

Dick laughed.

"Why, we had a very good dinner and passed a pleasant evening there," he replied.

"Waal, I swan!" ejaculated the storekeeper. "I reckon you're the only fellers, 'ceptin' Al Johnson, as is ever been inside the place. What's it look like? What'd you have fur supper?"

"It's just like any other house inside," the Yale man answered. "You ought to know what we had for supper, you furnished the supplies, didn't you?"

"I did not!" snapped Pettigrew. "I of'en wondered why this here Randolph don't git his stuff here. It's nearer nor anywhere else."

Dick hesitated a moment.

"Didn't Mr. Randolph leave a big order with you this afternoon?" he asked.

"No, nor any other arternoon," the storekeeper returned promptly. "He never bought a cent's worth offen me."

This was evidently a sore point, for the man displayed considerable heat.

"Well, we must be getting on," Dick said, as he let in his clutch. "Good night, Mr. Pettigrew."

As the car glided away, Merriwell was thinking over this new discovery. Randolph had certainly told them of getting in a large order of supplies from Pettigrew's that afternoon, and yet the storekeeper had just declared most emphatically that the man had never bought a cent's worth from him. Randolph must have been lying. Why had he done so? What possible reason could he have for wishing to deceive them?

The next instant he put his hand up quickly to his breast pocket.

"By Jove, what a chump I am!" he exclaimed in a tone of annoyance.

"What's the matter now, pard?" the Texan inquired.

Dick stopped the car with a jerk.

"I've left my pocketbook back at Randolph's," he explained.

"Are you sure you left it there?" Brad asked. "Mebbe you dropped it in the car."

"No; I left it in the library," Merriwell returned positively. "I remember now taking it out to get Frank's letter, which Randolph wanted to read. I laid it on the couch, intending to replace the letter when he had finished. Instead, I must have put it in my pocket and left the bill case lying there. We'll have to go back. It contains all my money and a lot of other things."

He jammed on the reverse and, by dint of careful manœuvring, turned the car around and started back. In a few minutes the path was reached, and they scrambled out and hurried along it as rapidly as they could.

Under the bright starlight they had no trouble in finding their way; but reaching the plateau and facing the grim, stone building, it seemed even more desolate and deserted than when they had left it half an hour before. Under the shadow of the towering cliffs, the house loomed up a vague, mysterious bulk.

It did not seem possible that there could be a living soul behind those dark, silent walls; but it had looked that way before, and the opening door had revealed a bright glow of cheerful comfort. Consequently the two hastened confidently to the entrance and Dick knocked loudly on the steel door.

The sound reverberated in a hollow manner which seemed loud enough to wake the dead, and they waited expectantly for a response. But none came. Their keen ears could detect no sound of footsteps within; the massive door remained closed.

After five minutes of patient waiting, Dick was raising his hand to knock again when Buckhart gave a sudden exclamation.

"By George, pard! I'll bet we can knock here all night without his coming. Don't you remember what he said about shutting himself in after we were gone, and paying no attention to anybody or anything?"

"Yes, I remember that, all right," Dick answered; "but I thought that, coming so soon after our departure, he would guess who it was and come down to——"

He broke off abruptly and looked swiftly upward.

"Listen!" he exclaimed in a low voice.

In the silence which followed there came faintly to their straining ears an odd, muffled humming. For a moment they both thought it was one of the pieces of machinery in Randolph's laboratory, but very soon they reached the conclusion that it was much farther away than that. It seemed to come, in fact, from high up among the cliffs which towered above the house.

Dick looked at his friend significantly.

"It's a gasoline engine," he whispered.

Buckhart nodded silently. It certainly sounded very much like one.

"What the mischief is it doing up there on the mountain?" he asked presently.

There was no chance for Merriwell to reply. The humming increased as though the engine was speeding up, followed by a strange rustling, creaking noise unlike anything they had ever heard. Suddenly before their astonished eyes, a vast, black, shadowy shape rose slowly from the cliffs and hovered an instant in the air high above them. There was a majestic sweep of great wings, as it made a wide, half circle; then it shot northward into the darkness, gathering momentum at every instant, and a moment later the muffled hum of the engine died away in the distance.

"Thundering coyotes! What was that?" the Texan exclaimed, when he had recovered from his surprise.

"An aëroplane, I should say," Dick returned quietly, though his voice quivered with suppressed excitement.

This new development added tremendously to the mystery with which the personality of Scott Randolph was surrounded, for it must belong to him. There could be no question of that. But why had he not spoken of it? What was it doing up on the cliffs? Above all, what did this silent, stealthy flight through the darkness mean?

"What in time is it doing up there?" Brad questioned.

"I haven't an idea. I suppose it belongs to Randolph and that he keeps it up on the cliffs somewhere."

Silently they turned and began to retrace their steps.

"Say, partner, mebbe that's what he's experimenting on," the Texan remarked presently.

"Perhaps it is," Dick returned absently.

Could it be that Randolph had deceived him? Was it possible that the amazing statement he had made was false, and that, instead of making diamonds, he was experimenting on an aëroplane?

Merriwell did not like to think that the man who had once been a friend to Frank, and whom he himself had found so attractive and likable, would stoop to a thing like that. It was so totally unnecessary, too. He need not have told any story at all had he desired to keep his work a secret. Dick had nailed one lie that night, and if there was one thing he despised above another it was a deliberate liar.

But there was the drawer full of diamonds. They were real enough and bore out the man's astounding statement. It was a most puzzling situation.

All at once Buckhart caught his friend's arm.

"Look," he cried excitedly—"look at the lights!"

Following the direction of the Texan's hand, Dick strained his eyes to the northward. There certainly were lights there. Brilliant, regular flashes came from high up in the air many miles away. As Merriwell studied them, it seemed to him that some one was signaling from the clouds. If they were really signals, the man was using a secret code and not the regular government system, with which Dick was perfectly familiar. Suddenly they ceased.

"Signals, weren't they?" Buckhart inquired.

"Looked like it; but I don't know the code."

They had reached the car and Dick stooped to crank it. The next instant he let go the handle and stood erect, his head bent back and his eyes upward, in an attitude of strained attention.

A faint humming sound came from the distance, gradually growing louder.

The aëroplane was returning.

Even as this conviction darted into his mind, the vast shape flashed by high in the air. For a second the shadowy form was barely discernible against the glittering stars, and then it vanished from sight among the mountains.

"Back again, eh?" commented the Texan. "What do you know about that? I tell you, pard, this here gent has sure got me guessing some."

Starting the engine with a flip of the crank, Dick took his seat at the wheel and Buckhart climbed in beside him.

"You're not the only one he has guessing," Merriwell remarked, after he had turned the car and started back. "He's a most perplexing mystery, and I rather think we couldn't spend to-morrow more profitably than in trying to solve that problem."

For several hours that night Dick tossed restlessly on the bed. His mind was working so actively that it seemed impossible to go to sleep. Theory after theory flashed into his brain, as he sought to account for the curious behavior of Scott Randolph, only to be rejected because of some serious flaw in his reasoning. Each of the important, vital facts he had gathered concerning this mysterious man were utterly at variance with the other.

The astounding statement that he had discovered a method of manufacturing diamonds seemed to be corroborated by the drawer full of the precious gems, and also by the scrap of conversation the two Yale men had overheard in the dining room of the Brown Palace. Besides, Dick knew that diamonds had been produced by scientists, though not on a scale which made the process a scientific success. But the thing was possible.

In the face of all this stood the lie Randolph had told and the presence of the aëroplane. Why had the man kept such absolute silence about the flying machine when he had been so communicative in a far more vital matter? And more than that, why had he told Dick a deliberate falsehood in the matter of the provisions? What had been his object? What had he gained?

At last the Yale man gave it up and fell into a troubled slumber.

Bright and early next morning the *Wizard* again left the city and spun out along Bonnet Trail. Merriwell had cashed a check at the desk before starting and so was supplied with funds. Yet he was anxious to obtain his bill case more for the papers it contained than for anything else; and besides, it would serve him as a sufficient excuse for trying to locate Randolph.

Again the car was driven over to the side of the trail and the coil plug removed. Again the two friends hurried up the narrow, mountain track which led to the mysterious house of stone.

In the bright glare of the morning sun it did not look so gloomy and desolate as it had the night before; but it was still quite grim and forbidding enough, with its blank expressionless windows and absolute lack of sound or life.

Merriwell had hardly expected any response to his repeated poundings on the metal door, and he was not disappointed. He might have spared himself the effort.

When he was finally satisfied that there was no possibility of effecting an entrance, he turned his attention to the cliffs above the house, from which the aëroplane had appeared. A glance told him that they were insurmountable. For the greater part of their height they were almost as smooth as glass, and the top ledges overhung the plateau in such a manner as to make an attempt at climbing them out of the question.

"I'd certainly like to get up there," he remarked. "But there's nothing doing from here."

"Do you think the flying machine is up there, pard?" Buckhart inquired.

"That's what I want to find out," Merriwell returned, "I shouldn't be surprised if it were."

He stepped to the edge of the ravine from which Randolph had appeared the afternoon previous, but though a faint outline of a path showed among the rocks, it turned abruptly away from the cliffs and followed the course of a little stream as far as the eye could reach.

"Let's take the car and go up the trail a bit," Dick said, as he turned from the ravine. "Perhaps we can find some way to climb up the mountains in that direction."

They went back to the car and Dick drove slowly on along Bonnet Trail. For perhaps a mile nothing favorable appeared, then his quick eye discerned the almost obliterated signs of where a path had once wound among the rocks up the steep slope. Drawing the car in to the side of the road, they stepped out and started their climb.

The path was rough and winding. Once or twice they lost it, but, after a little searching, struck it again farther up. The general direction it took was southeast, and Dick noticed with satisfaction that it seemed to lead with more or less directness, toward the heights surrounding the stone house. On the side of the mountains was a fair amount of vegetation—small pine trees and some underbrush. Presently, emerging upon a wide, fairly level spot surrounded by the higher reaches of mountain, they stopped stock-still in astonishment.

Quite near them was a small cabin, ruined and decayed. It had evidently been long deserted, and what its former use had been it was impossible to determine.

It was not upon the cabin, however, that their eyes were fixed in gaping amazement. It was a question whether they even saw it at first, so engrossed were they in the intricate mass of rods and metal, burnished copper and great, wide-spreading planes which lay on the ground near them, stretched out like an enormous, uncouth bird at rest.

"By George!" the Texan exclaimed. "It's the flying machine, or I'll eat my hat!"

"It certainly looks like it," Dick returned with much satisfaction.

Then a strange voice sounded from the cabin, and the two Yale men whirled around instantly in surprise.

"Guessed right the first crack, gents. It sure is a flying machine."

# CHAPTER XVIII.

## BERT HOLTON, SPECIAL OFFICER.

Standing in the doorway was a slim, wiry, alert-looking man of twenty-eight or thirty, dressed in a dark, serviceable suit, with leather leggings. He leaned carelessly against the sagging doorpost, a slight smile on his smooth-shaven face, watching them with keen, snapping black eyes.

"Is this your monoplane?" Dick asked quickly.

"I don't know anybody that has a better claim to it," the stranger answered promptly.

As he glanced again at the aëroplane, Merriwell gave a sigh of relief. This, then, was what they had seen the night before, and he had quite misjudged Randolph. The scientist had probably never left his house.

Dick had been so anxious to think the best of Frank's friend that he was rejoiced beyond measure to believe that his suppositions to the contrary were wrong. Then he remembered the lie Randolph had told him. That, at least, had not been disproved.

"You gents seem mighty interested in my little bird," the slim man remarked as he stepped forward and joined them. "Might I inquire if you've happened to see another one around here lately?"

Dick gave a slight start.

"Why do you ask that?" he questioned.

The stranger hesitated.

"I might as well tell you the truth," he said at length, with a slight shrug of his shoulders. "I'm about at the end of my rope, and you're not apt to help me any unless you know what you're doing. My name is Holton—Bert Holton. I'm a special officer from Washington. For about five months we've been trying to run down the cleverest gang of diamond smugglers that ever tried to beat Uncle Sam. Got on to 'em first through one of our agents in Europe. Glen is certainly a smart chap; I don't know how he smells out some of these cases, but somehow he got wind of a party that was having a big bunch of rough diamonds cut in Amsterdam. Didn't know where they came from, but he got suspicious at the amount of stones the duck had and wired us when he took passage direct to Canada.

"We had men on hand to meet the gent, and he was shadowed wherever he went. He didn't make any try to cross the border, but took the Canadian Pacific direct to a farm he had about two hundred miles the other side of

Winnipeg. It was a good seventy-five miles from the State line, and the fellows didn't have much difficulty shadowing him. They had their trouble for their pains, though. The old duck didn't stir away from his farm for six weeks, and then what do you suppose he did?"

Merriwell smiled at the fellow's earnest manner.

"Give it up," he answered. "What was it?"

"Took ship to the other side and went direct to Paris. This time the boys over there were ready for him. He stayed two days at one of the big hotels and then went to Amsterdam. While at Paris he was seen talking with a big, rough-looking fellow who looked like a Dutchman. After Carleton—that was the name of the Canadian guy—left Paris, this Dutchman was followed until he got aboard a steamer bound for South Africa. At Amsterdam, Carleton trots right off to his diamond cutter, leaves a lot of rough stones with him, and sails for home with another bunch of cut and polished sparklers. It was a cute game, and Heaven only knows how long they'd been playing it.

"Well, sir, that chap had the whole department guessing. Try as they would, they couldn't catch him with the goods. Of course, they couldn't touch him on British soil; he had a perfect right to have bushels of diamonds there if he wanted to. But there was a bunch of inspectors watching him and all his friends, that pretty near started a riot among the people thereabouts. Nothing doing, though. He never went near the line; and if he had, it wouldn't have done him much good, with the country a wilderness for hundreds of miles.

"Finally I was put on the job, and after the fellow's third trip across the pond—he must have brought back half a million in diamonds, all told—I got wise to their little game. It certainly was the slickest thing you ever heard of, though I'd been kind of expecting something of that sort ever since airships began doing stunts in the air."

A look of intense interest leaped into Merriwell's face.

"What!" he exclaimed. "You mean that they brought the diamonds across the line with an aëroplane?"

"That's what," nodded Holton. "Of course Carleton wouldn't let us on his property, so we couldn't look around much. He had a lot of fierce dogs, and the place was full of man traps and all sorts of riggings like that. But I found out afterward that the whole side of one of his barns was removable, so when the aëroplane came at night it landed in the upper part of the barn and nobody was the wiser. He'd load up with the sparklers and slide out the next dark night that came along. The only way I got onto the game was by keeping watch all night at the edge of the farm, and at last I saw the thing swoop down and land somewhere among the buildings.

"I beat it back home and had a talk with the chief, who decided that the only way to catch them with the goods was in another aëroplane. You see, nobody had the least idea where he went after he crossed the border. So he bought a good model on the quiet, and I took some lessons running it. In a couple of weeks I could handle it pretty fair, and it was shipped to Winnipeg and assembled there. I had the dickens of a job finding a place near Carleton's to keep it, but finally located an out-of-the-way barn that I rented and fixed up. When the machine was installed there, I went back to watching again.

"I hadn't been at it long before he slid in one night, and don't you believe that I wasn't ready for flight then. He stayed over one night, but the next he was off just after dark, and me after him. I thought he was never going to stop flying. We made about fifty miles an hour, and by daybreak I figured we must be somewhere in Wyoming. He landed in the mountains just as the dawn began to break, and I dropped down a few miles away.

"At dark I was ready again, up in the air circling around. He made for this place straight as a string, swooped down a little after midnight, and then blamed if I didn't lose him. Seemed as if the earth had just opened and swallowed him up, and I haven't seen hide or hair of him since. You see, I'm up against it for fair, and when one of you gents says, 'it's *the* airship,' like as though you'd seen one around here before, I thought perhaps you'd glimpsed the other fellow's, and maybe you could help me out."

As he finished, the young inspector looked inquiringly from one to the other of the two Yale men. He retained his air of careless nonchalance, but only by a palpable effort. Deep down underneath it there was an expression of anxious appeal in his eyes. It was quite evident that he was, as he had said, "up against it for fair"; otherwise he would never have confided so promptly in two total strangers, and Dick had a very strong inclination to help him out. But could he?

Not being in the least slow, Merriwell had at once sensed the entire situation. The mystery of Scott Randolph was a mystery no longer. Bert Holton's straightforward story had cleared it up completely. He was a smuggler, pure and simple. Amazingly clever, to be sure, and conducting his operations on a huge scale, he was none the less a smuggler, and his extremely plausible story of manufacturing diamonds had been made up out of whole cloth to cover his real doings.

A faint flush mounted into Dick's face as he realized how he had been duped, and for a moment he would have given a good deal to be able to put this clever officer on Randolph's trail. But could he? There was that unfortunate word of honor which he had given and which he could not break. Moreover, such was Scott Randolph's extraordinary charm of manner and likableness that, in spite of everything, Merriwell did not quite like the notion of turning him over to the law.

It was Buckhart who solved the problem. Bound by no promise of silence, knowing nothing of the diamond hoax, his mind was so full of what they had seen the night before that the consequence of his words did not occur to him before he blurted them out.

"Why, sure, bucko," he said quickly. "We saw an airship fly out of these very mountains last night."

A gleam of excitement leaped into Holton's keen eyes.

"You did?" he cried. "What time? Which way did it go?"

"About eleven o'clock," the Texan answered promptly, "It flew northward."

Holton made a despairing gesture with his hands.

"He's gone back to Carleton's," he exclaimed. "By George! He's given me the slip! If I'm not the worst kind of a lunkhead!"

"I reckon not," Brad put in quickly. "He came back again in about thirty minutes."

"Are you sure?" Holton asked doubtfully.

"Yep; we saw it plain. He must have gone twelve or fifteen miles, and then we saw him flash some lights like signals. Pretty quick after they stopped the machine came back again to the place where it started from."

"And where was that?" the officer asked eagerly. "Say, Jack, haven't you any idea at all who it belongs to?"

"We thought it was Randolph," Buckhart returned promptly. "He's the fellow that lives in that stone house with barred windows and a steel door."

"Never heard of him," Holton said quickly. "I'm a stranger here, you know. It sounds good, though. How do you get to it?"

"Go down to Bonnet Trail and walk toward Denver," the Texan answered. "In about half a mile you come to a narrow road on your right. Randolph's place is at the end of that road, not more than a quarter of a mile——"

He stopped abruptly as his eyes fell on Dick's face. It was calm and impassive, but there must have been something there which made the big Westerner think that perhaps he had been saying too much. He hesitated for a moment and then went on rather lamely:

"Of course, I'm not at all certain that it was his aëroplane. It came from near the house, but it might have belonged to some one else."

"All the same, I think I'll look the gent up," Holton remarked. "It's the only clue I've had, and it sounds pretty good to me."

There was silence for a few moments, then Merriwell glanced suddenly at the special officer.

"Are these monoplanes hard to manage?" he asked.

"Why, no, not very," Holton answered. "The control is very simple, once you've got the hang of it. I'd rather manipulate a monoplane than a biplane any day. Ever been up in one?"

"No, but I've always wanted to," Dick answered. "I've done something with gliders at college. The principle is pretty much the same, isn't it?"

"Exactly. Some people seem to have the idea that you get along by flapping the planes like the wings of a bird, whereas they are almost immovable. Of course, they can be deflected or depressed according as you rise or descend, but the only thing that keeps you going is the revolution of the propeller. If the engine should stop, you'd be turned into a simple glider. Even then, you wouldn't go down with a smash, but by a proper manipulation of the plane and rudders, you could glide on a long, easy curve, and could almost choose your own spot for alighting."

"I see," Dick said. "The two rudders are controlled by levers, I suppose."

"Sure."

Holton stepped to the rear of the aëroplane and Merriwell followed him interestedly.

"Here's the horizontal rudder," the officer explained, pointing out the two smaller, parallel planes which were attached to the extreme end of the light frame that protruded from the body of the aëroplane like an enormously long tail. "By a system of wires and pulleys, it is connected with the lever next to the seat. You pull that lever forward and the rudder is thrown upward, inclining the big plane so that the air strikes it underneath and drives it upward. In the same way when the lever is thrown back, the plane is deflected the other way and the machine descends. In flying it's always necessary to give the plane the least possible upward inclination, so as to get the full benefit of the air striking against it."

Merriwell nodded understandingly.

"This rudder above it is the vertical rudder, I suppose," he said. "It looks exactly like the rudder on a boat."

"It is like it, and acts the same way. You use that in making a turn, and it is controlled by the lever next to the other one. Pushed forward, it turns the rudder to the right, backward, to the left. When you're flying straight ahead it's kept upright, of course."

He pulled a worn, red leather notebook from his pocket and slipped off the rubber band.

"It's this way," he went on, as he drew a simple diagram on one of the pages.

Dick bent his head over the book, while Holton explained in detail the principle of rudder control, illustrating his meaning with rough sketches.

When he had finished, the Yale man straightened up and looked again at the machine.

"It's quite as simple as I thought," he said slowly. "I believe I could operate it with a little practice. Eight-cylinder engine, isn't it?"

"Yes, and it's a little beauty," the officer said enthusiastically. "I've never had a bit of trouble worth speaking about. It's a French make and only weighs a fraction under three pounds per horse power. It drives the crank shaft, which runs under the seat out to the propeller in front."

Dick examined the engine closely. It was beautifully made and took up a surprisingly small space.

Seeing his interest and his quickness of comprehension, Holton, who was an enthusiast, pointed out the various parts, and at the end of half an hour the Yale man understood it thoroughly.

"I suppose you'd have to have some kind of a start to make an ascension from here, wouldn't you?" he asked.

"All you'd need would be some one to loosen the anchor rope which I've tied to that tree over there, and give you a good, running shove," Holton said. "Of course, you'd get your engine going first and the plane and horizontal rudder inclined properly. You see, with these light pneumatic wheels underneath, it's no trouble at all for one man to give you the necessary starting velocity. Sometimes you don't even need that, but can start yourself, especially if you're on a slight incline. That's the sort of place I usually try to pick out when I come down."

He hesitated for an instant. He was plainly an enthusiastic aviator.

"I'd like to make a short ascension and show you how it works," he said, "but I don't dare to. That fellow doesn't know I'm anywhere around, but if I went up now, he'd spot me in a minute and be on his guard."

"Of course he would," Dick agreed readily. "Perhaps, though, after you've nailed him, you'd be willing to give us an exhibition."

"Sure thing," Holton grinned. "Come out and see me to-morrow. Maybe there'll be something doing by that time."

"I will," Merriwell returned promptly.

Then he turned to Buckhart.

"I guess we might as well be on our way, old fellow," he said quietly. "Now that we've mastered the principles of flying, there's nothing to keep us here. Good-by, Mr. Holton."

"By-by, fellows," the officer said warmly as they started down the slope. "Much obliged for the tip."

"Don't mention it," Brad called back.

They had almost reached Bonnet Trail where they had left the car, when he stopped suddenly and looked at his companion.

"Say, what about Randolph's aëroplane that we started to find?" he inquired. "I never knew you to give up anything as quick as that, pard."

Dick smiled.

"I gave it up because I didn't want to find it," he returned. "Randolph's a piker, all right, and deserves to have this fellow Holton land on his neck; but I'd rather not have anything to do with his capture."

The Texan grinned broadly.

"That's why you looked so blamed serious while I was chattering away like a dame at a pink tea," he remarked. "I sure put my foot into it, didn't I?"

"Not a bit of it," Merriwell returned. "I was afraid you were going further and put him wise to all this talk about diamonds and that sort of thing. There seems to be no question that he's the smuggler Holton is after, but somehow I'd like him to have every chance he can. We were his guests last night, and he was mighty nice to us; besides, he used to be a friend of Frank's, and —— Oh, well, let's just put him out of mind. If he gets pinched, all right; if he gets away it will be equally satisfactory."

This proved to be easier said than done. After a leisurely luncheon the two friends took the car again and went for a long drive out toward Castlerock, from which they did not return until past six. It is safe to say that half an hour did not pass during the entire afternoon in which one or the other of them was not thinking of Scott Randolph and wondering whether Holton had found him, or whether he had escaped, or what had happened.

Returning to the hotel, Dick drove around to the garage very slowly; and, instead of running the car in, he slid up to the curb and stopped. Then he turned in his seat and eyed Buckhart questioningly without saying a word.

"Well, why not?" the Texan inquired suddenly, apparently apropos of nothing on earth. "I'm sure curious to know how it all came out."

Dick laughed as he guided the car slowly down the street again.

"Evidently we haven't either of us been successful in getting Randolph out of our heads," he said. "We'll just take a run out and see if I can get hold of my pocketbook this time."

The swift twilight was just beginning to fall as they hurried up the narrow track and reached the open space before the stone house.

If they expected to find any signs of life about the place they were disappointed. The same grim, menacing wall of stone confronted them, from the same desolate, shadowy background. The steel door was as tightly closed as ever, the barred windows as expressionless. But wait! Were they quite the same?

Dick's eyes were fixed on the end window on the second floor.

"Take a good look at that shutter up there, Brad," he said in a low tone. "It looks to me as though it were open about an inch, but this dim light is beastly deceptive."

The Texan studied it for an instant.

"You're right," he said quickly. "It is open the least bit. Some one's been there since this morning, all right."

Merriwell stepped to the door and hammered loudly on it.

Five minutes passed in unbroken silence. Then he beat another thunderous tattoo on it, long and loud.

Still no response. The house was silent as a tomb.

The Yale man stepped under the window and looked keenly up at it. Was it possible that some one was watching them through that tiny crack? If so, the rapidly falling darkness hid him effectually. With a sigh of regret, Merriwell stepped back, his foot striking a small object on the ground.

Instantly he pounced on it and held it up.

It was a small, worn notebook, bound in red leather and kept together by a rubber band.

For a moment both men gazed in tense silence at the commonplace thing. Then Dick slipped off the band quickly and opened the book.

As his eyes glanced swiftly over the first page, even the semidarkness did not hide the sudden pallor which spread over his face.

"Heavens above!" he breathed in a horror-stricken voice.

"What is it, pard?" Brad asked anxiously. "What has happened?"

Unconsciously Merriwell clenched one hand tightly and his teeth came together with a click.

"Randolph has shut Holton into the air-tight room," he said slowly.

"What!" gasped the Texan, as though unable to believe his ears. "Deliberately left him there, you mean?"

"Yes," Dick said in a hard, dry voice. "Listen."

He bent over the notebook, barely able to distinguish the scrawling words, in the failing light.

"'He caught me by a trick,'" the Yale man read slowly. "'Says he's going to shut me in a room where the air will last two hours and no longer. If anybody finds this, for God's sake get me out. I've only a minute to write this and throw it out of the window. Don't waste a minute, but hurry. I can't die like a rat in a trap.

HOL——'"

The note ended in an irregular line as though the writer had been suddenly interrupted.

The Texan's ruddy face was pale as death and in his eyes there came a look of horror.

"Two hours," he exclaimed in a strange voice—"two hours to live!"

Dick threw out one hand in a gesture of despair.

"And those two hours may be up!" he cried. "No one knows how long ago this note was written!"

# CHAPTER XIX.

## THE RACE IN THE CLOUDS.

The words were scarcely spoken when, from the cliffs above them, came the familiar muffled purr of the gasoline engine.

Instantly a look of hope flashed into Dick's face as he quickly turned his head upward. Scott Randolph had not yet departed. He might be stopped—must be stopped—and induced to return and release his prisoner. He could not possibly realize what an awful thing he was doing.

The humming increased; there was that same rustling, creaking sound which had attracted their first sight of the aëroplane, and then the great black shape appeared slowly and majestically from among the mountains.

Dick placed his hands trumpetwise to his mouth.

"Randolph!" he shouted at the top of his voice. "Come back! You must come back! It is I—Merriwell. You must not leave that man there! Randolph! Randolph!"

His voice rang out clearly on the still night air, and the echoes came back mockingly from the gloomy, towering cliffs. But Scott Randolph paid no heed. The course of the black aëroplane did not waver by so much as a hair's breadth as it sped on with rapidity increasing momentum, presently vanishing to the northward.

Dick dropped his hands despairingly at his sides.

"What a monster," he exclaimed. "What an inhuman monster! I wouldn't have believed it possible."

"Isn't there something we can do?" Buckhart asked. "We just can't stand here and let that fellow suffocate. Don't you suppose there's some way of finding the spring? Or we might tear down the wall."

Though he spoke eagerly, there was not much conviction in his voice.

"By the time we'd found a way into the house the man would be dead," Dick answered. "We couldn't tear down the wall in time. No Randolph is the only one who can save him. He must be brought back; but how—how to do it?"

He was thinking rapidly. There must be way—some way. But there was so little time.

Suddenly he gave a quick exclamation.

"I've got it! By Jove, I've got it! Come along—quick! There isn't a second to lose."

He turned and flew toward the trail as fast as he could get over the ground, with Buckhart close at his heels. Into the car he sprang and started the engine.

"Never mind the lights!" he cried, as Brad hesitated. "Jump in—quick!"

The Texan leaped up beside him, and a moment later the *Wizard* was hitting the high places on Bonnet Trail, heading away from Denver.

To the bewildered Westerner it seemed as though they had scarcely started before Dick jammed on the emergency and leaped from the car. He darted up the steep, rocky slope, Brad still keeping close behind him. At last a glimmering of what his friend meant to do flashed into the Texan's mind and turned his blood cold.

"Say, pard," he gasped. "You're—not going—to monkey with—that airship?"

"I've got to!" came through Merriwell's gritted teeth. "It's the only way."

There was silence for a brief space as they climbed rapidly.

"But you'll be killed," Buckhart panted in an unsteady voice. "You've never run one in your life."

Dick laughed.

"Don't worry, old fellow," he said. "It isn't as bad as that. I may not catch Randolph, but I learned enough about the thing this morning to keep myself from being killed—I hope."

A moment later they burst through the bushes and Dick gave a sigh of relief as the shadowy bulk of the aëroplane loomed before him.

"I wasn't quite sure whether Holton had used it or not," he said, hurrying toward it. "Now, Brad, let's get busy. Just hold a match to that burner while I turn on the prestolite."

The next instant the bright light blazed forth, and Dick proceeded methodically to prepare for flight. He passed his hands swiftly over the steering levers to make sure which was which. Then he turned on the gas and plugged into the coil. Setting spark and throttle experimentally, he started the engine. She pounded a little at first, but he quickly pulled down the throttle a trifle and soon had her running smoothly.

That done, he pushed the lever governing the horizontal rudder forward. The vertical lever he left upright.

Swiftly he thought over Holton's instructions. There was nothing more to be done, and, with a last look at the engine, which was running perfectly, he climbed into the seat.

For a second he sat there motionless. It must be confessed that his pulse beat rapidly, and he felt an odd, unpleasant tightening at his throat as he realized what he was about to attempt.

Then the thought of Holton, slowly smothering in that air-tight room, made him press his lips tightly together as his left hand reached out and closed over the steering lever. The propeller in front of him was revolving swiftly with a whirring sound, and it seemed as though he could feel the aëroplane tugging gently at the anchoring rope, as if it were anxious to be off.

"Loosen the rope, Brad, and give me a good, running shove!" Merriwell said quietly.

The Texan stifled with an effort an almost irresistible impulse to drag his chum off the seat and prevent him forcibly from going to what he considered almost certain death. Then he made a last appeal.

"Dick, you ought not to do this," he said, in a low voice. "It's madness!"

"I must, old fellow," Merriwell returned quietly.

Somehow the confidence in Merriwell's voice seemed to put heart into the big Texan.

Turning, he walked to the rear of the machine and slipped the hook of the anchor rope out of the ring. Then he took a good hold of the framework and ran forward, pushing the aëroplane before him.

As it rose with a long, sweeping glide, Dick caught his breath suddenly.

For an instant he seemed as though he were standing still and that the earth was dropping swiftly away from him—dropping, and at the same time rushing backward. He wanted to look back at Buckhart, but he did not dare. It was as though the machine was poised in so fine a balance that the least motion on his part would upset the equilibrium.

The big Texan was left standing in the centre of the clearing, his hands clenched so tightly that the nails cut into the flesh, his face white and drawn, with great beads of perspiration standing out on his forehead, his whole frame trembling like a leaf. As he watched with a strained and breathless eagerness, the aëroplane soared upward and away, carrying the best friend he had in the world swiftly out of sight in that perilous race through the darkness for a human life.

It took but a moment for Dick to recover his coolness and presence of mind. Then he realized that he was headed in quite the wrong direction.

Instinctively he felt that it might not be safe to attempt a turn with the monoplane still gliding upward, so very slowly he drew the horizontal lever toward him until he was going nearly on a level. Then he clasped the vertical lever and pushed it forward, little by little.

Luckily there was scarcely any wind, and the aëroplane responded instantly by turning in a wide, majestic circle. As soon as the propeller was headed northward, he pulled the lever back into the upright position, with a sigh of satisfaction. So far, there had been not the slightest hitch.

Presently he noticed that the monoplane was steadily increasing in speed, but somehow, this did not trouble him in the least. He was rapidly gaining confidence in himself and in the strange air craft, which was momentarily proving herself so much more steady and controllable than he had ever imagined she could be.

Then, too, there was an extraordinary sense of exhilaration in that rapid flight through the night air. A delicious feeling of lightness, of buoyancy unlike anything he had ever known. And stranger than all else was the amazing lack of fear. It did not seem as though he could possibly fall, or if he did, he felt that he would float to earth with the lightness of a thistledown.

He leaned forward and deflected the powerful searchlight, but he could see nothing. He must have gone considerably higher than he had realized, and promptly he pushed back the horizontal lever.

The result was startling. The monoplane gave a swift downward plunge which nearly threw him from his seat, so unexpected was it. With a jerk, he thrust the lever forward, and the craft slowly regained its equilibrium and began an upward glide.

A little experimenting showed him the danger of dropping too suddenly, and he soon discovered how to reach a lower level by a series of short gradual glides, instead of too abrupt a descent.

After a little he tried the wonderfully powerful searchlight again and was relieved when he found that the earth was clearly visible. He must have been at an elevation of little more than a thousand feet, and as he swept along at the speed of an express train, the plains and isolated farms flitted by under him with the silent, uncanny unreality of a dream.

Then he flashed the light ahead, but could see nothing of Randolph's aëroplane. He increased the speed a little, and presently he foolishly raised his head above the wind shield. It cut his skin like alcohol from an atomizer on a raw surface and made him draw quickly back into shelter again.

"Not for mine!" he muttered. "A little more of that would flay a fellow alive."

He shot the searchlight before him and this time the powerful rays fell on something in the air far ahead of him—a black, indefinite shape, barely within the range of the reflector. His heart leaped joyfully.

"Randolph!" he muttered. "I'm gaining!"

Almost before he could realize it the black air craft leaped into vivid relief, he could distinguish clearly every rod, almost every tiny wire, even the white face of Randolph shown clear in the bright light. Then the black monoplane flashed by him with throbbing engine and was gone.

"Great Cæsar!" he gasped in amazement. "He's going back! What does that mean?"

His first natural impulse was to turn swiftly as he might have done in a motor car, but he caught himself in time and remembered the need of extreme caution.

First pulling down the speed of the engine, he moved the vertical lever slowly, and executed a wide, graceful curve. Once headed southward, he increased the speed and started on the return journey at a rate that made the air hum.

What could be the cause of this sudden change on the part of Scott Randolph? Was it possible that he had relented and was voluntarily going back to release Holton? Had he come to a full realization of the awful thing he had done? Merriwell sincerely hoped so, but he did not relax his vigilance in the least. He meant to follow the other aëroplane to the bitter end, and his searchlight still shot its bright rays straight ahead as he strained his eyes to catch another glimpse of the shadowy craft.

Before long he saw the lights of Denver far in the distance, but on his right. At once he throttled down on the engine and swerved to the west a little. In returning, he had gone too far east. When he was finally headed in the right direction, he throttled the engine still further and turned the flashlight earthward.

In an instant he had his bearings and shut off all power. The propeller slowly ceased its revolutions, and the aëroplane, with horizontal rudder depressed a trifle, glided downward.

Randolph's aëroplane was nowhere in sight, but the bright gleam of light from the door of the house, showed Merriwell that something out of the way had happened, and he resolved to waste no time, but drop down there. He landed in fair shape, but he had not calculated on the retained velocity of the monoplane, and the craft rushed forward on its light wheels, striking against the front of the house with a splintering crash which threw Dick headforemost out of his seat to the ground.

He was up in an instant. Running into the hall, he dashed up the stairs. The first person that met his eager gaze was Bert Holton, lying on a couch in the upper hall, gasping painfully for breath. Then, standing by the open door of the air-tight room, he saw Scott Randolph, his face pale, but seeming otherwise cool and collected.

"I'm very glad you've come, Merriwell," he said quietly. "You will be able to look after Mr. Holton. He is somewhat in want of air just now, but will soon recover."

He hesitated for an instant, still looking straight into Merriwell's eyes.

"I think I have you to thank for saving me from myself," he said slowly. "But for you I should have done something which would have made the remainder of my life a living hell."

There was a puzzled look on Dick's face.

"I don't think I quite understand," he said. "You came back of your own accord. What had I to do with it?"

"I did not turn until I saw your searchlight," Randolph explained. "It was that which brought me to my senses. The moment I saw it flash far behind me, I knew that another aëroplane was following me. I knew there was no other around here but Holton's, and he was—er—locked up. It puzzled me for a moment, and then the realization suddenly came to me that it must be you. I don't know just what made me think so, but the conviction was a very positive one.

"You had found out about Holton in some way, and had taken the only possible means of following me to bring me back. And at the thought of the tremendous risk you were running to save the life of a total stranger, I seemed to realize for the first time what a horrible thing I had done. I turned at once and started back. I was just in time, thank God! Holton was almost gone."

He paused and then went on in a lighter tone:

"I leave him to your care. I cannot stay. I can only say that I am glad to have met you, Dick Merriwell. You're a thoroughbred, if there ever was one, and I shall not soon forget you. After what I have done, you probably won't shake hands, so I'll just say good-by."

Without another word, he wheeled and started down the hall.

Holton struggled to his feet.

"Catch him!" he gasped thickly. "Don't let him get away! He must not get away!"

Dick ran down the hall with the officer stumbling after him.

"Stop, Randolph!" the Yale man cried.

The loud slam of a door was his only answer. It was the door at the end of the hall which Randolph had told them the night before led into a closet.

Dashing forward, Dick tore it open and tripped against the first step of some stairs leading upward. Without a moment's hesitation, he hurried up them. It was slow work, for the way was pitch dark and he had to trust to his sense of feeling alone. His outstretched hands touched the rough, uneven surface of rock on either side. He seemed to be in a natural tunnel which wound along with many twists and turns, but always steeply upward. It had been fitted with rough wooden stairs, but that was all.

On he went, and on and on. He felt as though he must be almost among the clouds before the cool night wind began to blow upon his face. At last he emerged on a flat, rock-floored surface, walled and roofed with timbers, but open in the front.

The hum of a gasoline engine was in his ears, the whirring purr of an aëroplane propeller; and, as he ran forward to the open front of the shed, he saw the shadowy bulk of the black craft spread out before him on the flat, rocky surface.

Even as it flashed into view, it began to move swiftly down a steep incline.

"Randolph!" the Yale man cried. "Stop!"

But Scott Randolph paid no heed. As Dick sprang out on the rocky platform, the great black aëroplane launched itself from the cliff, and, gathering speed with every moment, it soared upward and northward, vanishing into the night. Presently the muffled throb of the engine died away and all was still.

"He's gone!" almost sobbed a voice at Merriwell's elbow. "I'll never get my hookers on him again."

It was Bert Holton, weak and exhausted by his hard climb, but rapidly recovering in the cool night air.

"I'm afraid not," Dick answered slowly. "I don't think he'll ever come back here."

But somehow, deep down in his heart, he was not so sorry.

Presently he turned and looked about him. They were standing on the top of the cliff with only the glittering stars above them. It was a wide, rocky, flat surface—an ideal spot from which to launch an aëroplane, sloping sharply as it did, toward the outer edge.

Over a small part of this surface a rough shed had been built. The roof was completely covered with boulders, and when the great, gray painted doors, which closed the front, were shut, it would have taken a keen eye to detect the presence of that ingenious shelter for the aëroplane.

"How did he catch you?" Dick asked, turning to Holton.

"I was too blamed cocksure," the officer answered bitterly. "He was wise to me all the time. When I come snooping around the house I finds the door open, and like a fool, in I walks. Next thing I knew he had a gun at my head."

"But how did he know you were around?" Merriwell interrupted.

"One of his pals piped him off the other night," Holton explained. "That was the signaling you saw. The guy had seen me following, and put Randolph wise. That's why he came back so soon. Well, he politely tells me what he's going to do, and then locks me into a room while he gets his airtight place ready. I unfastened the shutter, but there was no way to get out through the bars. So I hauls out my notebook and scrawls a note. You got it, didn't you?"

Dick nodded.

"I hadn't more than tossed it out the window, when he comes back and makes me go into that room. I knew from the look in his eyes that he'd shoot me then and there for two cents. He was just itching to do it. Otherwise, I'd have made a fight for it. But I had a little hope that maybe you or some one would find the book and get me out."

He paused and wiped his face with a handkerchief.

"I can't describe the rest," he went on slowly. "It was awful. I never hope to go through a thing like that again. Say, Jack, was that straight what he said about your taking the monoplane and going after him?"

Dick smiled rather ruefully.

"It was," he acknowledged. "And I'm very much afraid I smashed something when I landed outside."

"Oh, that be hanged!" Holton exclaimed. "I don't care a rip if it's smashed to bits. But, by George! That was a gritty thing to do! You've sure got pluck. Did you have any trouble?"

"Not a bit after I got the hang of it," Dick answered. "But I certainly had a sinking feeling when I first went up. Let's go down and see how much damage has been done."

They felt their way to the stairs and slowly descended. About halfway down they were surprised to hear some one stumbling toward them. The next moment a big body bumped into Dick and a pair of arms closed around him with a strength that nearly took his breath away.

"Thunderation, pard!" came in the Texan's voice. "I'm sure a whole lot glad to get my paws on you. I could rise up on my hind legs and howl like a wolf. You had me near off my trolley till I saw your light coming back. I beat it over here quick. Did you catch him?"

"I did not," Dick returned, his hand resting on his chum's shoulder. "He came back of his own free will and let Holton loose. More than that, he was slick enough to get away again in the aëroplane before we could stop him."

They had reached the lighted hall by this time, and started down the main stairs.

"What do you know about that!" Buckhart exclaimed. "He's sure a slippery one."

He looked at Dick with a grin.

"Say, pard," he drawled, "tell us, honest, how you like flying?"

Four days later Dick Merriwell read the following item in a Denver newspaper with absorbing interest.

"Miles City, Montana:—Word was brought to this city last night of the discovery, by a party of prospectors in the mountains of Cook County, of a wrecked aëroplane. The affair has been the cause of a good deal of curiosity and speculation, since the presence of an air craft in this vicinity was totally unsuspected. The machine was completely wrecked, having apparently struck the rocks from a great height, so that scarcely a part remained entire. A curious feature which will, perhaps, lead to its identification, was the fact that every portion of the machine, planes, metalwork, framework, and even the engine, had been painted black. There were no signs of the unfortunate occupant, but it is hardly to be hoped that he escaped the fall alive, the supposition being that his body was eaten by wolves."

Dick gazed silently out of the window of the Denver Club, where he was taking lunch.

"I wonder!" he murmured presently. "Eaten by wolves, eh? I don't believe Scott Randolph was the man to be eaten by wolves."

# CHAPTER XX.

## THE OUTLAWS.

Bob Harrison, manager of the famous "Outlaws," was angry. His swarthy face expressing intense exasperation, he glared at the tall, quiet young man before him and flourished a huge fist in the air.

"Now, look here, Loring," he rasped, "what do you take me for? Do you think I'm an easy mark? I'm carrying around the greatest independent baseball team ever organized, every man a star with a reputation, and it costs me money. The expense is terrific. The terms on which I agreed to play your old Colorado Springs bunch were perfectly understood between us when we made arrangements over the phone—two-thirds of the gate money to the winner; one-third minus local expenses, such as advertising, the sum paid for the use of the park and so forth, to the losers. You know this was distinctly understood; now you're trying to squeal. You've got us here in Colorado Springs ready to play to-morrow, and you think you can force me into divvying up with you."

"I deny," retorted the manager of the Colorado Springs team, "that I entered into such an arrangement as you claim I did. If you can prove——"

"Blazes! You know I can't prove it. I took you for a man of your word. I had an open date for to-morrow; so did you. I phoned you, and after we had fixed it up you said to come on. Now we're here, and you want to make it dead certain that you're going to get one-half the pie. You've got something of a team, haven't you? You think your bunch can play baseball, don't you? Well, if you can beat us, I'm willing you should lug off two-thirds of the gate money. Such an arrangement as that makes an object to work for. With an equal division, either of us will be as well off financially whether he wins or loses."

"You called me on the phone, Harrison. You were mighty anxious for the game; I wasn't particular. The open date to-morrow meant an opportunity for my boys to rest up, and they know it. Hot weather and a long, grilling pull at the game threatens to make 'em go stale. My pitching staff is on the blink. There's only one slabman left in good condition—and he might be better."

Harrison looked the local manager up and down, as if taking his measure.

"You're just about built to run a third-rate bush league team," he sneered. "This is the first time I've got bitten by anything as small as you."

Loring flushed to the roots of his hair.

"You're an insolent, coarse-grained bully, Harrison," he said hotly; "but you'll find you can't browbeat me. The Springs will rest to-morrow, and you'll do the same as far as I am concerned. It's off."

"Quitter!" snarled Harrison, choking with excess of anger.

With a shrug of his shoulders Loring turned and left the furious man there in the lobby of the hotel, spluttering and snarling his wrath.

The Outlaws, managed by Harrison, was indeed a famous baseball organization, being composed entirely of men who had worn Big League uniforms. Harrison had been the manager of the Menockets in a certain Middle Western League, which had blown up in the midst of a season, the cause of the disaster being reckless extravagance and astonishing lack of business methods on the part of various managers in the league. The rivalry had been intense, and the salaries paid not a few of the players who had deserted the Big League teams, something to gasp at.

Stories of these "plums" waiting to be plucked had caused a host of fast players on the leading teams of the country to disregard contracts and hike for the land of promise. In most instances, it is true, these men had been disgruntled and fancied they were justified in their acts. Some claimed to have escaped from a slavery almost as bad as that which once nearly disrupted the Union. In almost every instance, doubtless, the lure which drew them like a magnet was the prospect of big money quickly and easily obtained. The get-rich-quick microbe lurks in the blood of almost every human being.

But the bubble had burst. The Outlaw League had gone to smash. Nearly a hundred clever baseball players had found themselves out of a job, with frosty weather and the end of the season far away.

Then it was that Harrison had conceived the idea of making up a nine picked from the cream of the different teams; and to encourage him he had been able to arrange in advance a game with St. Louis, in case he could bring such an organization of stars. Of the Menocket players he had retained Smiling Joe Brinkley, Nutty McLoon, and South-paw Pope, the latter being a wizard who had made an amazing record in giving his opponents only one hit in the two games which he had pitched for the New York "Yankees."

Then, with his head swelled, Pope had quarreled with nearly every man on the team, finishing up in a fist fight with two of them, which resulted in his suspension. Raw to the bone, he grabbed at the bait which Bob Harrison flung in his direction at that psychological moment.

Smiling Joe had worn a Boston uniform, and had declined to go back to the bush for another season when a veteran second sacker had crowded him out.

McLoon, a great hitter and wonderful centre fielder, was said to be a bit off in the top story, and for three seasons the brand of the Outlaw had been upon him, while he wandered from one unrecognized league to another. He was remembered, however, for his remarkable hitting and base running one season with St. Louis.

The other men, gathered up from the various disbanded teams, were Long Tom Hix, once with Cleveland; Gentle Willie Touch, who had worn a Louisville uniform; Grouch Kennedy, a former New York "Giant"; Buzzsaw Stover, from smoky Pittsburg; and Dead-eye Jack Rooney, who pretended to be not over-proud of the fact that he was an ex-"Trolley Dodger."

Among the reserves were Biff Googins, pinch hitter from Boston and general all-round man; Strawberry Lane, a pitcher who had lost his trial game for the Quaker City Americans and found it impossible to endure the gruelling of his teammates; and Wopsy Bill Brown, who had spent a season on the bench with the Chicago Nationals without being given a chance to pitch a ball over the plate.

With this aggregation Harrison had proceeded to make monkeys of St. Paul's representative nine. Indeed, the "Outlaws" simply toyed with their opponents in that game, winning at will.

Then it was that Harrison conceived the idea of touring with his team of wonders. Being a clever advertiser and press agent, he managed to get a great deal of space in the newspapers, and it was not long before immense crowds of baseball enthusiasts turned out wherever the Outlaws appeared.

To his deep satisfaction, Harrison found himself pocketing more money than he had dreamed of looking upon while representing Menocket. He was able to make a good thing, financially, while paying his players salaries which satisfied them.

In the matter of winning games the Outlaws seemed almost invincible. It is true that they dropped a game occasionally, but even then it was suspected that this came about through design rather than necessity. Through the Middle West, the Southwest, and along the Pacific Coast they toured triumphantly, boosted not only by Harrison's clever advertising, but by sporting writers everywhere.

Several times, through the efforts of minor league managers to gobble up certain men desired from the Outlaws, Harrison found it necessary to fight in order to hold his team together. He sought to impress upon the men the belief that by sticking to him they would eventually do far better than by accepting the bait of the minor league magnets. He was continually hinting of a "plum" that was coming to them.

Furthermore, he satisfied them that, one and all, they were Big League timber, and that he possessed the ability to put them back into the company where they belonged.

While Harrison stood there, snarling and glaring at the back of the departing manager, he was approached by Dick Merriwell, who was stopping at the hotel, in Colorado Springs, which was the first stop, after Denver.

"I beg your pardon," said Dick.

"Yah!" rasped the manager of the Outlaws, turning fiercely.

The other smiled upon him with serene good nature.

"I chanced to overhear a little of your conversation with Charlie Loring," said he. "It was quite without intent upon my part, I assure you; you were both speaking somewhat loudly. As your subject was baseball, I couldn't help feeling some interest, for I'm a baseball enthusiast."

"Yah!" repeated Harrison. "Perhaps you're one of Loring's cubs?"

"No, indeed."

"Belong here?"

"No, sir."

"Sorry. I wanted to tell you what I thought of that yellow quitter, for is he a quitter. I've been to the trouble and expense of bringing my team here to play a game of baseball to-morrow. Now it's off—off because that man won't stand by his verbal agreement. It will cost me a tidy little sum."

This thought added fuel to his rage, and he swore again, causing the hotel clerk to glower upon him from the desk. Fortunately, there were few guests in the lobby of the hotel.

The young man seemed more amused than disturbed by this burst of violent language.

"The best-laid plans of mice and men go wrong," he observed.

"I hope you don't call Loring a mouse," rasped Harrison. "He isn't big enough to be a mouse; he's a worm. If we could play every day it would be different; but I'm under heavy expense, and these long jumps add to the drain. I counted on doing fairly well here at the Springs, for the place is full of tourists who must be sick of seeing scenery and itching for diversion of a different sort. Think of that man going back on his word and trying to get an even split on the gate money! I told him over the phone that I would only play on the agreement that the winning team took two-thirds. That was pretty fair, too, considering that in lots of cases the contract has been for the winners to take three-fourths and the losers the remainder."

"Evidently you felt certain of winning."

Harrison's lips curled.

"There's nothing west of the Mississippi we can't beat three times out of four," he declared, "and I'd take my chances on an even break with anything the other side of the river."

"You must have a great team."

"Haven't you ever heard about us?"

"I think I've seen something in the papers about you."

"I've got the fastest independent team ever pulled together in this country. There isn't a man in the bunch who can't step into any of the Big Leagues and make good. They have played on the big teams, every one of them."

"Has-beens?" questioned the young man smilingly.

For a moment it seemed that the manager of the Outlaws would explode with indignation.

"Has-beens!" he rasped. "Not on your life! Comers, every one."

"But I inferred they had been canned by the big teams."

"Canned! Wow! You don't know what you're talking about. Not one big-league manager out of ten knows how to handle an eccentric or sensitive player. Most of them have the idea that the way to get baseball out of a man is to pound it into his head that he's a slob. They are afraid the new player will get chesty and conceited. Now, there's another way to take the conceit out of a youngster without breaking his spirit. I know how to do it.

"Never mind; it's my secret. You'll find my boys pulling together like clockwork if you ever see them play. They're fighters, just the same. They're out to win, you bet. Sometimes to see them you would think they were going to eat one another up. 'Sh! It's all a bluff. They do that, so they can turn on the opposing players the same way, and it generally gets the other team going."

Dick lifted a protesting hand.

"Don't let me in on too many of your secrets," he smiled; "for I am contemplating challenging you to play a game with a team of my own organizing."

Bob Harrison was astonished. He stepped back and surveyed the speaker from head to foot, an amused, incredulous grin breaking over his face.

"You?" he exclaimed. "You were thinking of challenging us?"

"So I said."

"I thought maybe I misunderstood you."

"Evidently you didn't."

"Where's your team?"

"Right here in Colorado Springs."

"Oh, some amateur organization, eh?"

"You might call it that; we wouldn't call ourselves professionals."

"Ha! ha! ha!" laughed Harrison. "Why, my boy, it would be a joke."

"Well, I don't know about that. I have an idea that I can get together nine college baseball players who will make it a fairly interesting game, if you dare accept my challenge."

"Dare!" spluttered Harrison. "Why, young fellow, I'd jump at the opportunity, if there was anything in it. It wouldn't be worth my time, however, to play a bunch of kids."

"You won't find them kids—not exactly. I presume you'll admit that there are some college men who can play baseball."

"In every way. But the finest college teams have no business with professionals; in proof of which, consider the result of the regular yearly Yale-New York game. The 'Giants' always have a snap with the college boys."

Dick nodded.

"That's the natural order of things," he confessed. "The New York team is made up of the best professionals in the country, and those men play together year after year until they become a machine. Yale picks from her undergraduates, and the personnel of the team is constantly changing. This prevents the collegians from working out a team organization with the fine points of a big professional nine.

"Nevertheless, year after year New York spots certain promising youngsters on the college team and attempts to get a line on them. If those same youngsters could play together season after season under a crackajack coach, it wouldn't be long before the Giants would have to hustle in order to take that spring exhibition game."

"You seem to know something about baseball," admitted the manager of the Outlaws, nodding his head slowly, "and there's more or less sense in what you say; but you're talking about picking up a team here in Colorado Springs to butt against the acknowledged fastest independent nine the country has ever seen. You haven't practiced together, and you would be rotten on team work."

"By chance," said the young man, "I happened to come to Colorado Springs. With me came some players from my own college team. To our surprise and pleasure, we found here at the Springs some other men from the same college team. We've nearly all played together. I'm confident that we can get together a nine that will acquit itself with a certain amount of credit. In fact. I think we can make you hustle to beat us."

"You don't look like a chap with a swelled head; but I'm afraid you've got a touch of it."

"In that case," was the laughing retort, "you might do me an eternal favor by reducing the swelling."

"I'm not working for the benefit of humanity in general; I work for Bob Harrison's pocket."

"You might be doing that at the same time. You have been well advertised. Wherever you go people turn out especially to get a look at your wonderful aggregation of stars. They would do it here, even if they felt pretty sure that the game might be one-sided. It's better than lying idle to-morrow."

"What's your name?" demanded Harrison suddenly.

"You may call me Dick."

"Dick what?"

"Well, Richard Dick—let it go at that for the present."

"Richard Dick? Odd name. Mr. Dick, what do you reckon you're going to get out of this?"

"Sport—that's my object. If we could beat you, we would get a little glory also."

"I should say so! Beat us? Why, boy, you couldn't pick up a bunch of college men in America who could do that trick once out of ten times."

"Did it ever occur to you, Mr. Harrison, that you might possibly have a slight touch of the swelled head yourself?"

The manager of the Outlaws gasped, frowned, and grinned.

"Of all sassy youngsters, you are certainly the smoothest."

"I'm not insinuating that you have; but such a thing is possible for a man of any age and station in life. It is true that young men are far more often afflicted by it. Now, look here, Mr. Harrison, you're up against the necessity of lying idle, accepting Charlie Loring's terms, or playing with some other team. I don't think Loring is anxious to play for some reason or other. He may have been; perhaps he was when he phoned you. Isn't it likely that advisers got at him after he phoned and made it apparent that he would place the Springs in a ridiculous light if the game was pulled off and your Outlaws buried him alive? If he could be sure of the soothing balm of an equal division and a big pull at the gate money, he might afford to let them laugh; but to be walloped and get the short end of the finances would make him ridiculous. Now I'm not afraid of anything of that sort."

"I should say not! Apparently you're not afraid of anything at all."

"I'll tell you what I'll do. I'll guarantee to pick up a team to play you to-morrow, and the winners shall pocket three-fourths of the gate money, the losers paying all expenses. Can you ask anything more satisfactory?"

"Nothing except an additional guarantee of two hundred and fifty dollars."

"Indeed, you are modest!" scoffed Richard Dick. "You seem to want it all, and a little something more. But if you think you're dealing with a blind sucker, we had better drop the business at once. I've told you I was out for sport, and that will satisfy me. Whatever share of the gate money might come to me, I'd agree in advance to donate to the Collins' Home for Consumptives. I don't want a dollar above expenses, and our expenses will be light."

"You're certainly not working this deal as a business proposition," agreed Harrison. "How do I know you'll get up the team? How do I know you'll play at all? Perhaps you'll squeal, as Loring did."

"I'll agree to place a hundred dollars in the hands of the proprietor of this hotel, as a forfeit to be paid you in case we don't play. I shall ask that you put up a similar amount as a forfeit. The game shall be advertised at once— as soon as I can make arrangements for the field. The announcement shall be spread broadcast that a team of college players will meet your Outlaws to-morrow afternoon. What say you?"

"It sounds better than nothing," admitted Harrison slowly. "Of course, you chaps wouldn't be much of a drawing card, but we might get out a fair crowd to see my boys work. Yes, it's better than nothing."

"Do you accept?"

"Three-fourths to the winners, and the losers to pay all expenses?"

"Yes."

"But the grounds—how can you get them?"

"Leave it to me. I happen to know Charlie Loring personally. The local team will not use the grounds to-morrow. I'm confident I can secure them."

"All right," snapped the manager of the professionals sharply, "it's a go. We'll sign an agreement right away. I have a regular blank form, which can be filled out in less than a minute. I accept your proposition that each of us shall place one hundred dollars with the proprietor of this hotel to stand as a forfeit in case either party backs down. Come ahead into the writing room."

# CHAPTER XXI.

## DICK MERRIWELL'S FIST.

When they came to sign the agreement Harrison was not a little surprised to note that instead of "Richard Dick" the name the young man wrote at the foot of the document was Richard Merriwell.

"Hey?" cried the manager of the Outlaws, gazing at that signature. "What's this? I thought you said your name was Dick."

"And so it is," was the smiling answer; "Dick Merriwell. While we were talking I told you that Richard Dick would serve for the time being."

"Merriwell? Merriwell? I've heard of a fellow by that name—Frank Merriwell."

"My brother."

"That so? He was a great college pitcher. He was one of the college twirlers the Big Leagues really scrambled for—and couldn't get."

"My brother always had a decided disinclination to play professional baseball. For him, like myself, it was a highly enjoyable sport; but to take it up professionally went against the grain."

"Oh, yes," grinned Harrison, "I understand about that. He didn't have to do it. If he had been poor, maybe he'd looked at it differently; but he was loaded with the needful, and, therefore, he could afford to pose."

"At one time, in the midst of his college career, my brother was forced to leave Yale on account of poverty."

"Really?"

"Really. He might have gone into professional baseball then and made money."

"Why didn't he?"

"Because of his prejudice against professionalism in that sport; because he hoped some day to return to Yale and finish his course, and he wished to play upon his college team."

"Oh, that rule about professionalism is all rot."

"It is useless to enter into a discussion over it. It may seem to work unfairly toward certain clean young college men who might make money playing summer baseball; but on the whole, it's an absolute necessity to keep college baseball from deteriorating into something rotten and disgraceful."

"It's pretty rotten now in some cases. Lots of college men play for money on the quiet."

"Some may, but not so many as is generally supposed. Those who do so are dishonest."

"That rule makes them dishonest."

"No, it doesn't. They might do something else. There are many ways by which a college man can earn money to help himself. If he's a good player or athlete, he will find hands enough extended to help him. He will be given opportunities of earning money honestly by honest work. The trouble with nine out of ten of the ball players who play for money is that they shirk real work. I said I wouldn't enter into a discussion over this rule, but you seem to have lured me into one."

"What did your brother do when he had to leave college and go to work?"

"He started in as an engine wiper in a railroad locomotive roundhouse."

"Engine wiper! A greasy, dirty, slaving job."

"Well, pretty near that; but he didn't stay at it long."

"Oh! Ho! ho!" laughed Harrison derisively. "It was too much for him, hey? He quit, did he?"

Dick Merriwell flushed a little.

"My brother never quit in his life," he retorted. "He was promoted. It wasn't long before he was a locomotive fireman, and the day came when his place was at the throttle."

"That wasn't doing so worse," admitted the baseball manager. "He must be some hustler."

"He's a hustler all right. He never yet put his hand to the plow and turned back."

"And you're his brother?"

"His half-brother."

"I haven't taken much interest in college baseball these late years," admitted Harrison. "Been too busy. What position do you play?"

"I pitch."

"Well, my boy, we'll try to treat you gentle and kind to-morrow. It would be a shame to spoil your reputation all at once."

"That's very thoughtful," laughed Dick. "Now, we'll put up that forfeit with the hotel proprietor, with the understanding that it doesn't stand if we can't get the park for the game."

"We? You said——"

"That I thought I could make arrangements with Charlie Loring. I do. I shall attend to that matter at once. Are you stopping at this hotel?"

"Yes; but my players are at the Sunset."

"I'll phone you as soon as I've secured the park."

"O. K. I've got a lot of paper I'll agree to scatter through this town, telling people just what sort of a team they'll see if they come out for the game to-morrow."

"And I'll attend to the rest of the advertising."

At the desk they called for the proprietor, who came forth, after a brief delay, from his private office. When the matter was explained he agreed to hold the forfeit money, which was placed in his hands.

As they were turning from the desk a lanky, hard-faced man with a hoarse, rasping voice approached and spoke to Harrison.

"What's this about the game here?" he inquired. "I hear it's off. If there's no go to-morrow, I'll run up to Denver this afternoon to visit an old partner of mine who's playing on the Denver nine."

"It looks now, Stover," said Harrison, "as if there might be a game to-morrow, but not with the regular Springs team."

The fellow with the harsh voice appeared decidedly displeased.

"I was counting on a lay-off," he growled.

"You get lay-offs enough, Stover. Out in this country we don't play more than four games a week at the most."

"Well, when we're not playing, we're pounding around over four or five hundred miles of railroad at a jump."

"Quit your growling. You have a snap, and you know it. Can't you shake that grouch you've had for the last ten days?"

"Who do we play with, anyhow?"

"A team of college men."

"What? Well, that will be a ripping old game! Them college kids can't play baseball. They don't know what it is."

"Perhaps you'll change your mind after to-morrow," smiled Dick.

The fellow gave him a contemptuous stare.

"Oh, I reckon you're one of the college guys."

"You're right."

"He's the manager of the team," explained Harrison.

"He looks it. Somebody picked him too soon. He isn't half ripe yet."

"Don't mind Buzzsaw, Merriwell," said the manager of the Outlaws. "This is his way when his liver goes wrong."

"He needs to take something for his liver," said Dick. "A shaking up would do it good. If he handed out enough loose tongue to some people he might get the shaking up."

"Well, blamed if you ain't a sassy young rat!" rasped Buzzsaw Stover, an ugly light in his eyes.

Harrison grasped the man's shoulder, turned him around, and gave him a push.

"Go away, Stover," he commanded. "You've been ready to fight with anybody for a week or more."

"By and by," laughed Dick quietly, "he will get what he's hunting for."

Stover walked out of the lobby.

A few minutes later Dick followed. He found Buzzsaw waiting on the street. The pugnacious Outlaw blocked Dick's way.

"What you need, my baby, is a first-class spanking," rasped Stover. "If you'd minded your own business, I'd had the rest of to-day and to-morrow to do as I please."

"If I was manager of your team you would have the rest of to-day and to-morrow, and the brief remainder of this season, and all the seasons to come, to do as you please," returned Dick quietly. "I would hand you a quick shoot that would land you at liberty to please yourself for all time."

"Oh, you would, hey?"

"That's what I told you."

"Well, I'll hand you something you won't forget!"

As he roared forth the threat Stover sprang in and swung a blow at the face of the seemingly unprepared Yale man.

Several minutes later Buzzsaw awoke to find Warwhoop Clinker and Gentle Willie Touch laboring to revive him, while a curious crowd stood around looking on.

"What's—what's matter?" mumbled Stover. "What happened to me—sunstroke? This blamed hot weather——"

"It was a stroke, all right," murmured Gentle Willie, "and it was the son of some proud father who passed it out to you. He was a nice, clean, sweet-looking young man."

"What's that?" snarled Stover, struggling to rise. "What are you talking about?"

"You got up against a polite gent and made one reach for him with a bunch of fives," explained Warwhoop. "Willie and I were over across the way and saw it all. We didn't know what was going to happen until it was all over and you had stretched yourself out to rest in the dust. He reached your jaw with the quickest wallop I ever saw delivered. There must have been chain lightning behind it, for you went down and out instanter."

Stover felt of his jaw and rubbed his head wonderingly.

"Who was it?" he asked. "I remember talking to that upstart who's made arrangements to put a college team against us to-morrow. He got sassy, and I decided to take it out of him."

"You made a slight miscalculation, Buzzsaw," murmured Gentle Willie. "He knocked you stiff."

"It's a lie!" snarled Stover. "Somebody hit me from behind."

"No," denied Clinker, "that young fellow ducked your blow and rose with a wallop on your jaw that sent you to by-bye land."

It was beaten in upon Buzzsaw at last that he had been knocked out in a flash by a single blow of Dick Merriwell's fist. He struggled to his feet a bit weak, but shook off the supporting hand of Warwhoop.

"He took me by surprise," he snarled. "I wasn't looking for it. Wait! I'll get him for that, and I'll get him good and hard!"

# CHAPTER XXII.

## ALL ARRANGED.

Having disposed of Buzzsaw Stover and seen him cared for by his two friends, Dick Merriwell quietly walked away and sought Charlie Loring at the Sunset House, a small hotel at which most of the Outlaws had found accommodations.

It fortunately chanced that Loring was there, and soon Dick was explaining his business. Surprised, the manager of the Springs nine looked Merriwell over with a queer smile on his face.

"What's this you're giving me?" he said. "You want to engage the ball park to-morrow? You've made arrangements to play Harrison's Outlaws? Why, my boy, where's your ball team?"

"I'll have one to-morrow," laughingly declared Dick.

"But I don't understand where you'll get it."

"Leave it to me, Loring. If I can secure the field I'll put a team against Harrison's bunch."

"Well, I think perhaps we can fix it about the park. When I entered into negotiations with Harrison, I had no idea the backers of my team would object, but in a way they're a lot of old women, and they got cold feet. You see, they have an idea that these Outlaws would make us look like fourth raters, and they've figured it out that there wouldn't be much of any profit in the game anyway if we got only one-third of the gate money and stood for all the expenses.

"Furthermore, it's a fact that my players are pretty badly smashed up. We've had rotten hard luck this season. I really couldn't blame Harrison for making a howl, though he barked it into me so hard that I had to get away in order to keep from punching him. You understand when the financial backers of my team got out from under me I had to find a loophole for myself. Never did such a thing before, and I hope I'll never be forced into it again."

"Well, if I get together a nine and play the Outlaws it will let you out all the more gracefully. Your backers ought to jump at this chance. They really ought to give us the use of the park without money and without price."

"That's right. Perhaps I can fix it that way. I'll put it up to them good and stiff and let you know inside an hour. I'll phone you at your hotel; I know where you're stopping."

"Thank you."

"Still, as a special favor, would you mind telling me where you expect to get your players?"

"Buckhart, the regular Yale catcher, is here with me. Two others of my party are Tommy Tucker, who once played short on the Yale varsity, and Bouncer Bigelow, who isn't much at baseball, but might fill right field on a pinch—though I hope I won't have to use him. Chester Arlington, an old Fardale schoolmate, is stopping here, along with his mother and sister. To my surprise and delight, this very morning I ran across old Greg McGregor, a Yale grad who once played on the varsity nine, and McGregor tells me that Blessed Jones, another Yale man, will be down from Denver this afternoon. They're out here on some sort of a business deal.

"There are seven men of the nine, if we count Bigelow in. Jimmy Lozier and Duncan Ross, two Columbia men, are here at the Springs, stopping at the Alta Vista. We sat out in the moonlight last night and talked baseball and college athletics for two hours. The fever is still burning in their veins, and they would jump at the chance to get into a game.

"So you see, Loring, old man, I'm confident that I can get a team together. I hope to find another man, so that I can keep Bigelow on the bench in case of accident. I didn't jump into this blindly; I had it all figured out in advance."

"Well, it seems that you can scrape up a team; but, oh, my boy! what chance do you fancy you will have against the Outlaws? They will make a holy show of you."

"Perhaps so," nodded Dick; "but you never can tell. We're not going into this thing for money. In fact, I've agreed to donate my share of the gate receipts to the Collins' Home for Consumptives. It's sport we're after, Loring."

"There isn't much sport in being wiped all over the map. However, if you fancy it, that's your funeral, not mine. I'll do what I can for you."

"Harrison has agreed to pepper the town with paper advertising his own team. I'm to look after the rest of the advertising."

"Leave that to me also, Merriwell. If I can get the park for you, I'll see that everybody at the Springs knows there's going to be a game to-morrow."

"Thank you, Loring. You're putting yourself to too much trouble."

"Not at all. I couldn't put myself to too much trouble to oblige the brother of Frank Merriwell."

True to his word, in less than an hour Charlie Loring looked up Dick at the big hotel where Merriwell was registered and informed him that he had found no difficulty in securing the ball park. The matter of advertising was discussed, and Loring hastened away to attend to it.

Having phoned Harrison and put him wise to the successful course of affairs, the Yale man looked around for Lozier and Ross. He found the latter in a short time, and Ross delightedly agreed to play, giving his positive assurance that Lozier would be equally glad of the opportunity.

Things were moving along swimmingly. On the broad veranda of the hotel Dick discovered Chester Arlington, who greeted him with a friendly smile.

Arlington pricked up his ears at once on hearing what Merriwell had to say.

"Baseball?" he cried. "A game with the Outlaws? Why, say! I thought they were to play the local team."

"So they were, but it's off—a disagreement over terms."

"And you've got it fixed to tackle them?"

"It's all fixed. The ball ground is engaged for the game."

"Will I play!" laughed Chester. "*Will* I! Ask me! I haven't touched a ball, it is true, since I played down in Texas with Frank's pick-ups. Oh, we gave the great Tigers a surprise down there! But say, I've been looking over the list of games played by these Outlaws, and they walloped the Tigers to a whisper. They must be the real hot stuff."

"I fancy they are," nodded Dick.

"Think we'll stand any show with them?"

"I don't know about that. We'll do our handsomest, and it won't kill us if we're beaten. Nevertheless, if they win we'll try to leave them with the impression that they've been in a baseball game."

"Surest thing you know, Dick. Say, old man, think of it! You and I playing together shoulder to shoulder—you and I, old foes of bygone days! I'm not especially proud of my record in those old days; but still, I can't help thinking of it sometimes."

"I think of it often, Chet. As an enemy you were the hardest fighter I ever got up against."

"Absolutely unscrupulous," said Arlington. "In those times it was anything to down you, Merriwell. I used to think you lucky, the way you dodged my best-laid traps and sort of ducked me into the pits of my own digging. After a time I got my eyes opened and realized that it wasn't luck—it was sheer superiority. I was sowing the wind in those days, and it's a marvel that I didn't reap the whirlwind. I was the lucky man, after all."

Indeed, Arlington had been fortunate; for a score of times, at least, he had been concerned in heinous plots and schemes which might have lodged him behind prison bars. His reckless career had carried him to the point of nearly committing homicide, and the shock of it, together with Dick Merriwell's friendly eye-opening words, had finally caused him to turn over a new leaf.

The fight to regain his lost manliness and win an honorable standing in the world had been long and bitter; but, with those words from Dick's lips echoing in his heart, he had struggled onward and upward. At last he had shaken himself free from the shackles of evil passions and bad habits, and, despite occasional falls and lapses, had risen to a man whom any one might proudly call friend.

In business, as in other things, Chester had shown himself to be a thoroughbred hustler and the worthy son of D. Roscoe Arlington, once known as the greatest railroad magnate of the country. This hustling had lifted him into financial independence, despite his youth, and placed him on the road to wealth. Mingled with remorse for his reckless past, there remained the regret that he had never been able to take a course at Yale.

"Buckhart, Tucker, and Bigelow are out somewhere with old Greg McGregor in my touring car," said Dick. "They will be ready enough for the sport. Tommy and Bouncer spent a week, with headquarters here at the Springs, while Brad and I hunted up Scott Randolph, an old college acquaintance of my brother. We found Randolph in the foothills west of Denver. It's a mighty interesting tale, Arlington, and I'll spin it for you sometime when we're sitting down comfortably at leisure."

"Good! Think of it—you and I sitting down comfortably at leisure and chatting! But say, old man, I wish you would have a little chat with my mother."

"Your mother?" breathed Dick, not a little surprised by the proposal.

"Yes. You know she's ill. It's pitiful, old man—she has almost completely lost her memory. I was speaking to her of you last night, and she tried in vain to recall you. She's sitting yonder at the far end of the veranda."

As Chester made a motion with his hand Dick's eyes discovered a woman, seated amid pillows in a big, comfortable chair. He was shocked. Was it possible that this thin, sad-faced, white-haired old lady was Chester Arlington's mother, the woman who, as an enemy, had been even bitterer and more venomous than Arlington himself?

There she sat with her pallid hands resting on her lap, gazing dreamily upon the mountains which rose majestically against the western sky.

"Will you come, Merriwell, old man?" asked Arlington softly, as his hand rested on Dick's arm.

"Yes," was the answer.

# CHAPTER XXIII.

## CHESTER ARLINGTON'S MOTHER.

Mrs. Arlington looked up as they approached, and at sight of her son a faint smile passed over her face. From her faded eyes the old fire had died, to be rekindled no more. There was no longer rouge upon cheeks or lips, and the hands which had once been loaded with jewels were now undecorated, save by a single heavy ring of gold, her wedding ring. Her dress was plain and modest, almost somber.

"Mother," said Chester tenderly, "this is Dick Merriwell. You remember, don't you, that we were speaking of him last evening?"

"Dick—Dick Merriwell?" she murmured. "Were we speaking of him, Chester? I'm so very forgetful. It's annoying to be so extremely forgetful."

"Yes, mother, I told you that he was my dearest friend—the fellow I esteem above all others."

She held out her hand, which Dick promptly took, bowing low, his head bared.

"You will excuse me, Mr. Merriwell," she said. "I would rise to greet my son's dearest friend, but I'm not very strong."

"I wouldn't have you rise for the world, Mrs. Arlington," said Dick, his voice a trifle unsteady in spite of himself, a slight mist creeping into his eyes. "I am very glad indeed to meet Chester Arlington's mother. It is a pleasure and a privilege."

"Thank you," she returned, looking at him earnestly. "You have a fine face, and you are a thoroughbred gentleman. My boy has to mingle with very rough characters, you know—his business demands it. His business is —it is—— Chester, what is your business?"

"Mining, mother."

"Oh, yes. Isn't it strange I can't remember such things? My daughter is here with me. Have you ever met my daughter, Mr. Merriwell?"

Had he ever met June Arlington! It seemed impossible that her mind could be blank to all recollection of the past, in which she had so intensely opposed the friendship between June and Dick.

"I have met her, Mrs. Arlington."

"You seem to have forgotten, mother," said Chester, "that June and Dick are quite well acquainted. They met for the first time several years ago at

Fardale."

"Fardale—that's the place where you attended school, I think you told me. It was your father's choice to send you there, was it not? Seems to me I opposed it; and that, I presume, was the reason why I never cared to visit you at Fardale."

She had spent months at Fardale!

Unobserved by Mrs. Arlington, Chester and Dick exchanged glances. Although Chet was smiling, Dick knew that deep down in his heart there was hidden a great sorrow for the affliction of his mother.

"My daughter is a very charming young lady," Mrs. Arlington continued. "In a way, I am quite as proud of her as I am of my fine, manly boy. Few mothers are blessed with such children."

"Few indeed," agreed Dick, accepting the chair which Chester had placed beside that of Mrs. Arlington. "I quite agree with you, madam."

"You see, mother," laughed Chester, "Merriwell is something of a flatterer."

"I am sure it is not flattery. I see nothing but sincerity in his face and eyes. Is he interested in your business affairs, my son?"

"Oh, no, indeed. He is still a student at college. He's the pride of old Yale, the college I would have attended had circumstances permitted."

A slight frown of perplexity settled upon her forehead.

"I can't understand how circumstances could have prevented you from attending any school you wished to attend, my son. Am I not right in thinking that your father was in a situation to give you the advantage of a course at any college in the country?"

He evaded the question.

"At the time when I was contemplating entering Yale," he said, "I saw a business opportunity that fascinated me."

"I shall never cease to regret that you chose to let business interfere with your education, Chester. You might have attended college, and been assured that your father would have set you up in any business or profession you chose to follow."

There was not the slightest recollection of the fact that appalling reverses had stripped D. Roscoe Arlington of wealth and power and made it necessary for him to husband the few resources left him, in order to provide for himself and his wife in their old age.

More than once Chester had wondered at the strength of the man who, in face of such calamities, had found it possible to hold up his head and resist the temptation to put a bullet through his brain. It is almost invariably the brave man who survives crushing adversity; it is the coward who commits suicide.

"Father was not very well, you know," Chester went on. "Besides, it is often the worthless chap who depends upon his pater to start him out in life."

"You are very independent, my son. I presume it's a spirit to be proud of. I can't quite understand why your father didn't come out here with us."

"He didn't wish to take the long railroad journey, mother. We're going back in a few days. A letter from the physician tells me that father is not at all well."

"Then we should return at once. If he is ill, my place is at his side. You must stay with us, Chester."

"I am going back with you, but I can't stay there long unless it is absolutely necessary. A man of business," he added, "makes a serious blunder when he neglects his affairs. In these hustling times, a fellow has to keep on the jump to gather in the shekels."

"Oh, but there's something better than mere money. Whoever gives himself wholly to the accumulation of wealth loses half his life."

The change in her was marvelous, for once her only thought had seemed to be of wealth and power and social prestige. A country girl, risen from the humblest station in life, she had slavishly worshiped false gods. After all, was it not a blessing of kind Providence that the page of the past had been turned down and sealed for her? There was no recollection of the years she had spent in a private sanitarium, separated from husband and children— and that was well.

They sat there talking for some time. Other guests of the hotel came forth in summer garments and scattered themselves in chairs along the veranda to get the cool breath which now came creeping down from the snow-capped Rockies. Parties of sight seers were returning from Manitou, the Garden, the Cañon, Monument Park, and other near-by places of interest. Nearly all the guests of that big hotel were tourists from the East.

Presently a large touring car containing four young men rolled up to the steps and stopped. Brad Buckhart was at the wheel. His companions were Tucker, Bigelow, and Gregory McGregor.

At sight of them Dick rose and excused himself, bidding Mrs. Arlington adieu.

Chester proposed to take his mother to her room, but she declined, saying that she preferred to sit there a while longer.

"Go with your friend, my boy," she urged. "I am all right. Don't worry about me. Such a friend as that young man is worth cleaving to."

"You've sized him up right at last, mother."

"At last?" she breathed. "Why, I've never had the opportunity before. I could only judge of him from what you told me about him."

"Oh, of course—certainly," said Chester hastily. "I'll return directly, mother."

Buckhart had turned the car over to a man from the garage, who took it away.

Tucker threw himself into a chair on the veranda.

"There," he said, "we've done up this old town brown. We've taken a peek from the top of Pike's Peak, we've gaped at the wonders in the Garden of the Gods, we've seen a man or two down at Manitou—likewise two or three girls. There isn't anything more to be done, and I'm ready to weep. Bigelow, lend me your handkerchief."

"Not on your life," said Bouncer. "I'm sick of paying laundry bills for you. I've been lending you handkerchiefs and socks and pajamas until the laundry man has got the most of my wealth."

"Now, wouldn't I look well rattling around in a suit of your pajamas!" scoffed Tommy. "Big, you're a heartless, unfeeling creature, and I repudiate you as a friend. In order to get up some excitement to kill the monotony, I'll have to kill you."

"There's a little excitement in the air," said Dick. Then he told them of the arrangements for the baseball game.

"Wow! wow!" barked Tucker delightedly. "You've saved my life, Richard. You've preserved me from a possibly fatal attack of ennui. Will we play the Outlaws? Oh, say, watch us!"

"But can you get together a team, pard?" asked Buckhart.

"I've figured it all out. We will have nine men, including Bigelow."

"What?" cried Tommy, jumping up. "Are you going to let Big play? That settles it. It's all off as far as I'm concerned."

"What do you mean?"

"I quit. I throw up both hands. Bigelow play baseball! Say, Dick, you're a subject for the dotty house."

"Oh, come now," protested the fat fellow. "I don't pretend to be a crack at baseball, but if you've got to have me, I'll do my best. One thing I'm proud of, I never was dropped from the Yale varsity."

"A stab at me," snapped Tucker; "a most unkind thrust. But, look here, it's a well-known fact that I got too fast for the varsity."

"Oh, yes," agreed Bouncer, "you got too fast all right. You certainly hit a fast pace, and it's a wonder you didn't get too fast for the college. All your friends expected you would be invited to chase yourself."

"Of course," said Dick, "if we can find a crackajack ninth man, Big will be willing to sit on the bench and look handsome. You see, we'll give the impression that he's a marvelous pinch hitter, and his size ought to awe the Outlaws."

"I'm a martyr," said Bigelow. "For the sake of any good cause I am ready to be benched. In fact, I'd really enjoy playing the game on the bench, for then I wouldn't have to exert myself and get all damp with perspiration and rumple my beautiful hair and scatter a lot of cuticule around the diamond sliding to bases. I love baseball, but oh, you cuticule!"

"You're sure a generous, self-sacrificing soul, Bouncer," grinned Buckhart.

Dick told of his encounter with Buzzsaw Stover.

"I opine," observed Brad, "that Mr. Stover thought something worse than a buzz saw had struck him."

As they were chatting in this manner two horsemen came riding along the street. One of them, the younger, was dressed in corduroy and woollens. He sat his horse beautifully. The other, however, was the most picturesque figure of the two: for both were Indians, and the older man, bent and bowed, wore, despite the warmth of the unclouded sun, a dirty old red blanket draped about his shoulders.

Tucker saw them first, and, uttering a yell, he grabbed Dick's shoulder.

"Look," he cried, pointing; "look there, Richard! What do you see?"

"So help me marvels," exclaimed Dick, astounded, "it's old Joe Crowfoot and young Joe!"

# CHAPTER XXIV.

## TWO INDIAN FRIENDS.

True enough, the newcomers were Dick's childhood friend Shangowah, and his grandson, young Joe Crowfoot, Dick's college friend. The young Indian's keen eyes had discovered Dick already, and there was a smiling look of joyous astonishment on his handsome bronzed face. Both redskins reined toward the hotel steps as the group of young men came charging down from the veranda.

Then the guests lounging on that veranda beheld a singular spectacle. They saw the young Indian leap from his horse and shake hands with one after another of those delighted youthful palefaces. They saw the old Indian let himself down slowly and painfully from the saddle to stand half bent and seemingly tottering, with arms extended, to give Dick Merriwell an affectionate embrace. This was a sight that caused many of the wondering ladies, and not a few spick and span gentlemen, to gasp and turn up their noses.

"Of all surprising things," young Joe was saying, "this is the greatest. Merriwell, Buckhart, Tucker, Bigelow—here in Colorado Springs!"

"Right here, chief," chirped Tommy, "and ready at sight of your beaming, dusky mug to execute a war dance, a ghost dance, a waltz, or an Irish jig of joy. Tell us, how doth it happen thou art gallivanting around these parts?"

"Shangowah, my grandfather, sent a message requesting me to meet him here," explained the youthful redskin.

Old Joe having released Dick, nodded his head slowly.

"The long trail," he said, "has led Shangowah's feet near to the place where he must lie down for the big sleep that has no end. Shangowah him mighty near polished off, finished up, cooked, done for. He think he like once more to put him blinkers on Wind-that-roars-in-the-night, his grandson; so he get white man to write talking letter that say for young Joe to come."

"Now, Crowfoot," protested Dick, "I've heard you sing this same song before, but I notice that you invariably come out of these spells with colors flying."

Nevertheless, in his heart Merriwell was pained to note positive signs of declining strength and vitality in the old redskin.

"Mebbe sometime old Joe he make bluff 'bout it," confessed Shangowah; "but no can keep up bluff always. Bimeby, pretty soon, time come when bluff is real thing, and old man he have to croak. He no think when he get paleface friend to write talking letter that mebbe he meet you, too, Injun Heart. He much happy."

"Come up onto the veranda out of this sun," urged Dick. "There are some chairs yonder, and you can rest while we talk a little."

"Sun him feel good to old Crowfoot," mumbled the bowed and aged chief. "Blood get thin in old man's body; sun he warm it up some. All same, Crowfoot like little powwow with Injun Heart and friends."

Pride would not permit him to allow Dick to assist him up the steps. With an effort he mounted them in a certain slow and dignified manner.

Surprised and not at all pleased, some of the guests upon the veranda stared at the aged redskin and the presuming young fellows who had brought him thither. The two saddled horses had been turned over to the care of a boy.

McGregor placed the easiest chair for old Crowfoot, but the chief declined to take it.

"No like-um chair," he said, as he slowly let himself down to a sitting posture upon the floor of the veranda, placing his back against the hotel wall. "When Shangowah get so he can't sit this fashion, he stand up till he flop over for good. He take little smoke now."

The old rank, black pipe was produced, crumbed tobacco jammed into the bowl with a soiled thumb, and Crowfoot lighted up. As the breeze carried the tobacco smoke from his lips toward some of the near-by guests they turned up their noses still further and moved away, making some low, uncomplimentary remarks.

"Dear me!" chuckled Tommy Tucker. "The dukes and duchesses seem disturbed by the fragrant aroma of the chief's calumet."

"Never mind them," said Dick. "Let's mind our own business and pay no attention to people whose delicate sensibilities are so easily disturbed. Tell me, Shangowah, how has the world been using you?"

"Ugh!" grunted Crowfoot, pulling slowly at the pipe. "Same old way. Knock-um Injun 'round like young palefaces kick football. Sometime old Joe he be up; sometime he be down in mud. No can seem to settle nowhere. Injun have no home now. Palefaces take it all; pretty soon, bimeby, he own the earth."

"That's practically his now," grinned Tucker, "and with flying machines he's preparing to set forth for the conquering of other worlds."

"I was doing well guiding this summer," said young Joe, "when I received my grandfather's letter asking me to meet him here. I need all the money I can earn to help me through college, but——"

"Shangowah he have little dough in his kick," interrupted the old man. "He have 'nough to pay bills for his grandson one whole year at white man's big school. He no take chances to send it by mails; he want to hand it over himself, so he send for young Joe."

"You must have made a lucky strike of some sort, chief," said Dick.

"Oh, old Joe he manage to scrape along. He play little poke' now and then. He get together some mon' 'bout time big fight come off in Reno. Never see big fight like that, so he think he take it in. He go to Reno. Ugh! Everybody there. Town plumb full, swelled up, run over; but old Joe he got 'long—he sleep anywhere, he eat anyhow."

"Well, what do you think of the old sport," cried Tucker delightedly, "taking in a big prize fight? Did you see it, Crowfoot?"

The aged Indian gave the little chap a look of pained reproof.

"You bet-um your boots," he grunted. "Old Joe he buy ring-side seat. He meet up with heap much fight men before scrap come off. He look-um John Jack over; he look-um Jim Jeff over. He like-um Jim Jeff, but when he hear how Jim go by, when he see John Jack in prime, he think mebbe Jim no come back good enough to whip Jack. He have little talk with Jim Cob, too. He hold small powwow with John Sul."

"Waugh!" laughed Buckhart. "You certainly got in with high society at Reno."

"Jim Cob," continued Crowfoot, "he tell old Joe, Jim Jeff sure to win. Him fine feller that Jim Cob, but he make big mistake. Old Joe he listen heap much, say nothing, think all the time. When he see big odds on Jim Jeff he think mebbe it is good chance to make fancy clean-up, so he bet last dollar on John Jack. He win fourteen hundred plunk, United States cash, clean dough."

"Well, what do you know about that!" gasped Gregory McGregor, in profound admiration. "But what would you have done if you had lost every cent you had in the world, chief?"

Old Crowfoot looked at him wisely.

"If so," he replied, "it not be first time Shangowah get skinned to him teeth. He take chance more than once. He go busted more than once. He always find some way to get on feet again."

"You blessed old soldier of fortune!" chuckled Tucker. "How I admire you! If I was not fearful you would rise up and take my scalp, I would slap you familiarly on the back."

"Back 'gainst wall," reminded old Joe, sucking at the gurgling pipe. "Rheumatiz in back. Anybody slap-um Shangowah on back, he get in heap much trouble."

"We're stopping at a small hotel called the Sunset House," said young Joe. "I knew some of the big hotels might object—or the guests might—if my grandfather should seek accommodations in them."

"The Sunset House?" said Dick. "Why, that's where Harrison's ball team is putting up."

"Yes," nodded young Joe, "they're there. To-morrow they play with the Springs' nine, and my grandfather wishes to see the game."

"They will not play with the Springs' nine to-morrow."

"Why not? That's what brought them here."

"But that game has been called off."

"Too bad," mumbled old Crowfoot. "Joe he get so he like-um baseball heap much. He like-um to see one more game."

"Well, you'll have the chance," smiled Dick, "for to-morrow Harrison's Outlaws will play a team picked up by yours truly, Richard Merriwell, and your grandson is going to be in that game as a member of my nine."

A light of joy leaped into the old redskin's beady black eyes.

"The Great Spirit is good!" he said. "Shangowah he like to see young Joe and Injun Heart play again, but he no expect to have the chance."

After a time the two Indians departed, young Joe having delightedly agreed to take part in the baseball game.

Even as the redskins were departing a tall, lank, insipid-looking young man in flannels detached himself from a group of guests and approached Merriwell's party.

"I—I say, m'friends," he drawled, "don't you really think it's rawther *outré*—rawther bad taste, you understand? You should realize that there are ladies and gentlemen here. You should understand that bringing such offensive persons onto this veranda is deucedly distasteful."

Dick smilingly faced the fellow and took his measure.

"I don't think," he said, "I've ever been introduced to you."

"Quite unnecessary—quite. My name is Archie Ling."

"Ting-a-ling-ling," chirped Tommy.

Mr. Ling gave the little chap a look intended to be crushing.

"I'm addressing this young man here," he said haughtily. "I'm remonstrating against bringing common, dirty, foul-smelling creatures like those Indians onto the veranda of this hotel, and I hope my remonstrance will be heeded. If it occurs again, the guests will feel it their duty to protest to the management."

"They may file their protests as soon as they please," said Dick quietly. "Those Indians are friends of mine."

"Aw, really, you ought to be ashamed to make such an acknowledgement. If circumstances of any sort made it necessary for me to know such characters, I'd certainly do my best to hide the fact from the general public. I'd never acknowledge that I was friendly with an Indian, never."

"Don't worry," returned Dick; "you would never have the chance, for I don't know an Indian who would care to be friendly with you. Look here, Mr. Ling, you're poking your nose into a crack where it's liable to get pinched."

"Or twisted," growled Buckhart. "Back up, Ling. Chase yourself, before somebody is tempted to put their paws on you and toss you over the rail."

"Such insolence!" sniffed Ling. "I don't understand how such cheap, common people ever could find accommodations here."

"Judging by appearances, your understanding is very limited," said Merriwell. "Really, I think it is dangerous for you to strain your meagre intellect to understand things beyond your narrow scope."

"Now, say, that's insulting—actually insulting! I shall hold myself in restraint, however. In behalf of the ladies and gentlemen who were offended, I protest again against a repetition of your recent behavior."

"Go away and play with your dolls," begged Tucker. "If you annoy people, somebody will give you a spanking."

Mr. Ling gasped and choked.

"How dare you talk to me like that, you little——"

Tommy was on his toes in a twinkling.

"Cut it out, Ting-a-ling-ling," he interrupted, "or I'll hand you the spanking myself, and I'll guarantee that I can do the job to the queen's taste."

"Sic him, Tommy," gurgled Bigelow delightedly. "For once in my life I'll bet on you."

But the lanky young man backed away.

"It's evident," he spluttered, "that you're a set of young ruffians. I shall inform the management what I think of you."

"If you try to think too hard you may get a pain in that upper story vacuum of yours."

Ling retired, still muttering, and reported to the watching guests, some of whom seemed amused, while others betrayed sympathetic indignation. Neither Dick nor his friends, however, gave any one of them further attention.

"I'll have to get suits for the bunch," said Merriwell. "Brad, Tommy, and I have ours, which we brought along with us on the tour. I'll find Loring and see if he can fit the rest of the crowd out with uniforms."

In this he was successful, and ere the dinner hour he had procured uniforms enough for ten men, one of which, according to Loring's statement, was fully large enough for Bouncer Bigelow. He likewise learned that Loring had set about advertising the game in a manner which promised to leave no one at the Springs uninformed concerning it.

An hour after dinner, Dick found Chester and June Arlington chatting on the veranda. Mrs. Arlington had retired to her room.

"Just in time to entertain sis, old fellow," laughed Chet. "I have a little business that I should look after. Make yourselves sociable."

He left them together, whistling on his way down the street.

For a time they spoke somewhat constrainedly of commonplace things. Finally June put out a hand and touched Dick's sleeve lightly.

"Dick," she murmured, "I have something that I want to say. I want to tell you just what's in my heart, but I can't. Perhaps you understand how happy I am. Perhaps you know that I appreciate all you have done for my brother."

"I never did much for Chester, June. It was impossible; he wouldn't let me."

"You did everything for him. He knows it, and he has spoken of it many times. It was you who made him what he is."

"Hardly that, June. If there had not been the making of a man in him, I could have done nothing. Really, I did nothing but——"

"Many a time you had it in your power to punish him as he justly deserved, and yet you held your hand."

"For your sake, June, not his," whispered Dick as his fingers found hers in the soft darkness.

Again it was impossible for her to find the words she sought, and their hands clung together.

"It's so strange," she said, in a low tone; "so strange that my mother should speak of you with such deep friendliness. She told me about meeting you this afternoon. She told me how glad she was that Chester had such a staunch and worthy friend. She's wonderfully changed, Dick."

"She is indeed."

"The doctors have given some encouragement that her memory might be restored, but I almost think it is better as it is. The recollection of the past would be bitter to her now."

"To all of us the past holds both sweet and bitter memories."

"I'm very glad fortune brought us together here at the Springs, if only for a few days. We must take mother back home soon, for father is ill and lonely. Poor father! In his heart he always admired you, Dick."

Thus drawn into reminiscences and memories of the past, they chatted until Chester finally returned.

Five minutes after the reappearance of Arlington, a tall, quick-stepping young man ascended from the street, and by the light over the entrance of the hotel Dick recognized young Joe Crowfoot.

Joe turned and came forward quickly at Merriwell's call.

"Looking for you, Dick," he said. "You can handle my grandfather better than I. He will listen to you when he won't hear a word from me. Unfortunately, he's started to celebrate the pleasure of our meeting here. You know what that means. He's found liquor. I've locked him in a room at the Sunset, but I can't get the whisky away from him. I wish you would come over with me and see what you can do."

"I will," said Dick. "I'll come, Joe."

# CHAPTER XXV.

## THE MAN IN THE NEXT ROOM.

Gentle Willie Touch, of the Outlaws, was an inveterate poker player. He was likewise a constant loser, but the more he lost the keener became his desire to play; and so whenever he was paid his salary or could borrow money to get into a game, he might be found trying to "hatch up something."

At the Sunset House, as the members of Harrison's ball team lounged around after dinner, Willie sought to inveigle some of his comrades into tempting fortune with the pasteboards.

"Oh, come on, you sick kittens," he pleaded softly. "Come ahead up to my room and rob me. I've got twenty bucks all in hard money that's too heavy for me to carry around. The weight of so much silver is a severe strain upon my delicate strength, and some one will be doing me a favor by taking it away from me."

"Get out!" growled Grouch Kennedy. "I'm ashamed to play with you, you're such a thundering mark. Every time I get into a game and you go broke I want to hand you back anything I've won, and that causes me intense pain; for I can't seem to give up money without distress. I've sworn off, Willie boy; I'll play with you no more."

"Cruel old Groucher!" sighed Touch. "Now you know you're welcome to my dough when you win it honestly."

"Talk about honesty in a poker game!" sneered Kennedy. "Who ever heard of such a thing?"

"You know there's supposed to be honesty even among thieves."

"'Supposed to be' is good! You'll have to find somebody else, Willie. Your twenty doesn't tempt me. I'm sore because these locals got cold feet, and I'd be poor company, anyhow. I might growl."

"Goodness!" said Willie. "If you didn't, everybody would think you sick. You're always sore about something, you old groucher. Tell you what I think, I have a notion that you're afraid of me. You're not willing to give me a chance to get even. That's a mean disposition."

But he could not taunt Kennedy into playing. Nevertheless, in time he found three men who were willing to sit into a game for a while—Buzzsaw Stover, Warwhoop Clinker, and South-paw Pope. They followed him up to his room, where the quartette peeled off their coats, rolled up their sleeves, and seated themselves around a table upon which Willie tossed a well-thumbed pack of cards.

"Too bad we couldn't find one more man," said Touch. "Five players make a better game than four. Shall we use chips?"

"Nix," said Warwhoop. "Let's play with real money, and then there won't be any disagreement and chewing the rag over settling up. Every time chips are used the banker finds himself short. Cold cash is better, and out in this country there's always plenty of coin floating around. I've got a pocket full of chicken feed."

"Haven't you better cards than these, Willie?" asked South-paw, looking the pack over disdainfully.

"Dunno," was the answer. "Mebbe I have in my clothes somewhere. I'll see."

Touch opened the door of a closet at the back of the room and went through a suit of clothes hanging inside that closet.

"Nothing doing," he called. "Those are all the cards I have. Perhaps I'd better go out and get a new pack."

"Aw, forget it!" rasped Buzzsaw. "These'll do. Come on, let's get down to business."

Seated at the table, they produced fists full of silver and gold money and cut the cards for the first deal.

"Dollar limit?" inquired Warwhoop.

"Let's make it a little lighter," urged Touch. "With that limit my twenty wouldn't last long if luck ran against me as usual. Luck—Grouch says you're all thieves. He doesn't believe there's such a thing as honesty among poker players."

"Grouch judges everybody by himself," said Stover, who had cut "low" and was shuffling the cards. "Still, I'm willing to call it a half, with a dime limit; there seems to be plenty of dimes. Cut, Clinker. Your ante, South-paw."

Touch piled up his silver dollars in front of him, kissing them, one after another.

"Good-by, boys," he murmured. "I know we must part. You'll soon be scattered among my good friends, these thieves. I love money, but, oh, you little game of draw!"

"Hark!" rasped Buzzsaw. "What's that?"

To a sad and doleful tune some one in the adjoining room was singing:

"We from childhood played together,
　　Heap fine comrade, Jack and I;
We would fight each other's battles,
　　To each other's aid we'd fly."

"Oh, cut it out!" roared Buzzsaw. "Go file your voice."

"That's the tune the old cat died on," cried South-paw.

"Something awful!" growled Warwhoop. "It would drive a man to murder."

"These partitions are very thin," said Gentle Willie. "I don't think much of the old man bunking us in this place, when he might have put us up at the Antlers, the Alamo, or the Alta Vista."

"Oh, what do you want, anyhow?" cried Warwhoop. "Do you want to be a howling swell? If he had put us up at any one of those places it would have cost him two or three times as much as it does here. Here the feed is good, the bed is fair, and I'm not kicking for some of the places we've bunked in. Let's play poker."

As the game got under way they were still further disturbed by a doleful, wailing chant which floated in from the adjoining room. Listening in spite of themselves, they heard something like this:

"No booka lo go dana,
No booka lo go dana,
No booka lo go dana—
Happy he away yah!"

"What the blazes is it," snarled Buzzsaw; "Chinese, Hottentot, or——"

"Injun," said South-paw. "If that ain't an Injun dirge I'll eat my hat."

"Sure it is," agreed Warwhoop. "They've put a couple of Injuns into that room, a crazy old brave and a tall young buck."

"They seem to be celebrating," laughed Gentle Willie. "I should say they had been indulging in fire water."

"Don't talk of it," entreated Warwhoop. "You make me thirsty, and I have to be careful to let the booze alone while the baseball season is in swing."

Clinker's besetting weakness was his taste for liquor. Started on a toot by a single drink, he invariably went the limit, which meant a protracted spree from which he always recovered in a shaky condition.

The doleful singing continuing, they yelled threats at the singer and threw things against the partition. The result was a sudden burst of fierce and startling whoops and yells, followed by a return thumping on that same partition.

"Wow!" gasped Warwhoop, his eyes bulging. "I think mebbe we'd better let that party alone. He may break through and attempt to scalp us if we continue to irritate him."

"Close the door to the closet, Willie," directed South-paw. "That's what makes us hear it so plain."

"I guess you're right," said Touch, as he rose and peered into the closet. "The old partition is only boarded up part way. There's an opening two feet wide at the top."

Closing the door, he returned to his seat and the game continued. To the delight of Touch, luck favored him from the first, and it was not long before his twenty became forty.

"I know my hoodoo now," he laughed; "it's old Groucher. I always lose with him in the game. We wanted a fifth man to play."

The door of the closet swung open, and old Joe Crowfoot stepped softly into the room.

"You like-um 'nother man to play?" he asked eagerly. "Shangowah, he play poke' sometime. He sit in now. He take little hand."

# CHAPTER XXVI.

## WHEN GREEK MEETS GREEK.

They started up in astonishment.

"Mercy!" murmured Gentle Willie.

"Great Scott!" gasped South-paw.

"Thunder!" rasped Buzzsaw.

"Wow!" barked Clinker.

"Whoop!" cried old Joe Crowfoot.

"How in blazes did he get into this room?" snarled Stover.

"Heap easy," declared the aged Indian sweetly. "Nice big hole in top of little room. Old Joe climb up on shelves, wiggle through hole, come right in. How, how. Much glad. You got 'nother seat, he take-um hand in little game."

"The nerve of it!" exploded Warwhoop.

"Kick him out!" roared Clinker. "Open the door, Willie. We'll drop him out on his neck."

But when Clinker and Stover took a step toward the old Indian, the latter silently produced a long, wicked-looking knife.

"Try to kick-um old Joe, he make nice mince meat of you," said Crowfoot.

They stopped.

"The old buck is drunk," said South-paw.

Shangowah's beady eyes twinkled.

"Come to meet grandson, young Joe," he said, in an explanatory manner. "Meet other friends. Heap glad. Celebrate some. Old Joe so old he no have time to celebrate much more, so he whoop it up now. 'Scuse-um me."

The knife disappeared, and its place in Crowfoot's hand was taken by a large, flat bottle containing a brownish amber liquor. Removing the cork, the redskin tipped the bottle and permitted two or three swallows to slide gur-glingly down his throat.

"Oh, murder!" muttered Warwhoop. "It's whisky. I smell it."

"Mebbe you have little drink?" invited Crowfoot cordially, as he extended the bottle.

But Stover seized Clinker by the shoulder.

"Don't you touch the stuff, Warwhoop," he warned. "You know what it will do to you. We've got to play to-morrow."

"Got to play a bunch of college kids," said Clinker. "We could beat them if every man on the team was jagged."

"You no take little drink?" asked Crowfoot. "Then old Joe he have to drink-um it all. Grandson, Wind-that-roars-in-the-night, he think old Joe jigged up now. He lock old Joe in room so he get no more joy juice. Waugh! Shangowah have bottle hid under blanket. Grandson no know it."

"He's a sly old duck," grinned Gentle Willie. "Really he's a most amusing specimen."

"But he's interfering with the game," complained Clinker.

"No interfere," said Crowfoot. "Play some—take hand."

"You don't know anything about draw poker," said South-paw.

"Not much," agreed the Indian. "Mebbe play little bit."

"Why, you haven't got any money," sneered Buzzsaw.

"Guess some more," invited the ancient chief, as he promptly dug up a fistful of clinking coins. "Got heap much cash. Make heap good haul on prize fight in Reno."

Gentle Willie laughed aloud.

"Well, now, what do you know about that! Here's an Injun loaded down with real money."

The deportment of the four Outlaws underwent a sudden change.

"Really," said Buzzsaw, "he looks like a nice, decent old brave. Perhaps we'd better let him into the game."

The others agreed to this, and, a chair being placed, old Joe advanced unsteadily and seated himself between Stover and Pope.

"The limit is fifty cents, chief," explained South-paw.

"Let's make it a dollar," urged Gentle Willie, success having given him confidence. "What do you say, Mr. Lo?"

"Make-um it anything," grunted old Joe. "No limit suit me."

"Well, he is a sport!" chuckled Clinker. "Tell you what, we'll call it a dollar limit and all Jack pots. Understand that, Tecumseh?"

"Lemme see. Mebbe so," answered old Joe. "You make little explanation."

"It will be like taking candy from the baby," whispered Clinker in Gentle Willie's ear; while Buzzsaw explained to the Indian, who listened in a dull, half-comprehending way.

But when the game was resumed old Joe seemed to catch onto the run of it in a manner which surprised the others.

"No play much," said the redskin. "Most forget how."

He was permitted to win one or two small pots, which seemed so to elate him that he took another long pull at the bottle. His tongue grew thick and his eyes seemed to be glazy. At intervals he insisted on singing, and always the tune was a doleful dirge.

"I've traveled about heap much in my time,
    Of troubles I've sure seen a few;
I find it heap better in every clime
    To paddle my own canoe."

"You're certainly a musical cuss," said Clinker; "but music and draw poker don't go well together. Cut it out."

"My cut?" grunted old Joe, reaching for the cards. "You no like-um music, hey? Shangowah he no sing much; he too old. He got rheumatiz in his voice. What you do 'round here?"

"We came here to play baseball," explained Gentle Willie. "Know what that is?"

Crowfoot scratched his head.

"Mebbe so," he mumbled. "Old Joe see game once. See men throw balls like bullet at 'nother man. 'Nother man hit it with big stick. Then everybody run, crowd yell, one who hit ball make quick foot race round in circle back to place where he start. There he scoot-um head first on ground. Somebody throw ball to feller who grab it and hit-um man on ground 'tween shoulders. Everybody yell: 'Kill umpire.' Old Joe he get out knife and start to do it. Next thing everybody jump on old Joe, kick him stiff. What make-um holler 'kill umpire' if no want him killed?"

"Haw! haw! haw!" roared Buzzsaw. "You certainly was going to be obliging."

"No understand it," sighed Crowfoot sadly. "Take-um knife from old Joe, kick-um him, put-um bracelets on him, yank him to lockup. Next day judge fine-um him twenty-five dol' and costs—say 'cause he break peace. He no break anything. He all broke up himself."

"Well, just come out to the game to-morrow," urged Stover, "and you'll see us eat a lot of kids up."

"Eat um—eat um kids?"

"I mean the fellers on the opposite team."

"You eat um?" repeated Crowfoot in a puzzled way. "You like-um baseball players to eat?"

"He's speaking figuratively, Powhatan," exclaimed Gentle Willie. "He means that we'll beat the everlasting stuffing out of them. We can beat anything that plays the game, and a chesty, conceited youngster by the name of Dick Merriwell had the nerve to challenge us to play. What do you think of that!"

193

"Heap much nerve," nodded Crowfoot, swaying slightly on his chair. "Old Joe come. He have great fun to watch you beat-um young fool Merriwell. Mebbe you no beat."

"It will be a cinch," said South-paw. "I'm going to pitch."

"You no got swelled head nor anything?" mumbled Crowfoot.

"Keep your eye on me," advised Buzzsaw. "I've got it in for that feller Merriwell. He hit me when I wasn't looking, and I'll hand him his pay if he ever gets round to third base. That's my position."

"What you do to him?"

"Spike him if I get a chance. Watch me. See him come up to third, and watch me if I get the ball. Will I tag him with it? Will I? I'll bang it onto his muzzle and send him to the dentist's for new teeth."

"You got heap bad grudge," said Crowfoot. "Much fun to see you knock-um teeth out of Merriwell feller. Old Joe he laugh when he see it. It give him big fun."

"Let's play poker and cut out the talk," urged Clinker.

Crowfoot took another drink, and the game continued, with the old savage nodding and blinking over his cards. Apparently he was half doped by the liquor; yet, strange to say, try as they might, they could not seem to win a great deal of his money. He had most astonishing luck. Repeatedly Stover, who could manipulate the cards, put up a hand to win, only to have Crowfoot drop out or show down a better hand. Gradually the third baseman of the Outlaws grew ugly and resentful.

"Rotten luck!" he growled.

"Ugh!" grunted Crowfoot. "Good luck for Shangowah."

"The old sinner is a shark at the game," muttered Warwhoop.

"Sharks should be harpooned," said South-paw under his breath.

They arranged it without spoken words to sink the harpoon into old Joe. Under cover Buzzsaw showed Warwhoop three aces in his hand, and Clinker passed him the fourth.

Then old Joe dropped out, although he had already pushed eight dollars into the pot. Gathering up the Indian's cards, Pope managed to get a look at them and gasped with amazement; for Crowfoot had put down three queens and a pair of ten spots. Thenceforth for a time South-paw felt certain it was sheer blundering luck which prevented the uninvited guest from losing his last dollar.

Once, as Crowfoot seemed dozing, Stover attempted deftly to purloin a stack of coins from the Indian's pile. Joe lurched forward and put out his hand as if to save himself; his fingers closed on Buzzsaw's wrist, and he woke up.

"Hello!" he muttered. "What you do? You make-um little mistake. You think mebbe my dough belong to you."

"I was just pushing it back from the edge of the table, so that you wouldn't knock it all over the floor," said Buzzsaw sourly.

"Heap much oblige," said Crowfoot. "Shangowah do as much for you sometime, mebbe."

Gradually they began to wonder and suspect. Finally there came a heavy pot, in which, at the start, every one lingered. Gentle Willie and Warwhoop were finally driven out; but, with Crowfoot between them, Buzzsaw and South-paw continued to raise. Again Stover had made up a hand, and this time, having discarded an ace, he felt confident that his four kings must win. At last it seemed that the old redskin had been lured into a trap.

When the show-down came Pope dropped his hand, and Stover triumphantly displayed the four kings.

"Pretty good," mumbled old Joe. "How you like-um these?"

He lay down four aces!

"Crooked work!" snarled Stover fiercely. "I discarded an ace myself."

"Oh, you make little mistake," protested old Joe. "You no have ace."

"Wait! Don't you touch that pot!" cried Buzzsaw, as he grabbed the discards and turned them. "Look—look at this! Here's the ace I discarded."

He picked the ace of diamonds out of the discards.

"Ugh!" gurgled old Joe. "Heap funny. Lemme see. Lemme look at back of that card."

Stover turned it over.

"Waugh!" exploded Shangowah, pointing a soiled finger at the pasteboard. "That no belong in pack. Back of that card not like others."

It was true, and before their eyes Crowfoot turned his own cards, revealing that they belonged to the pack with which they were playing.

"You try to soak-um me," he sneered. "You slip 'nother card in pack so you can make bluff old Joe cheat."

Stover was staggered for a moment, but, as Crowfoot reached out to gather in the pot, Buzzsaw uttered a yell and sprang from his chair, seizing the redskin. On the other side South-paw Pope did the same, and Clinker, upsetting his own chair, came quickly to their assistance.

Crowfoot had started to rise. As he did this a pack of cards slipped out of his clothes somewhere and fluttered over the floor. Gentle Willie grabbed up several of them and looked at the backs.

"What do you think!" he cried. "These cards are like the odd one in the pack we've been using! The Injun substituted that odd card!"

"Kill him!" raged Buzzsaw.

# CHAPTER XXVII.

## SHANGOWAH'S BACKERS.

When young Joe and Dick arrived at the room of the Indians in the Sunset House they were astonished to find it empty. The door had remained locked, but old Joe Crowfoot was not to be found in that room. Young Joe even looked beneath the bed in search of him.

"He's gone," said Dick. "He's not here."

"But how could he get out?" muttered the young Indian, puzzled and dismayed. "I had the key, and the door was locked, as you saw."

Merriwell thrust his head out of the window and looked down to the ground. The room was a second-story one.

"Perhaps he jumped."

"No," said young Joe positively, "he didn't do that."

"I'm not so sure of it. I've seen the time when he would think nothing of dropping out of a window this distance from the ground."

"That time is past. Really, Dick, my grandfather is getting old and feeble. He's not the man he was. I've seen a great change in him. I doubt if he could jump from this window to the ground without injuring himself."

"Old as he is," returned Dick, "I'll guarantee, if put to it, or pitted against a desperate enemy, he would astonish some people. I've seen him before when he seemed nearly all in, and I've likewise seen him 'come back.'"

Dick opened the closet door and peered into it. Suddenly he lifted his hand, with his ear bent toward the closet.

Young Joe stepped swiftly and noiselessly to the Yale man's side.

A faint smile crept over Dick Merriwell's face.

"We've located Shangowah," he said, in a low tone, as the sound of voices came to their ears. "He's in the adjoining room, and, so help me! I believe he's playing poker with a bunch in there."

Mingled with the murmur of voices they heard the clinking of money and shuffling of cards.

"You're right," whispered young Joe. "But how did he get in there?"

Even as he asked that question his eyes answered it, for he discovered the opening high up at the back of the closet, and he knew the old Indian had mounted the shelves, squirmed through that opening and entered the next room in a decidedly unusual manner.

"He will play poker and he will drink," muttered young Joe. "He says he's too old to abandon such habits, though he's rather proud because his grandson has listened to the counsel of Injun Heart and never become a confirmed victim of such practices.

"It's ten to one." Joe went on, as he closed the closet door, "that he's fallen in with a bunch of sharks, and he's in poor condition to take care of himself."

"If that is true," laughed Dick, "it will be something unusual; for, sober or otherwise, I've never yet seen Shangowah in such a condition that he could not look after number one. However, I think it will be well enough to get in there if we can and pry him away from that bunch."

As they reached the door of the other room the sound of loud, angry, and excited voices came to their ears, Merriwell's hand fell on the doorknob, but the door was locked.

"Kill him!" shouted a voice within the room.

Dick stepped back two strides, then he flung himself forward, and his shoulder crashed against the door, which flew open, the lock broken.

Into that room leaped the two youths red and white. In a twinkling they had seized old Crowfoot's assailants and sent them reeling right and left. The aged Indian was torn free from the hostile hands that had clutched him.

"Ugh!" he grunted stoically. "Heap much obliged."

"What's the row in here?" demanded Dick Merriwell.

Buzzsaw Stover gathered himself up from the corner into which he had spun from the hand of Merriwell.

"We caught that dirty old wolf cheating!" he howled hoarsely. "He substituted a card from a pack of his own."

"Ugh!" grunted old Joe once more. "You cheat. You put up one, two, three, and some more little job on old Crowfoot. You think he not see? You think he no have eyes? He see you monkey with pasteboards. He see other man pass you card under table. He see you try to swipe stack of money from him. Cheat? You biggest blame thief on two legs!"

"It's a lie!" panted Stover. "I'll choke the breath out of the old robber! Come on, fellows! Going to let these two kids come in here and bluff us?"

His companions answered with vicious cries, and, following his example, proceeded to attack the intruders.

During the next few moments there were lively times in that room. If those Outlaws fancied that by superior strength and overwhelming numbers they were going to have a snap with their opponents, they fooled themselves to the limit. Young Joe Crowfoot could use his fists with all the skill of a finished boxer; and, side by side with Merriwell, he took care of his share of the assailants. Gentle Willie Touch got a punch in the wind that promptly put him hors de combat, and Warwhoop Clinker was given a thump on the bugle that nearly drove his proboscis back into his face.

Meanwhile, South-paw Pope had "got his" from Dick, and once more Merriwell reached for Buzzsaw's jaw and found it. Stover dropped into the same corner from which he had lately emerged and sat very limp and dazed, prevented from keeling over by the angle of the partitions.

While this was taking place old Joe Crowfoot calmly proceeded to rake his own money off the table and take possession of the big jack pot which had brought about the clash. The money piled in front of the chairs at which the Indian's associates in the game had sat was left untouched.

"Now we puckachee," said old Joe; "we vamoose. We make a sneak."

He wabbled a bit as he passed through the open door. Dick and young Joe followed him, leaving the Outlaws to recover.

"Oh! oh!" gasped Gentle Willie. "I'll never draw a full breath again."

"My nose!" groaned Clinker, whose face was an unpleasant, gory spectacle.

Pope made his complaint, but for the time being Stover had nothing to say.

Having recovered a short time later, however, Buzzsaw raged like a lunatic.

"There'll be murder in this town!" he snarled. "I'll have that feller Merriwell's hide before another day is over."

"Are we going to let that old Injun get away with the money?" asked Pope.

"No!" was the furious answer. "We'll take it away from him. Come on, let's find him."

But they looked for Shangowah in vain. When they finally inquired at the desk they were informed that old Crowfoot and young Joe had settled and left the hotel for good. No one knew where they had gone.

# CHAPTER XXVIII.

## BATTED OUT.

To the satisfaction of Bob Harrison, an astonishingly large crowd of people turned out to watch that baseball game. The manager of the Outlaws realized it was doubtful if a bigger attendance would have appeared had Manager Loring stood by his agreement to put the regular Springs' team onto the field. Harrison could not appreciate the fact that a host of tourists in town knew about the college men who were to play, and had a keen desire to see what they could do against the dreaded Outlaws. He imagined the crowd had been drawn out solely on account of the reputation of his star team.

Mr. Archie Ling was one of the spectators, and for a time he sought in vain some one who had the courage to bet on the collegians.

"Really," said Mr. Ling disappointedly, "I've heard some people say they thought the youngsters had a chance in this game, but 'pon my word I can't find anybody who cares to back them. I'd like a little wager, you understand. That would make it interesting."

Some one touched him on the shoulder, and, looking round, to his disgust he discovered, an arm's length away, the same old Indian who had offended him by appearing on the veranda of the hotel the previous evening.

"Ugh!" grunted old Crowfoot. "You make little bet? How much you bet on Outlaw men?"

"Go away," said Ling, fanning old Joe off and turning up his dainty nose.

"You make bet talk," persisted old Joe. "You shoot-um off your mouth. How much you bet?"

"Why, you haven't any money."

"How much you bet?" repeated the old redskin. "You bet five hundred plunk, old Joe he cover it."

"Five—five hundred plunks!" gurgled Ling. "Why, you never saw so much money in your life. I doubt if you have five cents in your dirty clothes."

Then Crowfoot dug up a huge leather sack, which clinked significantly and seemed to be stuffed to overflowing. Pulling the strings of this pouch, the redskin showed that it was filled with gold and silver coins.

"How much you bet?" he again demanded.

"Why—why," spluttered Ling, aghast, "where did you get it?"

"None your blame business," was the answer. "You go five hundred dol' on Outlaw men?"

"Five hundred dollars! Why, no, indeed!"

"How much you bet?" again came the question; "one hundred dol'?"

"No, indeed! I—I'd like to make a little wager just to—just to have it interesting. I'll bet—oh—er—about five dollars."

With a grunt of unspeakable disgust, Crowfoot yanked at the bag strings, closing the sack, which he again stowed away upon his person.

"Five dol'!" he sneered. "You big piker. You tin horn bluffer. You make heap much loud chin. Old Joe no waste time to bet little candy money with dude."

Mr. Ling hastily retreated, his face crimson, his ears offended by the loud laughter of the spectators.

The practice of the Outlaws was of that accurate, easy, professional order which marks the work of big teams. The youngsters likewise practiced well, but they lacked the cool atmosphere of indifference and certainty which characterized the professionals.

A man known to be a fair and impartial umpire had been secured. Confident of an all too easy victory, the Outlaws permitted the captain of the opposing team to name this official, and Dick took the man he was advised to take by Loring.

The toss of a coin gave the Outlaws the choice, and they took the field. The umpire called "play," and the game began with South-paw Pope on the slab.

"Eat 'em alive!" roared Stover.

"Mow 'em down!" shouted Nutty McLoon.

"Be gentle with them!" pleaded Willie Touch.

"Wow! wow!" barked Warwhoop Clinker. "It will be an awful massacre."

"We've never had such a snap as this," laughed Smiling Joe Brinkley.

Now possibly four out of five of the spectators fully expected to witness a one-sided game, with the Outlaws making a runaway from the very start; and when Stover mowed down Arlington and Blessed Jones at the pan, neither of those batters even touching the ball, it seemed such a sure thing that some sporting individuals were willing to wager that the youngsters would not score at all.

Moving about, old Joe Crowfoot picked up bets here and there. With one man he bet one hundred even that the collegians would get half as many runs as the Outlaws; with another he wagered that Merriwell's pick-ups would make as many hits as their opponents; in fact, they found him ready, as long as his money lasted, to lay almost any sort of a bet on the youthful antagonists of the professionals.

It created universal surprise when young Joe Crowfoot got a clean single off Pope. Following this, however, Buckhart popped to the infield, and the collegians left the bench.

"Start right in on the kid, Clinker," urged Stover savagely. "Let's give him a drop to start with. Let's take the conceit out of him. Wait till I face him!"

Clinker tried to start things going, but he hit a ball on the upper side of his bat and popped it high into the air for Duncan Ross, who was covering first base.

"Rotten!" complained Warwhoop, seating himself disgustedly on the bench.

Kennedy banged a hot one against the shins of Tucker at short, and Tommy fumbled long enough for Grouch to canter easily over first.

"We're off! We're going!" roared Buzzsaw.

Tucker was saying a few uncomplimentary things to himself, but Dick Merriwell did not seem greatly disturbed.

Long Tom Hix bumped a Texas leaguer over the infield, and Kennedy, on the jump, crossed second, keeping on toward third.

Joe Crowfoot, coming in fast from center field, took the ball in the bound and whipped it like a whistling bullet to Jimmy Lozier at third.

The coacher yelled a warning at Kennedy, who suddenly realized that he could not make the sack. A moment later the crowd was filled with excitement, as the youngsters trapped Kennedy on the base line and attempted to run him down.

Again Tommy Tucker made a mess of it. He it was who fumbled a throw and gave Kennedy the chance to dash past him back to second base.

"Oh, I'm pretty good, I am!" said Tommy. "I'm playing for the Outlaws to-day. I'm afraid they won't get a score, and I'm doing my best to help them along."

The Outlaws scoffed and sneered at the youngsters.

His eyes gleaming viciously, Buzzsaw Stover walked to the plate, bat in hand.

"Hand one over, you young snipe," he rasped at Dick, "and I'll hit it a mile!"

He missed the first ball cleanly, with Merriwell smiling at him in an exasperating manner. The next one was wide, but, immediately following, Buzzsaw struck again.

Bat and ball met with a crack, and the sphere, shooting at Tommy Tucker, touched the ground once. The little chap took that hot one cleanly. Like a flash of light he snapped the ball to third for a force-out, and Lozier, making a beautiful throw, hummed it down to second for a double.

The spectators rose and shouted, while the Outlaws stared in wonderment. Stover could not find language to express his feelings.

"That's the way to redeem yourself, Thomas," laughed Dick, as he jogged toward the bench with Tucker at his side.

"You little no-good runt!" gurgled Bigelow. "I'd like to hug you. A few moments ago I had to hold myself hard to keep from rushing out there to kick you."

"I was fooling 'em, Bouncer," grinned Tommy. "They thought they could all pound the horsehide through me."

It was Merriwell's turn to hit.

"Get busy with that conceited bottle of buttermilk, South-paw," urged Stover. "Show him up."

Pope grinned and gave Dick one on the outside corner.

A moment later the crowd was yelling, as Nutty McLoon, far out in the field, went wildly racing after the sphere.

Over first and second and on toward third ran Dick. McLoon got the ball and returned it in the diamond, causing Tommy Tucker, dancing wildly on the coaching line, to make frantic gestures for Merriwell to stop at the third sack.

Fortunately, Dick had been warned by old Joe Crowfoot, and he had his eye on Buzzsaw Stover. As he came up to the sack he saw Stover, standing close by the bag, prepared for something. Then Buzzsaw did his prettiest to jab his elbow into Dick's wind for what might have been a knockout.

Stover never knew exactly what happened to him, but he found himself spinning end over end, and Tucker was compelled to dodge to get out of his way. He picked himself up off the turf, the most amazed man in Colorado Springs. He was likewise infuriated, and started to rush at Dick. When he saw Merriwell ready and waiting, however, he changed his mind.

"What in blazes do you mean?" he snarled.

"You want to be careful with your elbows and your spikes to-day, Mr. Stover," said Dick. "Likewise, I'd advise you, if you have occasion to tag me, not to attempt to knock out any of my teeth. I shall be looking at you all the time."

Some of Stover's companions were inclined to rush at Dick in a bullying manner, but the crowd rose and made it plain that sympathy lay with the youngster.

"Here, here!" shouted Harrison from the bench. "Let up on that business, boys! We won't have to scrap to take this game in a walk."

They knew the old man meant it by his tone, and they likewise knew it was policy to obey him.

Lozier, who followed Dick, took a signal from the Yale man at third and batted the ball into the diamond.

Merriwell came home like a streak, sliding safely, in spite of the effort to stop him from scoring. This attempt to get Dick at the plate gave Lozier time to reach first.

South-paw Pope was exasperated. He heard the crowd shout its delight and distinguished in the midst of that tumult the sound of a wild, shrill war-whoop that came from the lips of a well-satisfied old redskin who had bet his last dollar on the college boys.

Old Greg McGregor jogged into the batter's box and let two wide ones pass. Then he found one of Pope's benders for a safety in right that sent Lozier all the way to third.

The Outlaws were amazed and possibly somewhat rattled. At any rate, Dead-eye Jack Roony made a poor throw to second when McGregor attempted to steal, and the runner was safe.

Duncan Ross fouled out.

"The little flurry is over, Pope," cried Long Tom Hix. "We'll take 'em in order now. Let the two kids cool their heels on the sacks."

Tucker scarcely looked like a hitter as he stood at the plate twiddling his bat. He looked even less so when he missed Pope's first ball by a foot. But a moment later he bumped an easy hit through the infield, and both Lozier and McGregor raced home.

"Oh, my, how easy!" whooped Tommy. "It's pie! it's pie! We'll bat him out of the box."

Chester Arlington had caught the fever. He followed with a stinging two-sacker, which carried Tucker to the pan.

The crowd was cheering and laughing; Bob Harrison was astounded and furious. The exasperated manager roared at Pope threateningly, and South-paw vowed to stop the "doings" right away.

He vowed in vain. Jones hit safely, and Arlington scored. Then young Joe emulated Arlington in hitting, and old Blessed added another tally.

Manager Harrison had a fit.

"Come in here, Pope!" he thundered. "You're on the bum! Go out there and stop this business, Brown!"

The collegians had batted the great south-paw twirler off the slab!

# CHAPTER XXIX.

## THE FINISH.

Wopsy Bill Brown had better luck to start with. Buckhart hit the ball hard, it is true, but the sailing sphere was gathered in by an outfielder, and Crowfoot lodged on third.

Dick likewise banged the horsehide far into the outfield, but again it was caught, which retired the youngsters after they had made six runs.

The Outlaws went to bat determined to change the aspect of affairs in a hurry. Imagine their astonishment when Merriwell smilingly mowed down three men in quick order.

Up to the beginning of the seventh inning Wopsy Bill held the collegians successfully, although twice the youngsters pushed a runner round to third. The Outlaws fought savagely, trying in various ways to frighten their opponents, but failing utterly.

The seventh opened with Buckhart at bat, and he led off with a smash that netted three sacks.

Dick hit safely a moment later, scoring Brad. Lozier bunted and died at first, while Dick took second.

Old Greg McGregor showed his mettle by drawing a two-sacker that gave the youngsters still another tally. Merriwell kept his eyes on Stover as he crossed third, and Buzzsaw did not dare try any dirty tricks.

When Duncan Ross followed with a hit, Bob Harrison went into the air and yanked Wopsy off the plate.

Strawberry Lane, the only remaining pitcher of the Outlaws, went in to stem the tide.

"Too late! too late!" came the cry from the crowd. "They've got the game now."

Like Brown, Lane succeeded in checking the run getting for the time being, striking out Tucker and forcing Arlington to lift an easy fly.

In the last of the seventh the Outlaws obtained their one and only tally. Stover struck out to begin with and retired to the bench, his heart bitter with hatred for Dick Merriwell.

McLoon, coming next, hit along the third-base line, and the ball caromed off Lozier's bare right hand. Nutty ran wild over first, and Lozier, trying to get him at second, caught the ball up swiftly and made a bad throw.

Over third McLoon sped, and McGregor, who had tried to back up second, completed the unfortunate series of errors by throwing wide to the plate.

"Now," snarled Buzzsaw Stover, "let's keep right at it and make a hundred."

A few moments later, Merriwell had cut down Smiling Joe Brinkley and Gentle Willie Touch, and Buzzsaw went to third sore as a flea-bitten cur.

In the eighth there came near being a riot when Stover tried to spike Blessed Jones, who had reached third on a single, a sacrifice by Crowfoot, and a steal. The umpire promptly informed the vicious third sacker of the Outlaws that he would be put out of the game if he tried any more such contemptible tricks.

Jones scored on a safety by Buckhart.

Dick hit one into centre field and was out.

Lozier fanned a few seconds later.

There was no further run getting on either side. In the eighth and ninth innings Merriwell was invincible on the slab. Those amazed Outlaws could do nothing whatever with his delivery, and the delighted spectators simply shouted themselves hoarse. Never had Harrison's stars received such a drubbing, the final score being nine to one against them.

The college lads were congratulated on every hand. Old Joe Crowfoot found young Joe and looked him over approvingly.

"You make heap fair baseball player bimeby, mebbe," said the old chief. "You learn some, mebbe. Old Joe he clear up good thing to-day. He have money 'nough to-night so you pay two year at Yale school. He reckon he hand-um it over so he no lose it."

Bob Harrison shouldered his way through the crowd and reached Dick Merriwell.

"Look here," he called; "look here, young fellow, you certainly was loaded with horseshoes to-day. It was the biggest accident that ever happened. Play us again. Play us to-morrow, and we won't leave you in the shape of anything. I'll call off a date with Cheyenne in order to play you."

"I'm very sorry, Mr. Harrison," smiled Dick; "but it will be impossible for us to give you another game. My pick-up team disbands to-night, as business will make it necessary for several of the players to leave the Springs to-morrow."

"Yah! You're afraid!" cried Harrison. "You don't dare play another game."

"Go 'way back and set down," grunted old Joe Crowfoot. "He beat-um you any time you play. You have big team of stars? Waugh! No good!"

Then several of the bystanders stepped between Harrison and the old redskin to prevent the exasperated manager from laying violent hands on Shangowah.

---

That evening Dick and June sat talking in low tones on the hotel veranda.

"Buckhart," said Dick, "has an uncle on a ranch up North, and we're going up there. It was a great treat to meet you here, June."

"It was fine, Dick," she returned. "Oh, it was just splendid to watch the game to-day! It seemed like old times. We are leaving to-morrow."

"Going back home?"

"Yes. Chester and I decided that we ought to go right away. I'm sorry we can't all stay here a little longer, for it has been very pleasant—very pleasant ____"

His hand found hers and held it tightly.

"It has been the pleasantest feature of my summer, June," he declared.

In the shadows he lifted her hand to his lips.

"Till we meet again, June!" he whispered.

"Till we meet again, Dick!"

### THE END.